THE HILL OF THREE BORDERS

Also by Jefferson Flanders

CAFÉ CAROLINA AND OTHER STORIES
THE GIRL FROM RECOLETA AND OTHER STORIES OF
LOVE

HERALD SQUARE
THE NORTH BUILDING
THE HILL OF THREE BORDERS

THE HILL OF THREE BORDERS

A novel of the Cold War

Jefferson Flanders

Munroe Hill Press
Lexington, Massachusetts

Cover design and Budapest map by Mick Wieland Design

ISBN: 0-9887840-0-9
ISBN-13: 978-0-9887840-0-0
eBook ISBN: 978-0-9887840-1-7
Library of Congress Control Number: 2014912199

Munroe Hill Press
Lexington, Massachusetts

For my father, Stephen Carver Flanders

"And if ye go to war in your land against the enemy that oppresseth you, then ye shall blow an alarm with the trumpets; and ye shall be remembered before the Lord your God, and ye shall be saved from your enemies."
   – Numbers 10:9

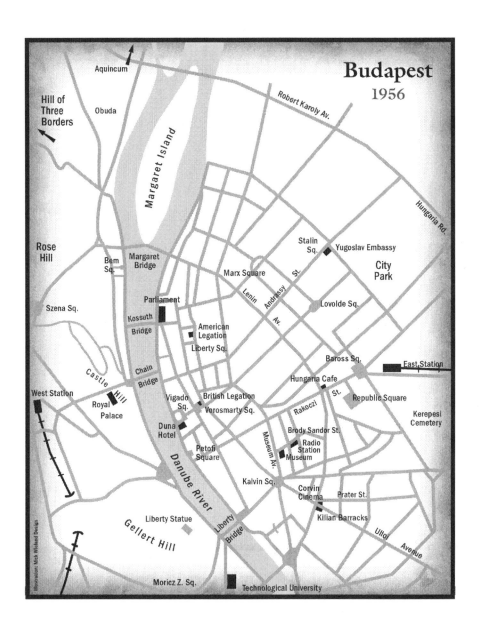

Budapest
1956

A Note on Hungary's History

Throughout much of the 20th century, Central Europe faced political unrest, economic deprivation, and war. Hungary was not exempt from these tribulations.

The defeat of the Austro-Hungarian Empire in World War I sparked a series of dramatic political and territorial shifts. In Hungary, Bela Kun's Communist regime—the Hungarian Soviet Republic—held power in 1919 for 133 days. Romanian troops drove Kun and his commissars out of Hungary, and the conservative nationalist Admiral Miklos Horthy became regent of Hungary. The Treaty of Trianon of 1920, imposed upon Hungary by the victorious Allies, reduced the size of the country by two-thirds and left a third of its ethnic Hungarian population living in other nations (including Romania, Czechoslovakia, and what became Yugoslavia).

Largely in the hopes of recovering lost Hungarian territory, Horthy joined the Axis Powers in their attack on the Soviet Union in 1941. In 1944, Adolf Hitler ordered the invasion and occupation of Hungary after Horthy entered into secret peace negotiations with the Allies. The Germans placed Ferenc Szalasi of the fascist Arrow Cross Party in power. Szalasi's followers assisted the Nazis in sending some 400,000 Hungarian Jews to Auschwitz. In Budapest, Hungarian fascists also shot thousands of Jews, dumping their bodies into the Danube River. Scholars of the Holocaust estimate that some 569,000 Hungarian Jews were murdered, 69 percent of the country's pre-war Jewish population.

In 1945, the Red Army defeated the Germans and captured Budapest. In 1947, Hungarian Communists effectively took power after a campaign of intimidation and fear. Communist leader Matyas Rakosi slavishly followed Joseph Stalin's lead, employing mass surveillance and terror tactics in seeking totalitarian control over the country. A popular saying at the time was: "When it rains in

Moscow, the umbrellas go up in Budapest." Rakosi's dreaded secret police (known as the AVO, for *Allamvedelmi Osztaly*, "State Security Department"*) crushed dissent, torturing and imprisoning thousands. Like his idol, Stalin, Rakosi sought to establish a cult of personality; John Gunther, the American journalist, described Rakosi as the most malevolent character he had ever met in political life.

After Stalin's death in 1953, the Soviet Politburo pushed Rakosi as premier aside in favor of Imre Nagy, a reformer. Hungarians welcomed Nagy's "New Course" of economic liberalization, but his emphasis on light industry and market-driven food production became an unacceptable challenge to Marxist orthodoxy. Nagy was ousted as premier in 1955, and Rakosi was returned to power.

In February 1956, Nikita Khrushchev gave his famous Secret Speech to the 20th Party Congress in Moscow, denouncing Stalin's crimes. In June, Rakosi was removed as General Secretary of the Party and replaced by Erno Gero, a fellow hardliner.

Despite some signs of political unrest in the summer and early fall of 1956, the consensus among Western intelligence agencies was that the Gero regime retained firm control over the country. In Washington, American foreign policy experts and intelligence analysts concluded in a June 1956 National Security Council report that open popular revolt in Hungary wasn't possible. Within a few short months, they were proven completely wrong.

*In 1950, the government changed the name of State Security to *Allamvedelmi Hatosag*, or AVH, but Hungarians continued to use "AVO" when referring to the secret police.

Part One

Budapest transformed into a golden city in late September, as beautiful and luminous as any other metropolis he had seen in Europe. Maxim gazed out his bedroom window at the Danube River far below, glittering in the afternoon sun, and his eyes were drawn to its east bank where blood-red flags on the spires of the massive neo-Gothic Parliament Building fluttered in the breeze.

He wanted to remember the city as it was on this Sunday afternoon, suffused with the slanting light that had always reminded him of Paris in the fall. From his top floor bedroom window in his house on Castle Hill the panoramic view gave little evidence of the gray drabness that, much of the time, seemed to envelop Budapest's streets at ground level.

When he turned from the window to glance back at the interior of his bedroom, he saw cascading light illuminating the graceful curves of Eva's naked body as she lay face down sprawled across his four-poster bed, the sheets tangled around her legs. They had made love earlier, and then she had curled up and fallen asleep afterward, as was her habit. She had thrown herself into their lovemaking ardently, pulling him close to her as she moved under him, gasping with pleasure.

But he had not joined her in sleep, for he was too aware of what lay ahead. He had donned his dressing gown and had restlessly paced in front of the window, gazing at the view of the river and the city, while he settled things in his mind. His eyes had strayed to the distinctive Hungarian Academy of Sciences building, an ornate Baroque beauty facing onto Roosevelt Square at the foot of the Chain Bridge and then he had shivered involuntarily when he recognized the nearby Ministry of the Interior building, the red star prominent on its top floor, an imposing fortress-like structure that had once housed a commercial bank. It was reminder enough that, while he wanted to let Eva sleep, he couldn't ignore the danger now confronting them and it was time for them to discuss the future, time to face what had to be done.

He leaned over and kissed her lightly on her neck and ran his finger gently down her spine, marveling at the beauty of its shape and the whiteness of her skin. It was strange that she moved him so, for he had slept with many other women and had never felt such a deep yearning for physical and emotional connection.

She rolled over, slowly opened her eyes, and smiled when she saw his face. "Do you want me again?" she asked in Hungarian.

"I do, but perhaps later," he said in English. "We must talk."

"You're too serious, Maxim." She switched to English without hesitation, and he smiled—she shared his facility with languages and they enjoyed the game of changing from language to language depending on the circumstances.

"It's time for you to talk to Hans Reisinger," he said.

She sat up in bed, clearly alarmed, instinctively drawing the sheet around her to cover her breasts, a sudden touch of modesty that he found endearing considering that they had been wrapped in each other's arms in the throes of passion only a short time before. "Have you heard something?"

"The Center wants me to return early in November," he said. "I'm told that it is for consultations."

"Consultations? What does that mean?"

"I don't know," he said. "Durov's the only one who could tell me the truth, and Mikhail is much too careful to say anything to me over the telephone. Even when I'm with him in Moscow, he won't speak frankly unless we're outside. He's wary of hidden microphones."

"You're worried."

"Yes, I'm worried. There's always a risk when I visit there."

Perhaps there was nothing sinister behind his recall. It might be a routine review of far-flung KGB personnel ordered by the Dzerzhinsky Square bureaucracy. Then again, it could be something else: would he be accused of wrongdoing, imprisoned, tortured, forced to confess to imaginary crimes? Would he be sentenced to hard labor in the barren reaches of Kolmya? Or quickly executed? He had heard that things had changed somewhat since Stalin's death—that some of the legal niceties were observed—but he had no interest in testing whether the "new face" of Soviet justice was humane and fair.

"You've done nothing wrong," she said.

He shrugged. "Who knows? If it has been decided that I'm a subversive or an enemy of the state...."

"Is there something you're not telling me?"

"Durov's silence worries me. Mikhail has been my protector. That's what concerns me. Has he lost favor? Because of my background, it would be easy for any of the hardliners to pin something on me. I believe that we must leave, now, while we have the chance."

"So it is time to talk to Reisinger? Once we do that, there's no turning back." She left the bed and began to dress, quickly hooking up her brassiere, stepping into her underwear, and then wriggling into her dress. Watching her made him desire her again, but, he thought ruefully, there would be no more lovemaking that afternoon.

"I'm well aware of that," he said. "I wouldn't take this step unless I was convinced that we have no other choice. The risk for me in Moscow is greater than the risk of leaving."

"Of defecting," she said. "Not just leaving. Defecting."

"You will be a defector, Eva. I will be a redefector, if that's even a word."

As they sat side-by-side on his bed, he quietly reviewed how she was to approach Reisinger in the dining room of the Hotel Astoria when he stopped for morning coffee and pastries, as was his habit. Once she was sure that he was alone, she should smile at him and make eye contact and then walk directly over to his table and sit down. She should flirt, playing with her hair and smiling at him as they talked so it would look to anyone watching that it was a romantic assignation.

She listened to him intently, asking him once or twice to repeat what he had said.

"Voros believes that you've been instructed to seduce Reisinger," he said. "To compromise him. So your meeting him at the Astoria should not raise suspicions."

"I'm to seduce him? He's an old man. Ancient." She grimaced in mock disgust.

"In your eyes, perhaps, he's ancient but he is a man and the lure of a pretty woman has worked quite handsomely with others. Voros understands this. It's an old trick."

"At least Reisinger knows me," she said.

"After you make some small talk at the table, invite him to take a stroll toward the National Museum. Tell him that you have something of importance to discuss, but you can't talk about it in the hotel. If he won't take the walk with you, then you must smile and say you must have made a mistake and get up from the table and leave. If he agrees to come with you, you must wait until you are alone at least a block from the hotel before you deliver my message."

He had her repeat what she was to say to the Swiss diplomat, making sure that she employed the correct turn of phrase in German. He told her that Reisinger had to understand that he should communicate directly with only one individual about the situation, Allen Dulles of the Central Intelligence Agency in Washington. Reisinger knew Dulles from the war years in Switzerland, when the American had run the OSS operation out of Berne.

"Only Dulles. Reisinger must not inform anyone in his own government. Under no circumstances should anyone in the American legation in Budapest be alerted. And should Dulles accept my offer, then he must send Dennis Collins here to bring me out. Collins must come or there is no deal. Make sure that Reisinger understands these conditions."

"Are you certain about this?"

"I'm certain. I'm staking our lives on it. I've thought about it a thousand times and this is the only way. I trust Denny. If he comes, then I'll know that Dulles understands and that everything is on the level."

"Does Dennis Collins work for them?"

"For the CIA? Lord, no. He's a newspaperman." He paused, reflecting. "My oldest friend in the world."

"You've never spoken about him before."

He gave her a forced smile. "He was part of a life that I was sure that I had left behind. I need him now."

"He is from New York?"

"From Brooklyn, like me. It's right across the East River from Manhattan, just like Buda is across the Danube from Pest. Except there are no hills. You'll see soon enough. You'll like New York, it's a wonderful city. I wish we could live there, but I don't think they'll let us. Too dangerous. Too easy for the Russians to find us."

"Where will we live then?"

"Someplace out of the way. It's a very big country. They'll help us start over in a new place. New identities. A new job for me. Someplace where they can protect us."

"We'll be together."

"We will." He took her hands in his, hoping to reassure her. "Tell Reisinger that I must have an answer back from Dulles within two weeks. If it is 'yes,' then they send Denny here and it must be before the end of October. I'm expected in Moscow the first Monday in November."

"How should he let us know?"

"If they agree to my terms, Reisinger should telephone you and inquire if you're available to interpret for a businessman from Zurich on a commercial mission to Budapest. Reisinger can give you the details when you go to the Swiss legation. If he doesn't call, we'll know the answer is 'no.'"

"I worry that someone in the Interior Ministry will learn about Reisinger's message to Washington. You have enemies, Maxim. Laszlo Kosa, for one. He knows that you're protected by Durov, for now, but he just waits for the day when he can move against you. He hates you."

"Kosa hates me because he's in love with you. Jealousy is a very powerful force, Eva. Some even say it trumps love."

"I don't deny that," she said. "It makes him a very dangerous man."

"All the more reason to get out of Dodge," he said.

"What does that mean? I don't understand."

"It means that we need to leave now, before Kosa comes up with something on me, or my luck runs out with Moscow Center."

"It will be very dangerous," she said. "With Laszlo watching you like a hawk, a *solyom*."

"I'll have a way to distract him when it becomes necessary."

"There's not much time."

"True, but there's enough, just enough."

She looked over at the clock on the bed-table and pulled her hands away from his. "And I have just enough time to get to my aunt's place for Sunday dinner. Are you sure you can't come?"

He shook his head. He was in no mood for company.

She kissed him on the lips, fiercely. "I love you," she said. "That will abide."

He smiled at her stilted English (he hadn't heard the word "abide" spoken in years) and kissed her in return, gently. "Take care when you approach Reisinger. Nothing sensitive said until you're on Museum Boulevard. You must be very careful, my love."

* * *

He lived well, as befitted a colonel in the KGB stationed in the capital city of the People's Republic of Hungary, a loyal satellite of the Soviet state. He chose Castle Hill for his residence because it gave him some privacy—or at least the illusion of it—after he finished work. He wanted to live at a distance from his colleagues. Most of the Soviet advisors found flats in Pest, near the embassy on Bajza Street, or around Lovolde Square, and the Hungarian party leaders preferred villas on the Hill of Roses in Buda.

He went into the small room he used as a study. He wondered what in his library could be used against him if things went bad. He had plenty of "subversive material" in the room—a few copies of the Paris edition of the *New York Herald Tribune* from the week the Dodgers won the World Series in 1955, some books of poetry by William Blake and Pablo Neruda, a copy of Khrushchev's secret speech in front of the 20th Party Congress.

And then there were his copies of Edward Everett Hale's *The Man Without a Country* and George Orwell's *Nineteen Eighty-Four* which he kept in the locked bottom left drawer of his desk. They were the most damaging books he possessed—subversive, dangerous.

The Man Without a Country told the story of a young U.S. Army officer, Philip Nolan, convicted of treason for joining Aaron Burr's scheme to carve out an empire in the West in the early nineteenth century. Nolan then bitterly renounced his country and had been sentenced to a lifelong exile at sea, with all news about the United States to be kept from him. Nolan came to regret his actions, making his cabin a shrine to his country complete with a portrait of George Washington and an American flag. His self-composed epitaph read: "*He loved his country as no other man has loved her; but no man deserved less at her hands.*"

The brief story was overly sentimental, embarrassing in its unabashed nineteenth century patriotism, but Maxim nonetheless found himself constantly re-reading it that fall. Why would he keep the slim leather volume unless he was questioning his transformation from Morris Rose to Maxim Rusakov? Why would he have Orwell's brilliant and telling attack on totalitarian regimes, an indictment of Stalinism, unless he had become disillusioned?

He had some feeble excuses for possessing the books. His job required staying current with happenings in the West—because he was tasked with collecting intelligence from the European diplomats in Budapest—but that wouldn't convince his interrogators. He knew that he should burn the books in his fireplace, but somehow he couldn't bring himself to destroy them, no matter how incriminating they were.

He could point to some successes from his time in Budapest. A French chargé d'affaires who traded sensitive information for a stack of forints to feed his monthly gambling habit; the Swedish political attaché who became indiscreet after too many glasses of palinka, the high-proof local fruit brandy; the Italian cipher clerk, a fervent Communist, who passed his legation's cable traffic to Maxim as a matter of conviction. According to Durov, Moscow Center greatly valued the intelligence that Maxim had funneled to Dzerzhinsky Square.

There were practical limits to his effectiveness. He could not approach the British or the Americans, of course. They shunned him, cut him dead. They refused to acknowledge him at diplomatic receptions, they crossed the street to avoid him, deliberately snubbing him. He understood it, of course. How else would you treat a man regarded as a traitor to his country? He shrugged off their disdain. Soon it wouldn't matter.

In a sense he *had* become a man without a country. He had to consider himself, for the moment, as a citizen of the world. That was going to change. He was going to become an American again. He knew that he would return to a completely different life. Many of his past friends would reject him; certainly his colleagues at State would, if he was allowed to have contact with them, which he doubted.

Maxim opened his copy of *The Man Without a Country* and found his bookmark, a treasured photo from the past. In the snapshot, he stood next to Dennis Collins and his father in the stands at Ebbets Field during the 1947 World Series. The three of them were relaxed, smiling, enjoying the late afternoon sun and the Dodgers' win over the Yankees in a series that the Bronx Bombers would eventually win in seven games.

Dennis had been his closest friend growing up in Brooklyn. They had both wanted more: for Dennis it meant plunging into the New York newspaper world after high school; for Maxim it had been Columbia and then law school followed by a career in the State Department. They had kept in touch over the years, always able to reconnect quickly, a friendship interrupted but never broken. Until 1949.

He didn't expect Dennis or anyone else to forgive and forget what he had done. He knew that he would be starting over without friends or family. But he had Eva and they were in love. He could see having children with her and they could fashion a good life together, a quiet life. He had sacrificed so much for a cause he no longer believed in and now, nearing forty years of age, he wanted to make up for lost time. He figured that if he delivered, the Agency would take care of him. Perhaps he could teach in a small college somewhere. He liked that idea.

He was confident that his plan would work. He had thought it through, forwards and backwards, and he had made the best preparations that he could.

He opened the top drawer to his desk and stared at the Makarov revolver and the pill box he kept there. He had decided that under no circumstances would he risk an interrogation—something he had not told Eva.

Now that they were approaching Reisinger, he would reserve one sodium cyanide tablet from the pillbox to carry in his wallet. Another he would secrete in a hollow pocket in the heel of his right shoe. If he was found out, he knew they would break him and that he would betray anyone with whom he had the slimmest connection. He would betray even Eva. Orwell understood—in the end didn't Winston Smith turn on his beloved when faced with the terror of Room 101? *"Do it to Julia!"*

It would never be like that for him. No softening up in the basement torture chambers that the AVO had inherited from the Arrow Cross at No. 60 Andrassy Avenue, no isolation cell at the Fo

Street prison, no one-way trip to Dzerzhinsky Square and Moscow Center. He promised himself that he would keep that final freedom—of deciding the day and time of his death—and never relinquish it, no matter the cost.

One

There was something vaguely familiar about the man's face, but at first Dennis Collins could not recall where or when he had met him. It was an occupational hazard of newspaper work. How many thousands of people had he met over the years? There had been too many routine interviews, too many casual meetings, too many encounters with contacts and sources in smoky bars and crowded restaurants. Collins had once foolishly prided himself on his memory for names and faces, but as he got older he found it harder and harder to connect the two.

Then, suddenly and unexpectedly, he remembered who the man was. They had met in Key West, just days after the 1952 presidential election, and Collins had spent a sunny November afternoon with the man, relating a strange story about a British spy ring in Washington and the CIA official, Matthew Steele, who had been determined to expose it.

The name of the man who had come to see him in Florida was Wittingham, Collins remembered, Cliff Wittingham. He had been an employee of Steele's Agency and a sometime diplomat, or at least that was what they wanted the world to believe.

Collins wondered what Wittingham was doing in the elegant, baroque dining room of the Hotel Bristol with its dark panels and elaborate chandeliers, and he figured it was one of those bizarre coincidences in life, one he would marvel about later with Maria: *You'll never believe who I ran into when I was in Vienna. The CIA man who came to Key West to interview me about Matthew. The arrogant one*

*you didn't care for. The man who promised they would never bother us
again once I had been fully debriefed.*

Then he saw the other man trailing slightly behind Wittingham,
a tall, handsome man in his mid-thirties with high Slavic cheekbones
and intense eyes, and Collins recognized him immediately as a British
counterintelligence official, a man named Feliks Hawes. Collins
realized then, with a sinking feeling, that the men were there with a
purpose and that it most likely involved him.

He rose to his feet as they approached his table. Wittingham
nodded to him, as if their meeting was the most natural thing in the
world, and reached out with his right hand. Collins reluctantly shook
hands with him, and then with Hawes. They sat down at the table,
silently, and faced each other.

"I caught your profile of Don Larsen in the *Washington Star* the
day after he pitched the perfect game," Wittingham began. "Larsen,
the good times guy from sunny California, an unlikely hero. A nice
angle. I liked it."

"Thank you," Collins said warily. "It was an entertaining Series,
even if the Dodgers lost."

"Norris Jennings tells me that you're here writing a feature on
the Vienna State Opera. The rebirth of free Vienna a year after the
departure of the last Soviet troops."

"That's the assignment," Collins said. Jennings, his editor at the
North American Newspaper Alliance, must have told Wittingham
where to find Collins. That made Collins uneasy, to say the least. He
raised his hand slightly, bringing the waiter, trained to be quickly
attentive, to the table. They waited while he poured coffee for
Wittingham and Hawes.

Collins turned to Wittingham after the waiter had left. "But
you're not stopping by to talk baseball or hear about the Opera."

"We're not. I'm here on behalf of Mr. Dulles. He would have
come to see you himself if he could, but that wouldn't be practical.
Since I'm the only other person in the organization who knows you

personally, they sent me." He turned to acknowledge Hawes. "And you're familiar with Feliks, I believe. He has volunteered to help out."

"I am," Collins said and then addressed the Englishman directly. "We met in London in the spring of 1951. The Britannia Pub, near the Kensington High Road, if I recall correctly."

"That's correct," Hawes said. "You were with Matthew Steele, hot on the trail of Kim Philby and Anatoli Yatov. Steele seemed close to rolling them up. A shame that didn't work out. It was sickening last year when our Foreign Secretary publicly exonerated Philby. They find it too embarrassing to admit that a Soviet spy was in line to run MI6. Then Philby called a press conference to say he wasn't the Third Man. The smug bastard enjoyed rubbing it in. Some long faces in my shop that day, let me tell you. Even longer when Maclean and Burgess showed up in Moscow this past winter and held their press conference."

"Still no sign of Yatov?" Collins asked.

"None," Hawes said. "No sightings in Europe."

"Nor in the U.S.," Wittingham added. "You'd think we'd pick up some scraps about him. He was the KGB's top covert agent in Washington."

Collins shrugged. "Perhaps Yatov retired to a dacha somewhere in the Russian countryside, and he's drinking vodka and eating caviar as we speak."

"Not bloody likely," Hawes said. "I'd wager he's in an unmarked grave, caught on the wrong side of one of their purges."

Collins considered the idea for a moment. "Hope springs eternal." He paused. "I doubt you're here to talk to me about Anatoli Yatov."

"Yes and no," Wittingham said. "It's one of his star recruits we're here about. Morris Rose."

"I haven't heard that name in years," Collins said. "I'd be just as happy not to hear it ever again."

"He was your friend, though," Hawes said.

Collins didn't respond. He didn't want to talk about Morris Rose. That was a closed chapter of his life as far as he was concerned.

"Rose was your closest friend once," Wittingham said. "That should count for something. And you see, we need your help."

* * *

October had been too good a month, he thought, and he should have known better—something had to go wrong. Maria kidded him about his dark Irish fatalism, but Collins had never trusted life when all went smoothly. So, in a way, the unwelcome appearance of Wittingham and Hawes didn't come as a complete surprise. It was the wrong turn he always half-expected.

He had spent the beginning of October in New York covering the World Series, writing feature stories about the stars of the Dodgers and the Yankees. It had been a marvelous seven-game series even if the Bronx Bombers had won. In the fifth game, Don Larsen had pitched the first perfect game in World Series history and Collins had written a profile of the lanky pitcher that had been picked up and carried by newspapers across the country.

Then Norris Jennings had called and offered Collins a lucrative assignment, to fly to Vienna and write about the city's rebuilt Opera House, and how its success symbolized Austria's emergence as a free, neutral country in the year since the Allied occupation ended. The Vienna State Opera had reopened on November 5th, 1955 and Jennings wanted Collins to finish the feature story in time to mark the anniversary.

Collins took the assignment. He had come a long way since he lost his newspaper column when the *New York Sentinel* folded in December 1950. He had pieced together a decent living by writing for the Newspaper Alliance, *Colliers*, and a few other magazines. Unless the money was good, he tried to avoid foreign assignments.

It meant being away from Maria and his sons and he fought homesickness whenever he was overseas for any appreciable period of time, missing his family and the distinctive, familiar sights and sounds of New York, the vivid green infield grass at Ebbets Field, the smell of roasted chestnuts near Central Park in the fall, the sight of the Chrysler Building and the Empire State glittering in the sun, the jostling, happy crowds that filled midtown on warm summer days.

After a week in Austria, he was more than ready to return to New York. He had finished his story and had filed it via telex with the London office of the Alliance earlier in the day. There was nothing keeping him in Vienna. He wanted to head out to Schwechat Airport on Tuesday and board his scheduled flight, knowing that, after a stop in London, he would be back home on Wednesday.

* * *

Wittingham carefully placed his cup onto its delicate saucer and leaned forward, lowering his voice. "I know that you and Morris Rose parted on less than ideal terms," he said. "So I understand that this discussion may be somewhat unwelcome."

"Somewhat? I'd say so." Collins was fully on guard now, even more wary of Wittingham and his reasons for approaching him. He hadn't warmed to the man when they met in Key West years ago, and he had no reason to trust him now. "What's happening with Rose? I assume you're telling me about him for a reason."

"He's been stationed in Budapest for the past few years or so," Hawes said. "Acting as one of the KGB liaisons to Hungarian State Security. He goes by the name of Maxim Rusakov now."

"I see," Collins said. "So what's caught your attention now?"

The men exchanged glances and then Wittingham spoke. "Last month Rusakov—Rose—had an associate make contact with a Swiss diplomat in Budapest. She made it clear that Rose had information of value and that he was willing to share it if we could help him return to the West."

It didn't make sense to Collins. "Why a Swiss diplomat? Why not come to us? We have a legation in Budapest, don't we?"

"It's a matter of trust," Wittingham said. "Rose apparently doesn't trust anyone from the legation. He insisted that his offer be communicated directly to Allen Dulles in Washington by this Swiss fellow, Hans Reisinger. A personal friend of Dulles, from the war. We think Rose researched the relationship and knew that. Reisinger dutifully passed the message to Dulles. Flew to Washington for a face-to-face meeting. Nothing in writing."

"It sounds like Morris," Collins said. "He's hedging his bets. Trouble in the Workers' Paradise? Maybe he's fallen out of favor with Moscow Center. I assume that Dulles told the Swiss that Rose was out of luck. No sale."

Wittingham took a long sip of his coffee. "Actually, Washington was intrigued by his offer."

"Are you kidding?" Collins asked. "Seven years later the bastard decides that he has made a mistake? He wants to waltz back to the safety of the West. Why would you ever reward him after what he's done?"

"We think he could provide very valuable and credible information about the workings of Moscow Center. Office politics. Their tradecraft. Names of any diplomats they've turned in Hungary and Poland. Leads on any cells in the U.S. The man can give us a detailed picture."

"If it was my call, I'd let him rot."

"Sometimes you have to hold your nose in this business," Wittingham said. "I don't deny it stinks."

"So why are you talking to me?" Collins asked. "If you want the bastard, I'm sure you have the means to get him out of Hungary."

Wittingham shook his head. "No, it's not that simple. Rose won't come in unless someone he trusts is there from the first contact. Matthew Steele might have been an acceptable option, but that's no longer possible, for obvious reasons. That leaves you. Unless you're involved, he won't play."

Collins looked across the table at Wittingham, trying to keep his anger in check. "He has balls, I'll grant him that, but he's in for a huge disappointment. Morris Rose is the last man in the world I'd lift a finger to help. What else did he ask for in exchange for his information? A date with Marilyn Monroe? A seat on the Supreme Court?"

Wittingham hesitated for a moment. "We've agreed not to prosecute him for any crimes he may have committed in the United States. After we've debriefed him, we'll help him in establishing a new life."

"A new life?" Collins snorted in disgust. "What does that mean?"

"He'll be given a new identity and assistance in settling somewhere out of the way. We'll find him a job, doing something that won't attract attention. Moscow Center will move heaven and earth to find him, and we don't want that to happen."

"They'll be eager to liquidate him," Hawes said. He had been listening intently. "Quite eager. They have an entire group dedicated to that sort of thing. Department Thirteen."

Wittingham grimaced. "Yes, that's typically how they handle traitors."

"While we resettle them and protect them," Collins said.

"Hard feelings, still?" Hawes asked.

"Hell, yes."

Wittingham again lowered his voice. "All we ask is for you to travel to Budapest, show your face, walk Morris Rose in for us, and be done with it. You don't have to do anything more." He paused. "Here's another way to look at this. Maybe Rose has realized the true nature of the Communist system. He wouldn't be the first to experience an epiphany. Khrushchev's speech changed a lot of minds."

It had been eight months since Nikita Khrushchev's denunciation of Joseph Stalin's crimes before the 20th Communist

Party Congress in Moscow. Collins had read recently that disillusioned comrades had continued to desert the European and American Communist parties in droves, not that there were many card-carrying Communists left in the U.S.

"I don't buy it. Morris does what's best for Morris."

"His motives are immaterial, in one sense," Wittingham replied. "We need him out, as soon as possible. This operation should be very simple, very clean. We've established a cover story for you. You'll visit Budapest as part of a newspaper feature that you're researching about the wonderful work of our diplomats overseas. Our press attaché there has already alerted the local authorities that you're coming. Norris Jennings has been briefed, and he's ready to back up the story."

"That's pretty damn presumptuous of you. I haven't agreed to anything." Collins wasn't surprised that Jennings would cooperate—Matthew Steele had introduced him to Jennings so he knew there might be some Agency connection. But Collins had never been approached to do anything other than write travel and sports features for the Newspaper Alliance.

"Why do you think Jennings asked you to write a feature about Vienna's Opera? On short notice?" Wittingham seemed amused at Collins' obvious discomfort. "You're here because we asked for you to be here."

"Even if I were willing to do this, it would take weeks for a visa."

"That's taken care of," Wittingham said. "We've expedited the paperwork. A letter from Jennings and an encouraging word from our embassy here. The Hungarians were receptive, in the spirit of Geneva, easing of tensions, that sort of thing. Feliks stopped by the Hungarian legation on Bankgasse Street this morning and picked up your visas."

"It doesn't change anything. I'm not willing to help Morris Rose."

"We have a very small window in which to pull this off. Rose has been recalled to Moscow. He's worried that it's a one-way ticket.

We need to get him out now. Believe me, we would never have approached you if it were our choice. Rose is calling the shots, though, and he insisted that you be there."

"He can insist until hell freezes over. I'm not going to help him."

"Then do it because you'll be helping us. Your country."

"They say patriotism is the last refuge of the scoundrel," Collins said. "I don't see helping Morris Rose as my patriotic duty."

"See it in more mercenary terms, then," Wittingham said. "We'd hate to have to inform Jennings that you refused to play ball. I think you're earning the bulk of your income from the Newspaper Alliance. That's so, isn't it?"

"You're going to hold that over my head?" Collins asked, feeling himself flush with anger. "My livelihood? You'd do that?"

"There's no time for your delicate sensibilities," Wittingham said. "I'll use whatever leverage I have. I don't like this any better than you, but I'm not going to let a high-value defector slip through our hands because you get the vapors over some ancient grudge."

Hawes studied his cup and saucer, head down, avoiding Collins' eyes. The Englishman clearly didn't care for Wittingham's tactics. Wittingham stared at Collins, his face composed, unyielding.

"So what's the verdict?" he asked. "Are you willing to help out?"

Collins hesitated before he responded. If he refused outright Wittingham might well follow through on his threat to choke off assignments from the syndicate. That would make things difficult for Collins; at one point after the events of 1949 he had been investigated by the FBI and the Red Squad of the New York Police Department, and even though he was blameless and had done nothing wrong, the question of his "subversive" past would make it hard to land a steady job at one of the newspapers or wire services in New York.

Although it had been two years since Senator McCarthy's censure and witch hunts and blacklists were out of style, publishers and editors could hire plenty of journalists who didn't bring any political baggage—real or imagined—with them. It was expensive to live in New York, and if his income dropped off Collins might have to move Maria and the boys back to Florida, and he didn't want to do that.

He knew that if the American defector with second thoughts had been anyone other than Morris Rose he would have most likely agreed to Wittingham's request. It would have been hard to refuse to help a fellow countryman in a jam. Except that it wasn't a stranger, it was Morris, and that made all the difference.

* * *

The Saturday before his flight to Austria, Collins had surprised Maria by taking her to lunch at the Rainbow Room. His older brother Frank and his sister-in-law Peggy had agreed to babysit the boys at their house.

Lunch had been a chance for unhurried conversation. They talked about how Caleb was doing in school, about Maria's plans to take another course at Brooklyn College in the spring, and about Collins' upcoming trip to Austria. Collins had waited until dessert—coffee with petit fours glacé, one of Maria's favorites—to tell her that there was a room waiting for them at the Plaza Hotel.

"Isn't that pretty lavish for an afternoon?" she asked. "Not that I'm complaining."

"We'll stay the night," he told her. "Dinner and dancing at El Morocco. Frank and Peggy know the drill with the boys. They'll be fine."

"This is all quite a splurge."

"We can afford it," he said. "They're paying me a small fortune for the Vienna story."

They spent the rest of the afternoon in a queen-sized bed in their hotel room. They hadn't been truly alone for months and they made love slowly, resisting the urge to rush, savoring the pleasure of their naked bodies connecting.

He had made reservations for dinner at El Morocco, and they enjoyed a light supper with champagne before Maria pulled him out on the dance floor. Collins had the waiter take a note to the band leader so he could play "Autumn Leaves," one of Maria's favorites. She kissed him hard on the lips when she heard the song.

"What a wonderful day," she whispered to him during the cab ride back to the Plaza. "Thank you for planning this. It's so romantic."

"I consider myself the world's luckiest man to be married to Maria Sanchez Highsmith," he said. "I want to keep it that way."

She had appeared in his life at a dark time, when he was drinking too much, haunted by the senseless loss of a lover and what he had seen on the battlefields of Korea. Maria made him believe that the universe wasn't completely absurd and that love and grace existed—what else could explain her willingness to accept him despite his past, when marrying him meant raising the child he had fathered with another woman?

In the four years since their wedding at Saint Mary Star of the Sea church on a perfect Key West summer day, they had grown even closer. It had made the somewhat superstitious Collins anxious, afraid that somehow their happiness would be suddenly snatched away. Maria had laughed at him.

She had embraced his son, Caleb, and had lavished warmth and affection upon him. By the time Matthew arrived, Caleb was secure enough to greet his little brother as a welcome playmate and friend.

Maria had encouraged Collins to engineer their move from Florida to New York, recognizing that for him to make a living as a freelance journalist, he needed to be near the magazine and wire service editors who could provide him with work. She loved visiting the museums, catching Dodgers games at Ebbets Field, meeting Collins in the city for lunch or dinner, heading to Shelter Island for a few weeks in the summer and then back to the Keys to see her father at Christmas time. Now with Caleb in school, and Matthew soon to follow, she had started taking courses toward a college degree.

Once back at the Plaza, they hurried to their room and made love again and then, exhausted, fell asleep, Maria's head resting on Collins' chest. They woke up early enough for a light breakfast before heading to Frank's to pick up the boys in time for church.

* * *

Collins realized that Wittingham and Hawes were waiting for him to respond.

"And if it goes wrong?" he asked. "I'm on the other side of the Iron Curtain once I'm in Hungary. What then?"

Wittingham gave him a confident smile. "We know you have family responsibilities, and we wouldn't ask if this was risky. It isn't. Your role is simply to be there, to be the familiar face from back home for Morris Rose. Nothing operational."

"Things go wrong," Collins said flatly. By continuing the discussion, he knew that he was edging closer to agreeing to the mission.

"They can," Wittingham acknowledged. "But even if the Hungarians connected you to an attempt to help Rose redefect, at the worst, they'd boot you out of the country. You'd be persona non grata, and they'd never let you back in. You wouldn't be able to make a living as a travel writer specializing in features on Budapest. Not such a loss."

Collins kept silent. He didn't believe Wittingham that the Hungarians would take it so lightly—they could throw him in prison, subject him to a show trial.

"You'll have Feliks along for company," Wittingham said. "He spent six months in Budapest in 1947 and he speaks passable Magyar, along with his Polish and Russian, so he'll be able to handle any issues with the locals. He's already got rooms booked at the Hotel Duna for the both of you. We're a bit thin on the ground ourselves so we appreciate the help."

Hawes grinned. "I'll say. You chaps have what, two agents in Budapest and only one who speaks Hungarian?"

"All eyes are on Poland at the moment," Wittingham responded, turning back to address Collins. "We're fortunate that our English friends have lent us Feliks."

Collins figured that the Agency had also requested Hawes because of their brief, but shared, history. It made sense. Collins would be more likely to trust men he had met in the past. Of course, the truth was that he barely knew either Wittingham or Hawes, but at Agency headquarters on E Street in Washington they probably reasoned that even a slight relationship was better than nothing.

"How much do you know about the situation in Poland?" Hawes asked Collins.

"Just what I read in the papers. They want more independence from the Soviets."

"And Khrushchev has responded by surrounding Warsaw with Red Army tanks," Wittingham said.

Hawes frowned; he clearly didn't agree. "But we've also heard that Khrushchev is actually negotiating with the Poles, with Gomulka. Apparently they don't want a bloodbath. Both sides want to save face."

"It will end with the mailed fist," Wittingham said. "With the Soviets that's second nature. They won't stand for not being in charge."

"I'm more optimistic," Hawes said.

"I'd bet you on the outcome, but I don't want to take your money," Wittingham said. He turned to Collins. "It's nothing like that in Hungary. You won't see the Hungarians rioting in the streets of Budapest. The Russians showed them their place in 1945 when they took the city. They smashed it into little pieces."

"No signs of dissent?" Collins asked.

"The writers and intellectuals have this group, the Petofi Circle, and they made a little noise this past summer when they debated free speech in one of their meetings. All talk."

Hawes nodded in agreement. "Their secret police, the AVO, have informers everywhere, and Erno Gero, the new premier, is a hardliner. He won't hesitate to order a crackdown if there's the slightest hint of unrest. The man before him, Rakosi, aped Stalin in the worst of ways. Gero's out of the same mold. The joke in Budapest was that they replaced a bald Rakosi with a thin Rakosi."

"So your worry is State Security, then?" Collins asked. "Don't they watch any visiting foreigners quite closely? How does Rose propose to defect if we're under close surveillance all the time?"

"That's the beauty of it." It was Wittingham, excited by the thought. "Rose is one of the watchers. His job is recruiting foreigners, diplomats, as possible assets. They expect him to have contact with visitors."

"So he has an excuse to meet with Westerners. That still won't get him out of the country."

Wittingham gave him a self-satisfied smile. "We have a plan for that. Simple, but we think effective. Hawes has been briefed and you'll have what you need for the extraction."

"I guess you could call it that," Collins said. "I haven't agreed to anything, you know."

Wittingham moved the chair back from the table and rose to his feet; Hawes followed suit.

"I know," Wittingham said. "You should think it over. I'll stop by the hotel's lobby tomorrow morning. Let's say eight o'clock. You can let me know then if you're willing to help out."

"What will you do if I won't help? About Rose?"

"There's always a Plan B," Wittingham said. "But I'm hoping that you'll make it a moot point. Better for all concerned if you do. Much better."

Two

Collins slept poorly. He awoke at dawn, aware that he was in a strange bed in a strange place. His dreams had been troubled, jumbled, confused—he remembered disjointed scenes from the past, troubling images of Karina, snatches of conversation with Morris, and underlying it all, a vague sense of dread and foreboding.

He checked his wristwatch—it was just after six o'clock, which meant it was past midnight in New York. Maria and the boys would be sleeping soundly. Caleb and Matthew shared a bedroom, just like Collins and his brother Frank had done. Once they were tucked in, Maria would have read them a Christopher Robin story from *When We Were Very Young*, a book which both boys had grown to love. After their prayers, she would have kissed them good-night and turned out the lights. Maria would have stayed up to read in bed, and if it had been a long day she might have dozed off with the bedside lamp still on.

Collins found himself thinking about his encounter with Wittingham and Hawes. He resented being pressured to take on a mission that would make him an intelligence agent—a spy—in the eyes of the Hungarian regime. His family depended on him, and Wittingham knew that. If something went wrong Wittingham and his Agency couldn't guarantee Collins his safety no matter what pious assurances they gave him now.

Wittingham clearly didn't care, even though he knew that Collins had very good reasons to detest Morris Rose for what had happened in New York in 1949. Morris could have warned Collins about the sniper waiting for them at the rendezvous point, a sniper who would kill Collins' lover, Karina Lazda, a sniper controlled by Anatoli Yatov. But he didn't. To ask Collins to help Morris in any way was asking too much.

But there wasn't anything Collins could do about it. If he wanted to keep his Newspaper Alliance assignments coming, he would need to cooperate with Wittingham and go to Budapest. Collins wouldn't waste his time appealing to Allen Dulles—Dulles no doubt would countenance Wittingham's pressure tactics if they were needed to persuade Collins. The mission came first.

At the same time, Collins had to concede that the risks involved were probably as Wittingham described, manageable, acceptable. Hawes, an experienced intelligence operative, would take the lead and Collins was, in a sense, just along for the ride—he was there to demonstrate to Morris that the Agency was acting in good faith, that it was safe to trust whatever promises had been made to him.

In the end, Collins might have an anxious day or two, but it would be worth the trouble if it kept him in the immediate good graces of Norris Jennings. He hated his vulnerability, his loss of independence, but he needed the money. He promised himself that when he returned to New York he would immediately pursue other freelance jobs. He wanted never again to be so dependent on one employer.

* * *

After a hasty breakfast, Collins composed two telegrams. The first was to Maria, alerting her about his delayed return to the United States. He labored over what exactly to say. He didn't want to alarm her, but he couldn't very well explain the actual reasons for the delay in a telegram (nor in an international phone call, which might not occur over a secure line), so he decided to stick to the cover story.

He kept his message as neutral as possible: DELAYED. STORY NOW BUDAPEST. STAY HOTEL DUNA. RETURN US 10/26. LOVE TO ALL. D.

Yet Maria would immediately understand the risk he would be taking by entering Hungary, even with his press credentials and a valid visa, because of his past connection with the CIA, no matter how involuntary much of that involvement had been. As the daughter of a Marine major, she would not complain or second guess his decision. That didn't mean she would be happy about it, because she wouldn't be.

Then he wrote out the telegram to Norris Jennings at the Alliance office in New York. Collins figured that his message would come as no surprise. He kept it brief—which he knew his penny-pinching editor would appreciate: DIPLO STORY BUDAPEST NEXT. HOTEL DUNA. RETURN US 10/26. COLLINS.

He gave the telegrams to the Hotel Bristol concierge and added a very large tip above the estimated per-word charges. He thought about scheduling a telephone call to Maria through the hotel operator but decided against it. It would only alarm her because she would hear the tension in his voice and know that something was up. He could tell her the entire story later, once he was back home.

He waited for Wittingham in a comfortable leather chair in the lobby. At a minute before eight o'clock Wittingham appeared, striding purposefully into the hotel—a man with the easy confidence of a card player with a winning hand, Collins thought bitterly—before sitting down in the chair opposite Collins. He wore a gray Brooks Brother suit and club tie, and his black dress shoes were polished to a high sheen.

Wittingham glanced around to make sure they were alone and then got straight to the point. "So what's the verdict? Are you in?"

Collins wasn't about to answer him directly. "The last time I saw you, in Key West, you explicitly promised me that the Agency would never darken my doorstep again. You're breaking that promise."

"This isn't coming from us," Wittingham said. "It's your buddy who specifically asked for you. It's his condition."

"He's not my buddy. But he isn't the only one with conditions. I have some. I'll want a thousand dollars a day for my time."

"Done," Wittingham said.

"The money doesn't go to me. You'll pay it to the International Rescue Committee in New York—a donation in the name of Karina Lazda. And once I'm done with this business, my second condition is that you'll inform Rose about the donation and explain that I made it a nonnegotiable condition for my involvement. I'll need written confirmation from you that you've made the donation and that Rose has been informed of it."

Wittingham nodded. "I'll agree to both of those conditions. Anything else?"

"Threatening me through my work was low. Shitty. I won't forget it."

"I did what I had to do," Wittingham said. "No apologies for that. Now we must move quickly. Hawes will meet you at the Westbahnhof for the 9:30 train for Budapest. There's enough time for you to pack a bag and get over there. No need to check out here—you should be back in a day or two."

"And if we need to reach you from Budapest?"

"You can't use the phone for anything sensitive. In an emergency, send a cable to me care of Colonel de Silva at the Vienna embassy. Approach our Budapest station chief, Gaza Katona, to have the cable coded and transmitted. He's the political attaché."

"Will you alert him in advance about us?"

"No, but Katona will recognize my name. Use him only if it's an emergency—we want to keep knowledge of this operation to as few people as possible. Is that clear?"

"It's clear."

"Rose's code name is 'Pilgrim,' by the way. If you should send a cable, use that to refer to him."

"You people love your cloak-and-dagger, don't you? Code names and ciphers."

"They work," Wittingham said. "The idea is to keep our adversaries in the dark about Rose and his intention to defect. We'll succeed in that if we protect his identity. So 'Pilgrim' it is."

Wittingham reached into his inside coat jacket pocket and handed Collins a small paperback book with an envelope tucked inside the front cover. "An English guide book to Budapest. Slightly out-of-date, but it should help orient you. There's pocket cash in the envelope. The equivalent of fifty dollars in forints."

Collins opened the envelope and glanced at the unfamiliar currency inside. "I don't plan on being in Budapest long enough to spend this," he said.

"That would be dandy, wouldn't it?" Wittingham's thin smile only reminded Collins of how much he had grown to dislike the man.

* * *

Collins found Feliks Hawes waiting for him in the departure hall of the Westbahnhof station. They took seats in the far corner of the station café away from the other patrons and drank strong coffee sweetened with sugar.

Collins found Hawes likeable. He had been impressed with him when they had first met in London in 1951. The son of a Polish father and an English mother, Hawes had been educated at Cambridge before serving in Britain's special forces. After the war, he had been recruited by MI5 to help watch Eastern bloc diplomats in London and was occasionally asked to work in Europe. Matthew Steele had considered Hawes a tough and reliable intelligence officer, and that assessment was enough for Collins to trust in his professionalism.

"I have your ticket," Hawes said. He glanced over at Collins' one battered canvas bag and portable typewriter case. "You're traveling light."

"I learned that as a combat correspondent," Collins said. "You take only the essentials. As little weight as possible. I'm used to it."

"We'll be in and out as fast as we can," Hawes said. "By the way, my passport identifies me as Felix Winters. That's Felix with an 'x.' I'm your photographer, hired by your newspaper syndicate for this project. How long have you been working for them?"

"Since 1952," Collins said. "I contributed some travel pieces about the Caribbean, and then they started giving me other assignments."

"Spent much time with their London office? Do you know Ivar Bryce or Ian Fleming?"

"Met Fleming a few times before he sold his piece of the firm. Isn't he writing spy novels now?"

"That he is." Hawes grinned. "I tried the first one. His hero is quite romantic in a Scarlet Pimpernel sort of way. That sells books, I imagine, but it's more than a bit removed from the prosaic reality of intelligence work."

Collins decided to ask Hawes the question that had been bothering him since their meeting the day before. "Why are they sending you into Hungary when the action is in Poland?"

"Good question. Apparently I'm not deemed objective enough. I don't think Radio Free Europe should be encouraging open resistance against the Soviets by the Poles. There's no future in that. My views have made me somewhat unpopular with your people. "

"I can see that," Collins said. "Our Secretary of State likes to talk about rolling back Communism and liberating the captive nations behind the Iron Curtain."

"That sounds bloody heroic in Washington, I'm sure, but the Polish army killed seventy workers in Poznan during the riots there in June and wounded hundreds. The leaders of the protest got a show trial and harsh sentences. That's why I don't care for the loose talk of liberation. Not when the regime has all the guns and tanks and the workers are unarmed."

Collins loosened his tie and collar. "With our presidential election in two weeks, it's unlikely the Republicans will back off from the rhetoric. Not this close to the end of the campaign."

"Isn't Eisenhower almost guaranteed reelection?"

"It looks that way," Collins said. "But politicians never take anything for granted. They'll keep beating the anti-Communist drums because they know it plays well with the voters." He checked his watch. They still had fifteen minutes before the train departed. "I'm curious, do you actually know anything about photography?"

"I know which is the business end of the camera," Hawes said. "It's where you screw on the lenses. For our purposes I just need to have the camera and equipment with me and to take a few headshot photos of the embassy people. Nothing fancy."

"What's the plan for returning to Vienna? Will we take the train back?"

"That's the idea. Wittingham has sent an American passport and press card for Rose by diplomatic pouch to the legation. We'll need to pick it up there. He travels back to Vienna with us as a colleague. Of course, his visa is forged, but the passport is authentic. It's a simple plan and that's the beauty of it." Hawes explained that Wittingham was playing it safe by using the diplomatic courier—there was no telling whether they might be searched on the way into Hungary, and there would be no convincing explanation for having an additional passport made out to another man in their possession.

"Wittingham must have been fairly confident that I would cooperate if he already had the credentials prepared for Rose."

Hawes shrugged. "There's a deadline, you know. Wittingham has to move fast. Rose needs to be out before the end of this month. The Agency seems to have considerable sway with your syndicate. They issued press credentials for Rose and myself. The three of us will be seen as bourgeois journalists eager to get back to the decadent nightlife of Vienna after a few days in drab Budapest. Quite familiar to the border guards, who secretly pine for a chance to be corrupted by capitalism."

"You seem confident about all this."

"Why shouldn't I be? As extractions go, this one is straightforward. The people you typically worry about—the secret police—are quite wary of offending the Soviets and in their eyes Rose hails from Moscow. Trust me that we'll be drinking Manhattans with Rose at the American Bar just off the Kärntnerstrasse before anyone even realizes that he's missing."

Collins didn't respond. He was certain of one thing—he wouldn't be drinking with Morris Rose when they returned to Vienna. Collins planned to spend as little time with Rose as possible, and he recoiled at the idea of celebrating anything with him.

★ ★ ★

The train trip to Budapest from Vienna proved uneventful. When they crossed into Hungary and stopped at Hegyeshalom, the border officials studied their visas for an uncomfortably long time (or so it seemed to Collins), but they eventually stamped their passports.

Hawes had warned Collins that some of the passengers would likely be Hungarian State Security plants, reporting whatever they overheard, so they kept conversation to a minimum on the train ride.

Collins spent the time reading the *New York Herald Tribune* and glancing through the Budapest guide Wittingham had given him. He occasionally glanced out the train window at the passing farmland. There were bales of hay stacked in squares and the green trees bordering the fields had started to change color to yellow and orange. Some of the fields had been plowed over, leaving stubble and furrows of black earth.

The train stopped once, in Gyor, where Collins gazed out the window at the run-down, dingy railway station and the grimy walls of nearby buildings. He could see a smokestack in the distance—Gyor was known for its manufacture of locomotive engines. He watched as a few passengers boarded the train.

Thirty minutes later the terrain became hillier as they moved closer to Budapest. Collins abandoned his reading and watched through the window as the countryside rushed past until, without any warning, the Danube River and then the outskirts of Budapest came into view. Once in the city, the train pulled into the Keleti, or Eastern, Railway Station. The train platforms were located in a cavernous space under an arched iron-and-glass ceiling that reminded Collins of Penn Station in New York.

Near the front-end of the platform, by the locomotive, a man in a dark blue suit with a bow-tie was holding a small placard that read "D. COLLINS." Collins walked over to him. "Looking for me?" he asked. "I'm Dennis Collins."

"Pleased to meet you," the man said. "I'm Brooks Lawrence, press attaché at the legation. Got the call from your editor this morning with your itinerary, Mr. Collins. We're very pleased you're here. Don't get too many opportunities to tell people about the conditions that we have to work under. Not that I'm complaining, but it never hurts if the public and the powers-that-be in Foggy Bottom have the picture of what we do here painted in vivid colors for them."

Lawrence was a slight man with unruly hair and a slightly puzzled expression. He reminded Collins of the sad-looking comedian Stan Laurel of the Laurel and Hardy act. Collins introduced Hawes to Lawrence as Felix Winters.

"I'm here to welcome you and give you the lay of the land," Lawrence said. He cleared his throat, ready to impart local wisdom. "Assume that you'll be followed from here on by some of the Hungarian State Security people. Those two men in the leather coats by the newsstand have been watching everyone arriving on the train. I'm sure they're taking note of us."

"We are behind the Iron Curtain," Hawes said easily. "Par for the course, correct?" He seemed amused by the young, somewhat foppish American diplomat.

"We are, Mr. Winters. The Gero regime rules the country in classic Stalinist style. A bit of a thaw when Imre Nagy ran the show, but if you ask me, Nagy was just a wolf in sheep's clothing, no different than the rest of the Reds."

"So no signs of unrest like Poland?" Collins asked, curious about Lawrence's views on the subject.

"Absolutely not," he said. "Nothing like that here. The secret police keep a tight grip.

Hawes didn't seem satisfied with the answer. "What about the reburial of Rajk? That seemed to stir things up a bit." He turned to Collins to explain. "Laszlo Rajk was the foreign minister, purged from the government and executed back in '49 for being a Titoist spy. They reburied him early this month at the Keleti cemetery, and his widow gave a bitter speech at the graveside, glaring at the Party functionaries responsible for his death. Thousands turned up for the ceremony. Rajk was brutal in his own right, but his trial was a travesty, and now the regime has admitted it."

Lawrence flushed slightly. "You've done your homework, I see. But it will come to nothing. The Hungarians can be quite dramatic, but they know the limits."

"Even a beaten dog can bite," Hawes said.

"Not this dog," Lawrence said. "Comrade Gero has it tightly on the leash." He turned to Collins. "They have foreigners stay at the Duna so it's easier to watch them. Assume there are listening devices in your rooms and that the hotel staff will report anything they overhear. Any friendly young women who approach you are working on behalf of the secret police."

"So the girls here won't be chasing after me because of my good looks and charm?" Hawes said. "Quite a blow to pride, that."

Lawrence didn't laugh. "We received a package in the diplomatic pouch addressed to you yesterday," he told Collins. "Do you want to come by the legation later today? We can also talk about arranging interviews with the staff."

"We'll stop by after we've checked into the hotel," Collins said.

"I've taken the liberty of arranging a driver to take you there. He'll report everything you say to the authorities." Lawrence sighed. "It does become tiresome. It's like living in a fishbowl."

"I'm afraid we'll prove a major disappointment to their security chaps," Hawes said. "The two of us are hardly imperialist spy material. Collins will get his story, I'll take some snaps, and we'll not darken their doorstep a moment longer than necessary."

Three

They rode from the Eastern Station to the Hotel Duna in an ancient black Ford with a backfiring engine that spewed noxious fumes from its tailpipe. Hawes had greeted the driver, a beetle-browed middle-aged man, in Magyar and had tried to start a conversation with him, but was only able to elicit a few surly grunts from the man.

The Duna, an aging structure located on Apaczai Csere Janos Street, just south of the Chain Bridge, was the only hotel of the string along the once-elegant Danube Promenade that had survived the Second World War. According to the guidebook, it was "a favorite with foreign visitors for its views across the Danube of Castle Hill, topped by the Royal Castle, and of the medieval portion of Buda."

Hawes glanced over at the street sign and shook his head in mock exasperation. "A mouthful of a street name," he said. "Never understood why the Hungarians insist on the last name first, like the Chinese. Janos Apaczai Csere was a mathematician, I believe. Wrote an encyclopedia back in the seventeenth century."

The clerk at the reception desk studied their passports, gave Hawe's camera a quick glance, and asked in heavily-accented English if they were journalists who had come to Budapest because of the student march.

"The march?" Collins asked. "No, haven't heard anything about it."

"This afternoon the students march to the statue of Sandor Petofi in Pest and to the statue of General Bem in Buda to show their support of the Polish people," the man said.

"Good show, that!" Hawes said with enthusiasm. He turned to Collins to explain. "Heroes of the 1848 uprising against the Hapsburgs. Petofi is the Hungarian national poet, and General Bem, a Pole, joined the revolutionaries. The Russians, who were allied with the Austrians, executed Bem along with the other Hungarian generals when they crushed the revolution."

"Not sure we'll have time for the march," Collins said to the desk clerk. "But thanks for informing us."

The man gave him a short nod and rang the bell for the porter. Hawes told Collins that he had arrangements to make at the British embassy and that he would be back in an hour or so. "I need to see about a vehicle and petrol," he said. "We need local transport squared away as soon as possible." He paused for a moment, remembering something. "By the way, Lawrence was correct on one thing. If you stop for a drink at the hotel bar, watch out for the Duna girls. By all accounts they're quite attractive—and our chaps in Vienna tell me the AVO has them cozy up to foreigners visiting Budapest and extract whatever information they can."

"I'm ready for lunch, not for drinks with Mata Hari," Collins said. "And I'm married."

"Mata Hari may have been a spy, but she wasn't actually that exotic, you know. Daughter of a Dutch shopkeeper. Married or not, forewarned is forearmed, as my mother used to say."

"I'll try not to disappoint your mother," Collins said, eliciting a smile from Hawes.

The Englishman called the waiting porter over to take his two leather bags to his room, waved at Collins, and then strode confidently through the lobby and out the revolving front door of the hotel.

As Collins was heading to the lift with his portable Royal typewriter and his canvas bag, he heard his name called aloud. When he turned back, he immediately recognized Lester Kane, a New York-based journalist who also worked for the North American Newspaper Alliance and wrote occasionally for *The Reporter* magazine. An attractive dark-haired woman with a Nikon camera on a strap around her neck was at his side.

"Didn't think the Alliance considered Budapest a hot spot," Kane said. He was a solidly-built man with close-cropped gray hair and hooded eyes. "Never thought they would spring for the two of us to be here at the same time."

"I'd been in Vienna researching a story about the revitalization of the Opera," Collins explained. "Then Jennings thought comparing the conditions for American diplomats in Vienna and Budapest would make a great feature, so here I am."

"The Opera?" Kane smirked. "A feature on diplomats? I could have sworn you were a baseball writer, Collins. Did you get on Jenning's wrong side or something?"

"Not quite. These days I'm a jack-of-all-trades. I'll confess that my German's not very good, but I had an excellent interpreter in Vienna. And Jennings did have me cover the Series a couple of weeks back."

"The Yankees won again, did they not?" the woman asked. She had a French accent and when Collins turned to look at her, he realized that she was quite lovely. Her flawless, lightly tanned skin and dark, slightly Asian eyes suggested to him that she might be Eurasian.

"They did, but the Dodgers took them to seven games," Collins said and introduced himself. Her name was Isabelle Lavalle and she was a photographer for Agence France-Presse. She kept her eyes fixed on his the entire time during their introductions. He decided it was just her way of sizing him up, but it made him slightly uncomfortable, nonetheless.

"Isabelle's got the eye of an artist, Denny," Kane said. "You might have seen her photos of the Algerian guerrilla fighters in *Life*."

"I did," Collins said. "They were quite good." He paused. "I'm working with a photographer, Felix Winters, a Brit, for this story on the diplomats."

"I've not heard of him," Lavalle said, shrugging. "He's not a regular."

"We're about to leave for the rally," Kane said. "The students and the intellectuals seem pretty stirred up about reform. They want Nagy back as prime minister."

"Brooks Lawrence tells me the government has everything under tight control," Collins said.

Kane made a face of disgust. "That figures. I see you've already been exposed to the State Department's propaganda. The right-wingers at the legation like Lawrence lack any imagination. Everything's black-and-white for them. A Communist is a Communist. They won't listen when I tell them that there are some decent Hungarians, Marxists, who support dramatic changes in the system."

"Are you going to the protest?" Lavalle asked Collins.

"Hadn't planned on it," Collins said. "But you're making me curious."

"You should come," she said.

"Perhaps," he said. "I have a few things to do first."

"If we miss you at the rally, we'll catch up with you later," Kane said. "They make a decent martini in the hotel bar. If you like martinis."

"I'm a beer drinker, but I'll be happy to buy the first round."

"Then you'll definitely see me later," Kane said. "As long as you promise to put that round on your expense account and make that skinflint Jennings pay."

* * *

Collins had been given a corner room on the third floor and its panoramic views of the river and the graceful towers of the Chain Bridge almost compensated for its stained floral wallpaper, ancient furniture, and lumpy mattress. He was glad that he would only be there for a night or so.

The large windows in the restaurant of the Hotel Duna also looked out onto the Danube. Collins was surprised by the shabbiness of the dining room with its faded wallpaper, worn carpet, and frayed tablecloths. The waiters were outfitted in dinner jackets that had seen better days.

Collins was the lone diner in the room, except for one table of businessmen from Austria or Germany, judging from their suits and the distinctive sounds of German that he overheard.

He found he was hungrier than he had expected and he ordered sausage lentil soup, the luncheon special. The soup and the freshly-baked bread served with it proved to be excellent, and while he ate, he skimmed through the Budapest guidebook. He had been there only a few minutes when Hawes entered the dining room and hurried over. The Englishman was beaming in triumph when he sat down across from Collins.

"We have a car," he announced. "An Austin Cambridge with Austrian plates, on loan from the commercial attaché. I've parked around the corner from the hotel. And there's excellent news from Warsaw. Khrushchev has agreed to respect the choice of Gomulka as the new First Secretary of the Party. The Red Army is standing down. It's staggering that the Russians have accepted a negotiated resolution. I don't think Gomulka will ever have Tito's freedom of action, but Poland will have some independence—national communism is what the FO chaps in the embassy are calling it."

Hawes called one of the waiters over and ordered tea. "I already had lunch at the legation," he said. He lowered his voice. "The Polish situation may be a bit of unforeseen luck for us. The Hungarian border police should be more relaxed." He leaned back in his chair, stretching his legs out in front of him. "Any word from our man, Mr. Pilgrim? Phone calls to the room? Messages at the front desk?"

"Nothing. I figure it will take some time before word gets to him that I've arrived."

"Any sign of the Duna girls?" Hawes asked. "They told me at the embassy that one of them is a dead ringer for Diana Dors."

"No Diana Dors, or Jane Russell, in sight," Collins said. "Sorry to disappoint. I did run into Lester Kane, a colleague. He also works for the Alliance. Kane says the legation staff is clueless about the situation here. Claims the Hungarians are eager for significant reform, just like the Poles."

Their waiter approached the table hesitantly and, after Collins acknowledged him, handed him a small envelope. Collins thanked him and glanced around to make sure that they were being ignored by the other diners. He carefully opened the envelope. The note read: *Come alone to the Hungaria Cafe at 3 PM. Find a table and wait. M.R.*

"I was wrong," Collins said. "Apparently Pilgrim is aware that I'm here." He handed the note to Hawes, who quickly scanned it and folded it over and placed it on the table in front of them.

"The Hungaria is over on Elizabeth Boulevard, which the Reds renamed after Lenin," Hawes said. "Not too far from here. Best-known restaurant in the city. It attracts the top *apparatchiks* and their young mistresses. It became famous as the New York Cafe in its salad days, but obviously that name wasn't going to last under the Communists."

"Perhaps it's Pilgrim's sense of humor," Collins said. "We're both from New York."

"Apparently he isn't worried about being seen with you in public. Quite cocky."

"I won't complain if he has things well in hand," Collins said. "The less contact with the local authorities, the better."

"Perhaps I should accompany you."

"The note says I should go alone," Collins said.

"I don't like it. It puts you in a vulnerable position."

"He's just being careful. It makes sense, considering the situation. Reduce the pieces on the chess board. Keep it simple. No strangers. He knows exactly what he's doing."

"Does he? You're more confident than I am."

"I'll chance it," Collins said. "I know him. I told you that he calculates the odds before he makes a move. This will be as safe as having a cup of coffee and a piece of apple pie with him at the Horn & Hardart in Times Square."

"Don't know Horn & Hardart," Hawes said. "A restaurant in New York?"

"They're called automats, and they display the food behind small glass windows along the wall of the restaurant. You put coins in a slot and turn a knob and the window slides up and you can get your food."

"On the level?"

"On the level. Next time you're in New York, I'll take you to lunch at one. My treat."

Hawes laughed. "Thanks. I almost can't wait." He paused, a serious look returning to his face. "We'll drive over together. While you're meeting our eager Pilgrim, I'll be nearby, taking a stroll in the neighborhood."

"Suit yourself," Collins said. "As long as you stay out of sight."

★ ★ ★

The Hungaria wasn't quite what Collins expected. On the ground floor of a baroque structure topped by a spire, the cafe was lavishly decorated in an eclectic style. When Collins saw the gilded columns, golden stucco work, ornate chandeliers and faded ceiling frescoes, he wondered how such conspicuous opulence had survived after the Communist takeover. It certainly didn't fit the classless society envisioned by Marxist purists.

The maitre d' escorted him to a table in the center of the room and Collins took his seat, glancing over at the statues of fauns that decorated the windows of the cafe, and at the few scattered patrons.

A surly waiter stared at Collins blankly when he ordered an espresso, and then disappeared through a side door. It was a good five minutes before the man returned with a cup and saucer, which he deposited on the marble table top. Collins glanced at his watch and saw that it was 3:05. The always punctual Morris Rose was late, a bad sign.

A woman slid into the chair opposite him. "Dennis Collins," she said. It was a statement. Under a gray beret, her curly, dark hair fell in ringlets around a narrow face. He guessed her age at thirty.

He nodded in acknowledgment. "Where's Morris?" he asked, blurting out the first thing that came to mind. He immediately regretted it—for all he knew, this woman could be a plant, an agent of State Security.

"No names, please. It was not prudent for him to come here today, so I'm here on his behalf." She spoke with a slight accent, but her English was fluent.

"How can I trust that?"

"He said to tell you that he hopes you have taken good care of Babe Herman."

Collins nodded again, satisfied that she had been sent by Morris. After his defection, Morris had mailed his prized Babe Herman baseball card to Collins in New York. It was an inside joke that only the two of them would appreciate; Herman had been a Dodgers slugger and one of Collins' boyhood heroes. The card now sat in Collins' safety deposit box in the Brooklyn Savings Bank.

"What about the police?" Collins asked. "Are we being watched now?"

"They're preoccupied today with the student march. Not a man to spare, so we should escape notice." She looked around the cafe. "I would like some coffee." She waved at one of the waiters, and when he came to the table spoke to him in rapid Hungarian.

"We love our *fekete leves*, our black soup, in Budapest," she said after the waiter had left. "The Party leaders come here for that, and for the food. Sometimes you'll even see Imre Nagy, our former premier, but he's more often at Gerbeaud's to talk football and bring his grandchildren for ice cream. I doubt that our famous *kulak* will be here today."

"You call him a *kulak*?"

"If you'd ever seen him you'd understand. He looks like a farmer, or a walrus. Perhaps both. At least he roots for Honved, the Army's club, not Voros Lobogo—Red Banner—the State Security team."

"You dislike him?"

"He's not a bad sort, but he believes that he can reform that which cannot be reformed."

"Your English is quite good," he said.

"I speak five languages," she said proudly. "Hungarian, Russian, French, Portuguese, and English. Some Spanish, too. I'm often called upon to interpret and translate for diplomats in Budapest."

The waiter returned, staring at her rudely after he had served her coffee. She ignored him and waited until he had left before speaking.

"He assumes that I am sleeping with you," she said. "For money. It's not uncommon."

"What shall I call you?" Collins asked.

She glanced around to make sure there were no eavesdroppers. "My name is Eva Nemeth," she said. "It will be better, should you be asked, that you say that you've hired me as your interpreter."

"When will I get the chance to meet our mutual friend? To arrange what needs to be arranged?"

"Tomorrow, in the afternoon, at four o'clock you will meet him at Harmashatarhegy, the Hill of Three Borders. It's where the borders of Buda, Pest, and Obuda—three cities—once met. We'll travel there together for the meeting."

"Why there?"

"It's well out of the city. Anyone arriving there can be seen from a distance."

"Won't State Security follow us?"

"That has been taken care of."

"It has?" Her certainty annoyed him. "Are you sure?"

She laughed. "I'm sure. You see, I'm expected to report on all of your activities to the police."

"You work for them?"

"In a way." She grew serious. "I sometimes do things for them. I report what I have interpreted." She paused to sip her coffee. "Don't worry. If our friend spots any surveillance, there won't be any meeting. Have you arranged for a car?"

"That's been taken care of."

"Good. Then we can drive to the meeting." She stared at him for a long moment. "You're not what I expected."

"Excuse me?"

"Our friend has told me about you. I expected someone taller, older."

It was his turn to be amused. "Sorry if I've been a disappointment."

"I pictured you differently, that's all." She shrugged expressively. "Our mutual friend praised you. How you were a famous newspaper columnist in New York, how you covered the war against the Japanese and then the imperialist war America fought in Korea."

"All of that is accurate, except for the part about imperialism in Korea and me being famous. Well-known, maybe."

She glanced at the gold band on the ring finger of his left hand. "You're married, Mr. Collins?"

Collins took a sip of his coffee. He didn't want to talk about his personal life with a stranger, especially one connected to Morris. "I am, but that's immaterial. Can we focus on the meeting tomorrow? The idea is to wrap this up as quickly as possible."

"The two of you will have much to talk about."

"I doubt that. We'll discuss the arrangements for his departure. That shouldn't take very long."

"He's eager to see you."

Collins grimaced. "I just want to get this done quickly."

"And you're not eager to see him, Mr. Collins? Maxim thought you might still stand in judgment of him. A harsh judgment."

"No more harshly than he deserves. But I'm not here to judge him."

"Do you plan to cover the student march this afternoon?" she asked.

"Cover it? No, I might stop by, out of curiosity."

"I should come with you," she said. "As your interpreter. It would be strange if I did not."

Collins didn't like the idea. "Wouldn't it better for us to have as little contact as possible?"

"That's not what Maxim wants. As long as you are in Budapest, I'm to be your interpreter and go where you go."

Collins didn't say anything in response. He called for the waiter and they sat in silence until after he had paid the check. On the way out of the dining room, he noticed a stocky, dark-haired young man in a khaki military uniform waiting near the entrance to the Hungaria, hostility evident in his face. Eva muttered something under her breath and marched over to confront the man. She spoke rapidly, angrily, and the man stepped back, his face flushed, and after shooting a hard stare at Collins, left through the front door.

"Who was that?" Collins asked. "I got the distinct feeling he didn't like me."

"He was a boyfriend," she said. "Before Maxim. He'll not accept that we will never be together again. He has become a nuisance."

"He's in the army?"

She looked at him critically. "No, he's a captain in State Security. You can tell by the blue epaulettes on his shoulders."

"State Security? You're sure he's not here because of me?"

"No, Laszlo's not here on official business. It's jealousy. There have been other incidents in the past, when he has followed me. He flies into a rage if I am with a man. He would have made a scene just now, but he's afraid of Maxim. No need to worry. I have told him that if it happens again, there will be hell to pay."

Looking at the scowl on her face, Collins didn't doubt that for a moment, but he was still unsettled by the episode. The last thing they needed was a jealous State Security officer skulking around, and it meant that the sooner they could remove Eva from the picture, the better. As it was, Morris was taking a large risk by involving her. She obviously knew something about his plans to leave Hungary—she had more-or-less said that she was his lover—and Collins wondered what would happen to her in the aftermath of Morris' defection. Morris must have found some way of protecting her even after he was gone. Collins wasn't going to worry about it—Eva Nemeth was Morris' problem, not his.

★ ★ ★

They found Hawes stationed by the parked Austin two blocks away from the Hungaria, a cigarette dangling from his lips, waiting patiently. He raised his eyebrows when he saw that a young woman was accompanying Collins.

"Eva Nemeth, meet Felix Winters," Collins said, as way of introduction. "Mr. Pilgrim sent Eva as a go-between. He wants us to employ her as our interpreter while we're in Budapest."

"Mr. Pilgrim?" Eva asked, confused.

"That's what we call our mutual friend when we're in public," Collins explained.

Hawes looked her up-and-down, clearly suspicious. "We don't need an interpreter," he said. The relaxed, devil-may-care Hawes of the Duna dining room had been replaced by a humorless, wary field agent.

"You may not," she said, "but Maxim insists. He says we need to give State Security a reason for my contact with Mr. Collins until matters are resolved. I'm your means of staying in touch with Maxim and vice versa."

"We were told he could meet with us openly," Hawes said. "What's changed?"

"I don't know who told you that," she said coldly. "No public contact is best."

"I'm to meet with Pilgrim tomorrow in the Buda hills," Collins said. "A place called the Hill of Three Borders."

"At least it's a decent spot to rendezvous," Hawes said. "You'd know if you were being tailed, almost immediately." He looked critically at Eva. "So what are you to Pilgrim?"

"What business of yours is that?" she asked.

Hawes wasn't pleased with her answer. "The more people involved, the more chance for a cock up. We were supposed to be dealing with Pilgrim directly."

"Tomorrow you will. Mr. Collins will meet him. You must be patient."

Hawes said something to Eva in Hungarian that made her flush with anger.

"We're lovers," she said. "If you must know. And there is no need for you to be crude."

Collins wondered what Hawes had said to her, but judging from her reaction it had been something vulgar. It was a side of the Englishman he hadn't seen before, but he could understand why Hawes was on edge.

Collins checked his wristwatch. "Felix and I need to stop by the American legation," he told Eva. "Can we drop you off somewhere?"

"Why don't you let me off at the Duna? I'll wait for you there. We should have tea in the dining room, make a show of it. I'm your interpreter now, and the more we're seen together in public, the better."

Collins didn't like that idea. On the other hand, he had to trust that Morris knew what he was doing. That was cold comfort for Collins—Morris had attempted to manipulate him before and it had ended badly. He could only hope that this time it would be different, and wasn't that the flimsiest of hopes? Burn me twice, shame on me. He didn't want to be burned again.

Four

The American legation in Hungary, located on the north side of Liberty Square, occupied what had been a turn-of-the-century mansion, which once had been a showy residence for an affluent Budapest merchant. The building, designed in the ornate Secessionist style, a variation of Art Nouveau, faced a lovely park with benches and trees that filled the center of the square. After they had passed through the black, wrought iron gate at the front entrance, a bored Marine guard gave Collins' passport a cursory review and Hawes' dark blue-covered British passport a slightly longer scrutiny before waving them into the building.

They were directed to Brooks Lawrence's second floor office, where they found the American press attaché behind a desk clear of paperwork. The rest of his cramped office was fastidiously clean. Lawrence stood up to shake hands and directed them to sit in wooden captain's chairs.

"Your editor only had time for a brief discussion on the phone," he told Collins. "He said that you'd want to interview some of our staff."

"That's the plan," Collins said with a slight smile. Lawrence needed to think that Collins' sole motive in coming to Budapest was to write about the challenges faced by American diplomats working there. "The story will be about the people who handle the everyday business of the legation. I'd like to get their thoughts on what life is like for them. If they've served in other embassies, they can talk about how different it is to work behind the Iron Curtain." Collins motioned to Hawes. "We'll want Felix to take some photos."

"Absolutely," Hawes said. "Perhaps a few atmospherics. Staff walking along the Danube Promenade, by the entrance to the Parliament building. Capture the visual flavor of the place."

Hawes certainly looked the part of the freelance photographer: his Nikon camera hung on a strap around his neck, and he had a green canvas gear bag slung over his shoulder.

"I can certainly draw up a list of the legation personnel for you to interview," Lawrence said. "The ambassador, Christian Ravndal, just left for the States. Spencer Barnes, the acting chargé d'affaires, will hold down the fort until Ravndal's replacement, Tom Wailes, arrives. Wailes is due in any day now. When would you want to conduct these interviews?"

"Tomorrow, if possible. Early afternoon? Just after lunch?" Collins could always call the legation and cancel if they were able to leave Budapest before then. Lawrence might be miffed, and the legation staff disappointed, but Collins could claim that his editor had changed his mind and spiked the story.

"We'll be ready for you at one o'clock," Lawrence said. "And Mr. Winters can take his photographs then." He adjusted his bow tie, as if prepping for a photo; Collins noticed the derisive smile on Hawes' face—Lawrence was certainly living up to the worst stereotype of the pompous, striped-pants diplomat.

"What do you know about this student demonstration today?" Collins asked.

"There won't be one. The Interior Minister, Piros, announced this morning a ban on any marches. End of story. Spencer believes there may be a reform movement brewing, but I've tried to dissuade him from reporting that to Washington. Gero and his ministers are all Stalinists at heart. They're not looking for reform."

"What does the average Hungarian, the man in the street, think about it?" Collins asked.

Lawrence shrugged. "It doesn't matter. I grant you that the students and the intellectuals have been more vocal recently, but that's only because the regime has allowed them more rope. And we know the Reds can tighten that rope whenever they like."

"Do you speak Hungarian, Mr. Lawrence?" Hawes asked, the smile still on his face.

"A few words. Hardest language in the world to learn, they say. A few of the legation staff speak it and we have translators for any government documents. The party newspaper, *Szabad Nep*, makes for boring reading—it just parrots whatever slogan Gero is peddling."

"Not speaking the language must make it difficult to know what's actually happening," Hawes said. "Flying blind, you might say."

"We know what we need to know," Lawrence said dismissively. He opened his desk drawer and retrieved a manila envelope. "This arrived in the diplomatic pouch," he said to Collins. "Apparently your editor, Mr. Wittingham, dropped it off at the embassy in Vienna and they forwarded it. A bit surprising. We don't usually convey private mail. Strange timing. You would think he could have given it to you in person."

Collins smiled ruefully as Lawrence handed the envelope to him. "Beats me. I just show up and write the story."

Collins thanked the young press attaché—ignoring Lawrence's obvious curiosity about what had been sent to Collins from Vienna—and promised to return the following morning to begin his interviews. Lawrence awkwardly got to his feet and walked them to the door.

Once back in the square, Collins and Hawes found an empty bench in the park. Hawes lit up a cigarette and took a long drag. Collins glanced around to make sure they weren't being watched before he carefully opened the envelope, noting that the seal hadn't been disturbed. Inside, he found a worn-looking passport and a press card from the North American Newspaper Alliance, both carrying Morris Rose's name. It was a younger Morris, posed stiffly, in the passport photo, and Collins figured it had come from his employment file at the State Department. The pages of the passport bore numerous border control stamps and visas.

Collins passed the documents to Hawes, who quickly reviewed them and handed them back. "They're well executed," he said. "The passport's authentic and the stamps should pass scrutiny."

Collins put the passport and the press card back in the envelope and then slid it into his inner suit jacket pocket. While carrying the documents represented a risk if he were to be stopped by the police, he couldn't trust the Hotel Duna's safe and he had to assume his room would be thoroughly searched at the first opportunity.

Hawes noticed Collins eyeing his cigarette. "Want one?" he asked. "I smoke Player's Navy Cut. They're fairly mild."

"Haven't smoked in a while," Collins said. "But one can't hurt."

When Collins took his first, long drag on the cigarette, pulling the smoke into his mouth and throat, savoring the taste, he remembered how much he'd enjoyed smoking. His last cigarette had been more than a year ago, and he had never smoked in front of Caleb and Matthew because he didn't want them to pick up the habit. But he had to admit that there was something calming about puffing away. He grinned when he remembered Mark Twain's old joke about how easy it was to quit smoking—Twain boasted that he'd done it thousands of times.

★ ★ ★

They found the Duna's lobby nearly deserted when they returned, except for Eva Nemeth, who sat waiting for them, a book on her lap. Zoltan, the clerk on duty, a distinguished-looking man with silver hair, shrugged eloquently when Collins asked him where all of the guests had gone.

"The student rally," he said. "Everyone's curious, not just the reporters and photographers." He looked at his watch. "They announced on Radio Budapest that they'd lifted the ban on the march. Now the crowd is headed toward Parliament."

"We'll want to take a look," Collins said. He turned to Eva. "We'd appreciate it if you would come along to interpret."

"If you wish," she said, noncommittally, careful—Collins noticed—not to express any opinion about the march in front of Zoltan.

Hawes pulled Collins to the side, out of earshot of Eva and Zoltan.

"Is this prudent?" Hawes asked. "Shouldn't we lose her? I think having her around is a mistake. It calls attention to us that we don't need."

"It's the way Pilgrim wants it. He must have his reasons."

"Attending the rally puts us on the local radar, too."

"But it fits our cover, you know. It's what journalists and photographers do. If we don't go, we'll raise questions about our bona fides."

The truth was that Collins welcomed the chance to observe the protest—it represented actual news, an authentic story, unlike the bogus assignment that Jennings and Wittingham had fabricated for him. For a few hours, Collins would feel like a real journalist. If he was honest with himself, that was why he wanted to cover the march.

"As long as we stay out of the thick of it," Hawes said. "If the police come in to break it up with billy clubs flying, we need to be on the periphery, out of harm's way."

"You won't get an argument from me on that. I have a healthy respect for police night sticks. Don't want them anywhere near my skull."

Outside the Duna, it had cooled somewhat from earlier in the day, but it was still pleasant. They walked north along the street, parallel to the river. Collins noticed that there were posters plastered on building walls and trees. Eva walked over and quickly scanned one.

"It's a list," she said. "Sixteen demands for reform from the students at the Technical University."

Hawes read the poster over her shoulder and whistled. "Amazing. The first demand is for the withdrawal of Soviet troops from Hungary. They're also calling for free elections, and a trial of Rakosi, the former prime minister, for his crimes."

"I never thought this day would come," Eva said. "They're asking for what so many of us want."

They could see that a huge crowd had begun crossing the Chain Bridge, and the marchers in front were turning north, heading toward the distinctive neo-Gothic Parliament building. They marched in rows, ten and twelve across, with arms interlocked. Most were young students, but Collins noticed some older men in overalls. Many of the young men wore jackets and ties and light overcoats; the women students were in blouses and long skirts and Collins spotted numerous lapel ribbons of red, white and green, the national colors. Some marchers carried Hungarian flags—Collins noticed that there were holes in the middle of the flags, and he turned to Eva for an explanation.

"They've cut out the Soviet emblem, the red star above a hammer and corn stalk," she said. "It's risky for them if they're seen by State Security."

"A lot of risks are being taken today," Hawes said. "Do you hear what some of them are chanting? 'Nagy in the government, and Rakosi in the Danube,' and 'Russians Go Home.' That's provocative as hell."

"They must believe that there's safety in numbers," Collins said. "I hope that's true."

Further north they could see another large crowd was filling the temporary Kossuth Bridge that spanned the Danube closer to Parliament. Thousands of people were streaming in the direction of Parliament, chanting and singing. The scene reminded Collins of a soccer game in London he had attended between Arsenal and Tottenham Hotspur where the fans had entered the stadium at White Hart Lane singing and chanting and hadn't stopped for the length of the match.

As they approached the Parliament building, a line of empty trams and parked vehicles bore witness to the lure of the protest.

The immense square facing Parliament had filled up with thousands of people, carrying flags, signs, and banners. A few proudly held up large photos of Imre Nagy. It surprised Collins that many in the crowd around him were factory workers, still wearing their dirty overalls and sporting flat caps. The protest had spread well beyond the students. He wondered what that meant—did it reflect a broader and deeper disenchantment with the current regime? The crowd had grown so large that Collins did not see how the police could break it up without considerable violence.

Twilight began settling over the square, and the nearby street lamps came on. The neo-Gothic spires and the central tower and dome of the Parliament building were now silhouettes against the darkening sky. Scattered lights began appearing in the windows of Parliament and the other buildings facing the square. The atmosphere reminded Collins a bit of Times Square on New Year's Eve—except that New Yorkers gathered to celebrate the ball dropping and the advent of a new year and he wasn't quite sure what the Budapest crowd expected to happen. Perhaps they didn't know themselves.

Crowds could be unpredictable and Collins had always been wary of such large congregations of people. There was always the danger that they could turn into a mob. Yet those around him seemed relatively happy, chanting and singing, as it grew darker. Some of the people around him began chanting the name of Imre Nagy.

"Nagy's their best hope for reform," Hawes said. "Hard to believe that he'll be brought back into the government in any capacity."

Then the street lamps suddenly went out, plunging the square into darkness, provoking an angry roar of dismay from the vast crowd. Collins heard a new chant start, and it was quickly picked up by everyone around them.

"What are they saying?" Collins asked.

"'We've had enough of darkness,'" Eva said. "The chant is 'We've had enough of darkness.'"

In moments, the demonstrators had folded newspapers and leaflets and set them on fire. The square was illuminated by thousands of makeshift torches. There was a haunting beauty to the scene, Collins thought, and he found himself hoping that somehow the protest would have an impact and improve the lot of the Hungarians around him.

The lights of the square suddenly were switched back on, and there was a massive roar of approval from the crowd. Then someone in authority decided to turn on the light in the red star that topped the dome of the Parliament building, some three hundred feet above the square. The crowd began chanting. "They're saying 'Down with the red star!'" Eva said. In a minute or so the illuminated red star went dark, again prompting a huge cheer from the crowd.

Above them in the night sky, Collins could see the first stars and a waning moon starting to emerge. For the moment, the crowd seemed content to express itself through chanting and whistling. Collins glanced at his watch and was surprised to see it was already almost eight o'clock. He had been so caught up in the march and demonstration that he hadn't noticed the passage of time.

Hawes tugged on his coat sleeve and pulled him toward the edge of the crowd where a radio was playing at a high volume in a parked car, a white Skoda. Eva followed them through the crush of people.

"They're broadcasting a statement from Gero," Hawes said. "The government's response to the march."

Collins could see from the look on the faces around him that whatever Gero was saying wasn't being well-received. Other radio sets were playing the speech and much of the crowd in the square listened intently.

Next to Collins, one man wearing overalls spat on the ground, and two other younger men, most likely students, angrily repeated the same phrase in Hungarian several times.

"They're calling him a liar," Eva said. "Gero is saying the demonstrators are a mob. Subversives. He has rejected the demands. No concessions to hostile elements."

When Gero finished speaking the crowd responded with whistles and catcalls, followed by a chant that rapidly grew in volume. "They want Imre Nagy to speak," Eva said.

Twenty minutes later, there was movement on a second-story balcony of the Parliament building. Several men appeared along with a short man with a mustache and when Collins heard the cheers he figured it was Nagy. Someone in the crowd had run an electrical cord from the building and rigged up a spotlight and trained it on Nagy. The crowd quieted, eager to hear him speak. To Collins's surprise, however, Nagy's first words were greeted with whistles and boos.

"He began by calling them 'comrades,' a mistake," Eva explained. "Then he switched and addressed them as 'citizens.'"

Hawes translated Nagy's halting, impromptu speech for Collins—the former premier talked about democratic socialism and constitutional order and discipline and how the Central Committee would address the crowd's concern. Nagy finished by counseling patience, and after limited applause, began singing the traditional national anthem. The crowd joined in and the entire square was filled with the sound of thousands of voices singing the banned song.

"I think the demonstrators have misread the man," Hawes said. "Nagy sounds like a Party man, tried and true."

"I don't agree," Eva said. "He wants to take a different route."

"The Russians sent packing? Free elections? Prosecution of Rakosi? Those aren't even remotely realistic demands. If Nagy regains power—and who knows if that will happen—he'll find himself in a Lubyanka prison cell before you can say Jack Robinson if he tries to act on those demands. And he knows it."

"Khrushchev has accepted Gomulka," Eva said. "Khrushchev has denounced Stalin. Who would dream that either of those things would happen? One of our poets, Janos Arany, wrote 'In dreams and in love there are no impossibilities.'"

"You can have your poets," Hawes said. "If you want independence, you'll need a lot more than pretty verses."

Collins could tell that Eva didn't like Hawes' comments, but he agreed with him—the Soviet leaders didn't care about dreams or love. They were grimly practical men focused on keeping power.

"Shall we get back to the Duna?" Collins asked.

Hawes nodded and Eva made no protest; the crowd had begun to disperse—a few people were hanging Hungarian flags on the facade of the Parliament building—and there didn't seem to be any point to standing in the cold.

* * *

A furious Lester Kane waved them down on Apaczai Csere Janos Street in front of the Hotel Duna. "I'm missing the damn story," he said angrily. "I can't get anyone to drive me over to the Radio Budapest studios on Brody Sandor Street. Some of the students have marched there to ask that their list of demands be broadcast."

"What do you think?" Collins asked Hawes.

"We could head over there and check it out. Steer clear if the police decide to intervene."

Collins nodded—he was curious to see what might be happening. Kane got in the Austin's backseat. Hawes drove south onto Rakoczi Street and then onto a side street near the National Museum, a massive structure that loomed above them in the dark. As they neared Brody Sandor Street, where Radio Budapest's studios were located, Collins heard the distinctive sound of gunfire. He could feel himself tensing at the sound—it had been nearly five years since he had been under fire.

Hawes parked the Austin two blocks from the radio station. When they moved closer on foot they found Isabelle Lavalle, the French photographer, had taken shelter in the entryway of a nearby apartment building. They joined her there and Kane quickly introduced Hawes and Eva to her.

"It's been very confused," she told them. "State Security is defending the building. The AVO threw tear gas into the crowd when they first demanded entry. The students responded by throwing stones and roof tiles. There were shots and two students were killed. Then the Hungarian Army arrived, but there was some sort of dispute and the AVO killed one of the tank commanders. *Salauds*. Bastards. That's when it became very intense, with the soldiers joining the students in attacking the building."

"The AVO killed an Army officer?" Hawes asked, clearly surprised at the thought.

"They did. The Army and city police began passing guns to the students. Now the sides have been firing back and forth." She shrugged. "It's too dark to tell exactly what is going on. I think there may even be some tanks supporting the students."

"It has the makings of a full-scale revolt if the city police and the military sides with the students," Kane said. "Incredible. Never thought I'd see that."

"It may just be this isolated unit," Collins said.

"Are we going to try to get any closer to the action?" Kane asked.

"We should stay here, on the perimeter," Hawes said. He shot Collins a quick glance. "Too much crossfire. Any closer puts us in harm's way."

Collins had no illusions about the danger just up the street. There were some war correspondents who couldn't get enough of combat—they secretly craved the thrills of facing death, the rush of adrenaline when they survived a close call. Later, they would make too-casual jokes at dinner about their good luck. Or perhaps they just had a death wish. Collins wanted none of it.

Hawes pulled out his package of cigarettes and offered them around. Collins and Lavalle each took one, and Hawes produced a lighter. Soon the three of them were puffing away.

Suddenly, two young soldiers in Hungarian Army uniforms appeared out of the dark and moved quickly across the street. They were carrying rifles and they positioned themselves so they could aim up the street toward the radio station. They both shot off a round or two and then pulled back when their fire was returned.

Hawes hugged the wall of the apartment building as he made his way closer to the soldiers. He called out to them and they held a brief conversation.

Hawes worked his way back to his spot inside the entryway. "Their unit was sent to defend the radio station from the demonstrators," he explained. "Their commander stood on one of the tanks with the national flag and tried to persuade the men in the radio station to let the students in, but the AVO shot him down. That's when many of the soldiers went over to the rebels. These two have ripped off the red stars on their uniforms."

The soldiers passed them as they walked to the other end of the block and disappeared around the corner. Hawes watched them until they were out of sight. "There's no leadership," he said. "No organization. It's spontaneous. More likely to quickly burn out."

They waited in the entryway for another twenty-five minutes listening to the sounds of the gun battle a block away. Kane poked his head around the corner of the building once and reported that he could see muzzle flashes up the street. There would be brief periods of silence followed by renewed gunfire.

"They'll be at this all night," Hawes said. "Until the men inside run out of ammunition."

"I agree," Kane said. "We can check back on the situation in the morning. See whether the shooting match is still going or whether the students have taken the building."

Hawes glanced over at Isabelle Lavalle. "I suspect that the photos will be better when we have some light."

"That is so," she said.

"Back to the hotel, then," Kane said. "Time to catch some shut-eye."

While Collins wanted to see whether the students and their new allies from the Hungarian Army could force their way into the radio station, he reluctantly had to agree with Hawes. They weren't there to cover the demonstrations or street fights.

Eva, who had been silent, spoke up. "The regime will not be able to contain this. It will not burn out quickly." She gave Hawes a challenging look. "You heard them. They won't live in darkness any more."

"The government does have more guns," Collins said, hoping to forestall an argument between Eva and Hawes. "It's been my experience that usually carries the day."

"Not always," she said. "Someone has to pull the trigger on those guns. There will be few volunteers after tonight."

Collins remained silent. Unlike Eva, he believed that when the sun rose, the police and soldiers would follow the orders of their superiors and the regime would retake control of the city's streets. It would be a sad coda to the day's events, but that was the reality.

* * *

The five of them crammed into the Austin, with Kane, Lavalle, and Eva sharing the back seat. Hawes drove carefully back to the Duna. The streets were filled with excited people, many carrying flags and signs, singing and chanting, unwilling to end their night of freedom. Collins heard sporadic gunfire in the distance, but he couldn't place its origin.

It was well after two o'clock when they reached the hotel. Eva declined a lift home from Hawes, and told Collins she would return to the Duna the following afternoon.

"Tomorrow we will meet as we agreed," she said to Collins, choosing her words carefully with Kane and Lavalle within earshot. "I will return at one o'clock."

Collins watched as her slight figure disappeared into the darkness to their south. In the distance Collins heard the "pop" of a single carbine, followed by the rattle of submachine guns—more evidence that skirmishes were continuing in Budapest's streets.

Once back in the hotel, Hawes stopped Collins and handed him a few cigarettes. "You may want these," he said, and Collins thanked him.

"Not quite what we expected," Hawes said. "We'll need to sort things out in the morning. Figure out if we need to make any changes."

When he got back to his room, Collins took his typewriter out of its hard case and set it up on the small hotel room desk. He fed a sheet of paper into the machine and began typing notes, describing what he had seen over the past several hours. He wrote for fifteen minutes, smoking the cigarettes Hawes had given him, until he had a fair summary of the evening's events.

There were only sporadic gunshots now, and Collins figured that the intense fighting had died down. He realized suddenly how tired he was. He kicked off his shoes and crawled into bed, too exhausted to remove the rest of his clothing.

He thought of Maria and the boys, and wondered how the New York newspapers would play the rioting in Budapest—for that was how it would most likely be characterized. Buried on an inside page? Or headline news on the front page? He knew that after she got Caleb off to school in the morning that she would read the papers, starting with *The New York Times*. He knew that she would worry about his safety. He debated whether he should send her a telegram in the morning and decided that he would and then he felt himself drifting off to sleep.

Five

The harsh sound of diesel engines and the metallic clatter of tank treads on cobblestones woke Collins from a fitful sleep just after four o'clock in the morning. He found his way to the bathroom, splashed some lukewarm water on his face, and hastily got dressed. He rode the lift down to the ground floor to see if he could find out what was happening.

There were already several journalists in the hotel lobby clustered by the windows facing the street, peering out into the dark. The lobby chandelier was off, but with the reflected light from the street lamps outside, Collins recognized two of the men: Lachlan Ferguson of *The Daily Telegraph* and Joe Branson from the *Chicago Tribune*. He had met Ferguson in 1950 when they both covered the Inchon landing in Korea, and Branson had stopped by the *Sentinel* newsroom a few times when he was in New York. The third man introduced himself as Abe Kaufer of the United Press.

"We drove in from Vienna and got here after midnight," Ferguson said in his soft Scottish burr. Ferguson's short dark hair had turned gray since Collins had last seen him. "We'd been monitoring Radio Budapest and could tell that things were heating up. It appears that the regime has brought in Russian forces from all over Hungary to put down the rioting. We're just in time for the *coup de grâce*."

"You're sure they're Russian tanks?" Collins asked. He looked out into the street and saw, in the distance, the silhouette of a large tank. "Not Hungarian?"

"Based on the markings on the turrets, they're Russian," Branson said. "T-34s."

Ferguson offered Collins a dusty glass and then filled it with whisky from a half-full bottle. "Straight up, I'm afraid. The Duna's bar closed up at two. Fortunately, I had the foresight to borrow some glasses. Sorry about the lack of illumination, but the Sovs are shooting at any building with lights on."

"Cheers," Ferguson said, raising his glass; Collins followed suit, as did Branson and Kaufer. Collins felt the alcohol warming his throat and chest.

"Perhaps we should drink a final toast to the demonstrators," Kaufer said. "To the brave but doomed. I'm afraid it becomes quite ugly from here on. Gero won't fool around. Like any doctrinaire Stalinist, he's ready to use deadly force to crush his adversaries."

"If he can," Collins said.

"He can," Kaufer responded with certainty. He wore wire rim glasses and a small, neatly trimmed mustache in the style of Clark Gable. "Those kids in the streets can't hold off the Red Army for long. This will all be over by nightfall if not earlier. Once they see the tanks, the rebels will realize it's hopeless to keep resisting—that's how it went in East Berlin in '53 and in Poznan last summer."

"I'm not as sure," Collins said. "It wasn't only students in that crowd in front of the Parliament and at the radio station. There were workers, too. And soldiers from the Hungarian Army were helping, passing them weapons."

"The Hungarians had the daylights beaten out of them in '45 by the Ruskies," Branson said. "The Reds raped nearly every female over the age of ten, just like they did in Berlin, when they 'liberated' the city. I imagine they figured it was only fair because Horthy sent his troops to fight with the Wehrmacht against them. I can't believe that the Hungarians want that episode repeated."

Ferguson poured himself another drink before speaking. "After the demonstration at Parliament, some of the crowd migrated to Dozsa Gyorgy Square and toppled a huge bronze statue of Stalin. Brought in an acetylene torch, cut the legs off just above the boots. I'd say the symbolism won't be lost on the Reds."

"The Russians will have to show restraint, if only for propaganda purposes," Collins said. "They didn't have a hotel full of journalists and photographers reporting on the situation in 1945."

"I hope you're right," Branson said in his flat Midwestern accent. He tossed back the last of his drink. "It could be very nasty, otherwise. Massive reprisals."

"Only a few hours until first light," Ferguson said. "All shall be revealed then. We'll discover whether Comrade Gero wants the Russians on their best behavior or whether he wants blood and it's woe to the locals."

* * *

The dining room was crowded when Collins and Hawes met for an early breakfast. Newspaper, broadcast, and wire service journalists had begun arriving at the Duna at first light, drawn by the reports of unrest in Budapest.

After they had finally been served tea and some pastries, Hawes surveyed the new faces in the dining room and cursed softly in disgust.

"Carrion birds," he said. "That's what they are. Here only because very bad things are going to happen."

"That's part and parcel of the newspaper business," Collins said. "Not much demand for headlines that read 'Another Peaceful Day in Budapest.' News is when something very bad happens, or sometimes when something very good happens."

"What's something very good?"

"The Dodgers beating the Yankees in the World Series. Or England winning the World Cup."

"We lost to the Uruguayans in the last one. Imagine that. And the Germans won over the Hungarians. So that would count as bad news in both London and Budapest." Hawes put his tea cup down. "So what's our plan? What about the rendezvous with Mr. Pilgrim?"

"The fighting has been on this side of the river, from what I can tell," Collins said. "We're supposed to meet in the hills to the west, far from the center of the city. If anything, it's the safest place to be."

"So you're going to meet him?"

"We're here to bring him out, aren't we?"

"Good show. As long as you can get back to the hotel by dark."

"That's the plan," Collins said, with more confidence than he truly felt. The rioting had come as a complete surprise and he wasn't sure whether it would help or hinder their plan to take Morris back with them to Vienna.

"Perhaps we should take a stroll around outside and see what the Ivans are up to," Hawes said. "Get the lay of the land. Can't hurt, can it?"

★ ★ ★

Before they left the Duna, Collins dropped off a hastily scribbled telegram for Maria with Zoltan, who he learned also doubled as a concierge, at the reception desk. He kept the message brief: TENSE BUT OK IN BUDAPEST. HOME SOONEST. LOVE ALL. DENNIS. Collins added a generous tip to what he calculated would be the cable charges and handed Zoltan the paper and the money. Zoltan told him, apologetically, that the telegram would be sent from the General Post Office as soon as "conditions permitted."

A light mist hung in the air as Collins and Hawes exited the hotel for what Hawes called "a light reconnoitering." The streets around the Duna were empty of traffic—no buses or trams were running—and Collins saw only a few pedestrians. There were two dusty Russian tanks parked in Petofi Square, with nervous-looking crew members standing guard with Kalashnikov assault rifles at the ready.

At Hawes' urging they quickly left the square, and walked up a side street. A few national flags, with holes where the Soviet emblem had been cut out, hung limply from silent office buildings. Shops were shuttered and few buildings had lights on. Scrawled on walls and painted on store windows in block letters were the words RUSZKIK HAZA!, Hungarian for "Russians Go Home."

They turned down another side street and saw two bodies lying on the sidewalk, with Hungarian flags covering them. A few flowers had been placed on top of the flags. Further down the street, a crowd of Hungarians circled around a small fire, throwing books and pictures into the flames. One man spat on a red flag before tossing it into the fire. When Collins moved closer he saw that the pictures were of Stalin and Matyas Rakosi, the deposed Hungarian leader.

Hawes stopped a squat, middle-aged woman in a formless winter coat and asked a few questions in Hungarian before turning to Collins. "She says they're burning the Communist propaganda that's been crammed down their throat since the Reds took over," he said. "I don't care for book-burning, but it's understandable in this case."

He had just finished speaking when they were surprised by a sudden deafening roar as several MiG-15 jet fighters—Collins recognized their distinctive sweptback wings—flew over them, banking sharply to the north. Hawes waited until the sound had died down before he spoke. "A show of force," he said. "Standard operating procedure when your goal is to intimidate."

They retraced their steps to the hotel and, when they reached the lobby, found a group of journalists clustered around a large radio set.

Lachlan Ferguson glanced over at them. "It appears there's a general strike under way in response to the crackdown," he said. "According to Radio Budapest, the government has declared a state of emergency and imposed martial law. Gero stays as first secretary of the Party but Imre Nagy has been appointed prime minister."

Collins checked his watch; it was just after eight o'clock. The regime had wasted no time in cracking down on the rebels.

"The Nagy announcement's a sop for the crowd," Hawes said. "Declaring martial law and calling in the Red Army tells you what they really want."

"Gero can't rely on the Hungarian military to put down the insurgents," Ferguson said. "They apparently won't fire on their countrymen. He needs the Russians and the AVO for his dirty work."

Lester Kane entered the lobby through the revolving doors and walked over to join the group. "The students and workers did take over the Radio Building," he told them. "The government moved the equipment, though, and Radio Budapest is transmitting now from a studio in the Parliament building. And I don't think the Russians will let the students occupy the radio facility for very long."

"What's happening in the streets?" Collins asked.

"Sporadic fighting. Pockets of resistance. You'd think that things will quiet down now. The presence of the Red Army should give the hotheads pause."

"At least the world will know that the people of Budapest don't want this regime," Collins said. "And they don't want the Russians here, either."

"That's true," Kane said. "The world will know. I'm afraid that the Hungarians may pay a very high price for sending that message."

* * *

Eva Nemeth met Collins in the lobby of the Hotel Duna at the appointed time, one o'clock. She wore a long dark wool overcoat and a Basque-like beret, and Collins noticed there were dark shadows under her eyes.

She waited until they were on the street before she informed him that the place for their rendezvous had been shifted with the Russians controlling all of the Danube bridges. "No guarantee we can cross to Buda and get to the Hill of Three Borders. Instead, Maxim will meet with you here in Pest."

"How far away is the meeting place?"

"Too far to walk. The Eighth District, Josephtown. I've arranged for bicycles. We can't be sure that the trams will be running, and some of the Russians are firing on cars. With the bicycles, anyone trying to follow us on foot won't be able to keep up, and any automobile tailing us will be very obvious."

She led the way around to the back of the hotel, near the service entrance. A young, very thin auburn-haired boy, no more than ten, waited there with two bicycles propped against the wall. Eva handed him some coins and the boy smiled and motioned for Collins to take the larger of the two bicycles.

Collins followed Eva as she pedaled away from the hotel. She headed south, parallel to the river, before swinging east, avoiding the city's wide boulevards in favor of tree-lined side streets. Twice she stopped and they reversed direction, once when she spotted overturned trams in the street ahead, and a second time when they heard the sound of Soviet tanks and armored cars in the near distance.

Many of the young men and women they passed on the street carried weapons. Some of them waved to Eva and Collins as they pedaled by. An attractive woman with long raven hair and dark eyes smiled at Collins and he immediately thought of Maria—back in New York it would be just after seven in the morning, she would be making the boys breakfast and getting them ready for school.

They crossed a main thoroughfare and passed a striking white-and-red brick building in the Byzantine style that was topped by two onion domes; Collins recognized it from his guidebook as the Dohany Street synagogue, a landmark in the Jewish quarter of the city.

After another fifteen minutes of pedaling they reached a shabby neighborhood. Eva slowed down and then stopped at an intersection. Collins took note of a sign on the building next to them, *Koris utca*—Koris Street. Paint peeled from the walls of the nearby buildings, potholes dotted the street, and the few people Collins saw walking about were dressed in cheap, ill-fitting clothing.

"We're almost there," she told him. "We're to meet Maxim in a flat in the next block."

Collins exhaled slowly, suddenly tense. His meeting with Morris would surface bitter memories, ones better left undisturbed. The last time Collins had seen Morris had been on the first day of October 1949, at a furtive meeting in lower Manhattan within sight of the Brooklyn Bridge, a meeting that ended with the death of Karina Lazda.

Collins could not forgive Morris for his complicity in what happened that evening. He promised himself that he would keep his emotions in check when he saw Morris—and could only hope that he could keep that promise.

* * *

Eva slowed her bicycle halfway down the block and then stopped in front of a four-story tenement building with the number 9 over the doorway. The building's stone facade was weather-beaten and the windows facing the street were streaked with soot and grime.

Eva knocked on the door and when it swung open, they found themselves facing a short dark-haired woman dressed in rough men's clothing who pointed a carbine at them. Eva immediately said something to her and the woman stepped aside, lowering the rifle, and motioning toward the steps of a long staircase. The interior of the building smelled of unwashed clothing, paprika, and fried onions.

Eva took Collins' elbow and pulled him toward the stairs. "Top floor," she said. "I'll wait here. Maxim wishes to meet with you privately."

When Collins reached the fourth floor, he found a thin, dark-haired man carrying a Thompson sub-machine gun standing watch in the corridor. The man wore a turtleneck sweater with an armband of the national colors, corduroy trousers, and heavy leather boots.

"We've been expecting you," the man said in slightly-accented but excellent English, fixing his brown eyes squarely on Collins. "I'm Viktor Toth."

A door at the end of the dimly-lit hallway opened and Collins immediately recognized the handsome features of Morris Rose, his childhood friend. Rose wore a well-tailored fawn-colored suit and polished brown shoes.

"Hey, Denny," he said, raising his right hand in welcome.

Collins remained silent, not acknowledging the greeting.

"You've met Viktor, I see," Morris continued. "Unfortunately he's a Yankees fan, but since he lived in New York for a while I forgive him that."

"The Bronx," Viktor said. "And now I live in Chicago, the roughest part of the Eighth District, home to the class enemies and thieves and whores and gamblers. The only truly free people left in Budapest."

"We've heard there's been heavy fighting in the district," Collins said.

Viktor smiled. "I should hope so. I've gathered a few of my Chicago friends to play some music with our guitars." He held up his submachine gun. "Lots of scores to settle."

Morris nodded to Viktor and ushered Collins into the room, closing the door behind him. It was a squalid little place. Shades covered the windows and a faded floral wallpaper was peeling from the walls. A narrow, unmade bed sat in the far corner. Two chairs were positioned by a wooden table with a hot plate, a coffee pot, and two cups on its scratched surface. Morris motioned Collins to one of the chairs and sat on the edge of the bed.

"What does Viktor do?" Collins asked. "When he's not settling scores."

"Viktor's a janitor," Morris said. "As a class enemy that's the only job he could get. He's a fence on the side, but he claims that he's a Robin Hood since the Party bosses are the only ones with anything worth stealing. They have the luxury villas and access to the special shops with the best goods."

"How did you get mixed up with him?"

"Happenstance." He found a pack of cigarettes in his jacket pocket and offered one to Collins, who declined. Morris fumbled in his pockets and found matches and lit one, taking a long drag before he spoke. "I wondered whether you'd be willing to help me out." He looked over at Collins. "It was wild last night. I watched from my flat on the other side of the river as the crowds crossed the bridges to head over to Parliament. And now we have Nagy back in the government and the Red Army here in force."

Collins shrugged in response. He wasn't about to make conversation. After what had happened, after all of Morris' betrayals—small and significant—Collins found it hard to be civil to the man.

"Can we get down to business?" Collins asked. "I'd like to get this over with."

"I'm aware that we have some difficult history between us. I don't blame you for hating me, Denny. I deserve that. But you have to know it wasn't what I wanted. Things just spun out of control at the end, in New York. Yatov made it clear that I had to follow his lead if I wanted his help in leaving the country."

"You followed his lead, I'll grant you that."

"I had to. I never imagined that he would order Karina's execution. You have to believe me about that. I thought that he would honor his side of the bargain."

"I can only hope that her death has been on your conscience. If you have one. You involved her. You brought her in."

Morris sighed. "That was a mistake. I should have left her out of it. You, too. I regret that." He paused to take another drag on his cigarette. "No one was playing fair. That CIA official, Matthew

Steele, was setting me up. That list of agents on the microfilm wasn't on the level. It was meant to make Moscow Center believe that some of their penetration agents hadn't been detected. The ones missing from the list were the men that Steele had turned and planned to use to feed Moscow false information."

Collins didn't say anything in response. Morris got to his feet and walked over to the table and took one of the coffee cups. He tapped the ashes from his cigarette into it and then brought it back with him when he returned to his seat on the bed.

"The bogus list caused me some problems," he said. "It raised unpleasant questions. Could I be trusted? Was I a double agent? I had to convince them that I wasn't part of some elaborate conspiracy cooked up by Steele. I realized that the further I could distance myself from Dzerzhinsky Square, the better. So I asked to be sent to Warsaw to be a liaison between Moscow and the local security forces. I knew the landscape, the Western diplomats—those who we might be able to recruit. Then later I went to Budapest, same job. I was good at it."

"Are you proud of that?"

"It removed me from Moscow." He finished his cigarette and stubbed it out in the coffee cup. "Then I got a break. Sometime in the summer of 1951 Anatoli Yatov disappeared. It wasn't clear whether he'd defected or decided to go underground and take his chances in the land of milk and honey. It raised questions about Yatov's motives, which took the spotlight off me. For a while, at least. You can never be secure."

"And now you want out," Collins said flatly. "Why now? Why are you so red hot to defect?"

"Just look around, Denny. Who's betraying the revolution? Not the students and workers in the streets. It's the same in Poland. How is the Red Army anything other than the arm of Russian imperialism?"

"You've lost your faith?"

"Only in the Russians," he said sharply. "I believe in socialism. I believe that it is the best hope for the masses, for the people. I think it is possible to construct a society where workers aren't exploited and the sick are healed and the hungry fed, where fat cat capitalists don't lord it over the rest of us. I've concluded that Stalinism isn't going to fashion that society. It's a distortion of socialism."

"You always loved theories," Collins said. "It's a shame that you backed one that has created a hell on earth."

"That's an easy cheap shot, Denny. Do you think that the minimum wage and Social Security and a five-day work week would exist without socialists, progressives, standing up to the big money boys? It's only because we fought for them that the capitalists gave in. I don't regret for a moment believing in these things and for doing what I could when I was in Washington to make them happen."

"Spare me the sermon."

"I see," Morris said. His face hardened. "So that's the way you want to play it. Fine. What's the plan?"

"I have your American passport and a press card from the North American Newspaper Alliance. You'll join me and my photographer—an Englishman named Winters—on the train to Vienna."

"The passport is in my name?"

"Morris Rose. I understand that's not what you're calling yourself now."

Morris ignored the dig. "The plan is sound. We shouldn't attract any notice traveling together." He paused. "You'll need to tell the Agency that I have two requirements, two additional conditions, for my return. The first is that you stay by my side until we reach an American airbase and I'm safely on a military aircraft headed back to the States. The second is that Eva must come along with us and she must be granted asylum when we arrive in Washington."

"The deal is to bring you out, not her."

"They'll go for it," Morris said confidently. "It's a package deal. No Eva, no Morris, no juicy secrets."

Collins wasn't completely surprised. It was one of the continuing mysteries of life, the attraction between a man and a woman. He wouldn't have figured that Morris would have fallen so hard for Eva—but he had—and demanding that she accompany him to the West made sense.

Morris reached under the bed and located a leather valise. He took an envelope from the bag and handed it to Collins. "Photos of Eva," he said. "For her passport and any other papers they'll need to forge. I'd suggest that they give her a cover as a journalist, since she will be traveling with us. I'll rely on you, Denny, to explain the situation to them. Eva will contact you later tomorrow. She'll have our next meeting place."

"I'll pass your message," Collins said. "I don't know what they'll say and what's more, I don't really care. I'm not here because I want to be—they strong-armed me into coming. As far as I'm concerned, I'd be happy to return to Vienna without you."

"It doesn't matter what you think of me," Morris said. "I needed you in Budapest because I could trust you. If you say you'll do something, you'll do it. That's no small thing for someone in my situation. So get me an answer from Washington."

.

Six

On their circuitous ride back from Josephtown to the Duna, Collins was struck by the beauty of the city's long boulevards, the leaves scattered on the sidewalks, and the resplendent fall colors of the maple, locust, and ash trees in the small parks that they passed. Other than the distant rumble of tank cannons and light artillery firing, there was nothing to suggest it was anything other than a normal autumn Wednesday in Central Europe, God in His Heaven, all's right with the world. Except that all certainly wasn't right.

Eva led them west back toward the Danube, and then north along the streets parallel to the Promenade. When they reached the hotel and dismounted, the boy with auburn hair who had brought the bicycles was waiting for them. Collins noticed that his eyes were slightly bloodshot, as if he had been crying, and that he averted his gaze when Collins looked at him. When Eva gave him her bicycle, he whispered something urgently to her. She straightened up and spoke to Collins.

"Milos says there's been trouble in Vigado Square. We should go and see."

Collins followed Eva as she purposefully strode up Apaczai Csere Janos Street. A small crowd was clustered in front of the Vigado concert hall, a massive building in the Hungarian Romantic style of architecture with scaffolding covering its upper floors. Their attention was focused on the square, which was dominated by a stone obelisk, a memorial to Soviet pilots. On the pavement near the memorial was what looked to Collins like a very large stylized aluminum model plane with one of its wings badly bent.

An elderly woman in the group sobbed softly, tears streaming down her cheeks, while another woman attempted to comfort her. Several of the men in the group were glancing toward the Danube side of the square. Collins realized that they were looking at the bodies of young men hanging from ropes tied to the lamp posts and flag masts.

"What has happened?" Collins asked Eva.

"I'll find out," Eva said. She engaged one of the older men in a brief conversation. She sighed deeply before beginning her explanation. "Twelve students were shot and strung up by State Security. It's in retaliation for the crowd toppling the sculpture of the airplane from the memorial obelisk. This is their response."

A sudden breeze swept through the square and the bodies swayed grotesquely in the wind. The elderly women moaned softly in despair at the sight, and another averted her eyes.

"It's so ghastly," Eva said. "It's meant to act as a warning to all of us." She shook her head slowly. "It's too late."

"Too late?"

"There's too much bottled-up rage," she said. "Rage against the AVO, at the Party, and at the Russians. Hanging students will not stop the fighting. Too many people feel they have nothing to lose."

"There's nothing we can do here," Collins said, taking her arm and steering her away from the square.

He wished they hadn't stumbled upon the macabre scene. He had already witnessed enough of man's casual inhumanity to man in his years as a journalist to last him a lifetime. Maria had reminded him more than once that humans were capable not only of great cruelty but of great love. Sadly, Collins didn't believe there'd be much of that love on display in Budapest in the days ahead—he didn't consider himself a cynic, but a clear-eyed realist.

They walked back in silence to the hotel. Before they went inside, Eva spent a few minutes outside talking to Milos, her arm around his shoulder, consoling him. It was clear that the boy had been badly shaken by what he had seen in Vigado Square. It didn't take long, Collins knew, for feelings of shock and anger to turn into a fierce and violent desire for revenge, even for ten-year-old boys.

* * *

Collins welcomed the sudden warmth and noise of the Duna's bar, the sound of glasses clinking and of animated talk and laughter. The room, crowded with journalists, was vibrantly alive, in stark contrast to the deeply disturbing scene in Vigado Square.

"I need something strong," Collins said to Eva. "And you?"

She nodded. Collins ordered two glasses of brandy from the bartender, a small, dark man with watchful eyes. He carefully poured the drinks and slid them across the marble counter to Collins.

Eva drank half of the glass in one try, and then, after a pause, finished it. "Another, please," she said.

Collins ordered another brandy for her and heard his name being called. It was Lachlan Ferguson, who with a wave beckoned them over to his table. Isabelle Lavalle and a middle-aged man with a receding hairline and prominent nose were already sitting, drinks in front of them. Ferguson made the introductions—the man was Indro Montanelli of the *Corriere della Sera*.

"You've been out and about?" Ferguson asked.

"We have," Collins said. "We've seen some ugly things today—bodies in the streets, reprisals just down the way in Vigado Square."

Ferguson wrinkled his nose. "I heard about that," he said. "Public hangings. Barbaric. We've stayed in the Duna for the most part. Decided that the better part of valor was discretion, just as Falstaff advises. Keeping off the streets for a bit seemed prudent."

"The insurgents are resisting in several spots," Lavalle said. "In the Eighth and Ninth Districts, near the Corvin cinema and on Tompa and Berzenczey streets. I plan to take some photos later today of the fighting near Baross Square."

"History in the making," Ferguson said. "The start of a revolution. There's always an initial spark of violence. Then, after the shots have been fired and enough people killed, there's no turning back."

"A revolution?" Collins asked. "Isn't that overstating the situation?"

"Not at all. This is more than an uprising. The rebels have gone after the telephone exchanges, the police stations, printing presses, the offices of *Szabad Nep*—just the places revolutionaries target. They've also seized arms from the barracks in Bem Square and from some of the arms factories on Csepel Island. And mark my words, there will be no mercy for the Communists as this continues. No room left for the old regime."

Montanelli frowned. "There should be room left for socialism," he said. "Socialism as it was meant to be. They're forming workers' councils in the factories and many of the fighters I've talked to believe they can build a truly socialist society."

Lachlan Ferguson laughed. "The last time they held a free and fair election around here, back in '45, your socialist friends didn't get many votes. The people wanted the Smallholders Party."

The Italian journalist shrugged. "It will be an unmitigated tragedy if reactionary elements seize power and the workers are betrayed."

"We'll never return to the days of Horthy or the Arrow Cross," Eva said, with a quiet fierceness that surprised Collins. "That will not happen. We want an independent, modern Hungary."

"Sadly, I don't think it's in the cards," Ferguson said "I'd put the odds at three-to-one on the Red Army remaining here, in control. Uncle Joe may have found a warm spot in Lucifer's pub, but the chaps in the Kremlin learned too bloody well from him that might makes right. That's a lesson they won't forget."

"What about the West putting some pressure on the Soviets?" Collins said. "Bringing the Hungarian situation before the United Nations?"

"You won't find the British or the French enthusiastic about that," Montanelli said. "The British have Cyprus and the French have

Algeria to consider. The day may come when they want to send troops into Nicosia or Algiers at the request of the local government. They'll make the same argument the Soviets are making today—that they acted to restore order."

"France should leave Algeria," Isabelle Lavalle said. "It's colonialism at its worst. You would have thought that the Quai d'Orsay would have learned its lesson from Dien Bien Phu."

"I can't second you on the question of Cyprus," Ferguson said. "The Turks and Greeks are a rather quarrelsome lot and they'd be at each other's throats without British rule. They're better off with us and they know it."

The Frenchwoman shook her head. "Rule Brittanica? Quite the loyal Tory, aren't you, Lachlan? Or perhaps that should be Sir Lachlan."

"The sun is setting on your Empire, Ferguson," Montanelli said. "You're apparently the last to know." He rose to his feet as a well-dressed, handsome man approached the table. Montanelli introduced him as Endre Marton, the resident Associated Press correspondent in Budapest. Collins knew the name—Marton, a Hungarian, had angered the regime with his accurate and unvarnished reporting and had been jailed for a time. Marton gave them a quick nod.

"My apologies for taking Indro from you," Marton said. "We're hoping to catch Imre Nagy for an interview, if we can. Wish us luck."

Ferguson watched as the two men left the bar. "Marton's top-notch," he said. "AP's lucky to have him. He's local, knows where all the bodies are buried. Understands the palace intrigue. Montanelli's a different matter. Muddled politics. Covered every war known to man. Roomed with Kim Philby when they were traveling with Franco. Later, he was with the Finns during the Winter War. In 1943 he joined the Partito d'Azione and the partisans, but the Germans caught him and threw him into prison. Somehow he escaped to Switzerland."

"Montanelli was a colleague of Philby's?" Collins asked. He wasn't completely surprised by the connection—Philby had covered the Spanish Civil War for *The Times* of London—but he hadn't expected to hear his name.

"I've heard his Philby stories," Isabelle said. "Montanelli says that Philby was a proper Englishman, except that he helped himself to a pair of Indro's warmest socks. Sent a note apologizing later."

"Proper Englishmen aren't traitors," Collins said sharply.

"So you don't believe Harold Macmillan when he says that Philby's not the Third Man?" Ferguson said.

"I don't," Collins said. "But let's not argue about it."

"No argument from me," Ferguson said. "I agree with you. There's something quite dodgy about the man. No clear explanation for his friendship with Guy Burgess."

Collins could tell that Isabelle Lavalle was studying him with renewed interest. He regretted his outburst—he shouldn't have said anything about Philby. While he knew firsthand that Philby had been spying for Moscow Center, it was a mistake to express an opinion, to draw attention to himself.

He was saved from having to reply to Ferguson when Lester Kane joined them at the table with the latest news. The natural history section of the National Museum was on fire and the smoke from the blaze could be seen from all over the city. Tass, the Soviet news agency, had announced that the "counter-revolutionary uprising" in Budapest had been defeated.

"Tass may think it's finished, but it's not," Kane said. "Not by a long shot."

"Whatever happens, as soon as they resume the trains to Austria, I hope to be on my way," Collins said.

"And miss whatever might happen here?" Lavalle asked, puzzled. "Even if the fighting continues?"

"The Newspaper Alliance already has Lester here," Collins said, nodding at Kane. "One of the best reporters around. I'm here in

Budapest by accident. The truth is that I don't really want to cover combat ever again. I've lost my stomach for it."

There was an awkward silence around the table. As a rule, war correspondents rarely expressed public doubts about their calling, but Collins didn't care—it was the truth. He had already seen enough. At the same time, he knew his comments established a reason for his departure from Budapest in the middle of a major news story.

Collins rose to his feet, and Eva followed. He was about to make his farewells when he felt a hand on this shoulder. He turned, expecting it to be Feliks Hawes but instead found the State Security officer from the Hungaria—Eva's former boyfriend, Laszlo Kosa—standing next to him. Kosa wore a dark sweater and a leather coat and he smelled strongly of alcohol.

"It's you and your lies that have caused this," Kosa said directly to Collins.

"Laszlo, please don't do this." It was Eva, clearly anxious, her face drawn.

Kosa ignored her and stared at Collins. "Your Radio Free Europe tells lies to the people. It's your American arrogance, your belief that we should all live like you with your chewing gum and your baseball."

"I can't say I like chewing gum," Collins said, hoping he could defuse the situation with humor. "Baseball's a great game, though."

Kosa glared at him. "You can joke, while outside the counterrevolutionaries and Horthyites are killing Party members. It's because you Americans are encouraging them."

Eva said something to Kosa in Hungarian but he ignored her and continued to glare at Collins.

"We just don't see things the same way," Collins said.

Kosa moved closer to Collins and then suddenly pushed him in the chest with both of his hands. "Americans are cowards," he said. "They let others do their fighting for them."

"I don't want any trouble," Collins said. He could feel his temper rising and hoped he could control it.

Lachlan Ferguson interposed himself between the two men. "There's no need for this," he said to Korda. "Collins is just trying to write a story or two, like the rest of us."

Kosa pushed Ferguson out of the way and grabbed Collins by the shoulders and shoved him, driving Collins back into the table and scattering glasses, ashtrays, and plates onto the floor.

The room fell silent. While Collins had been staggered by the push, he managed to keep his feet. He stepped to side and put his hands up, ready to defend himself against the attack he figured was coming.

"Stop this, Laszlo," Eva said. "Stop, now."

"Where is your courage?" Kosa asked Collins. "You're a coward."

"I'm not here to fight you or anyone else," Collins said. He could feel his heart racing and the blood rush to his head.

"Come outside if you have the courage," Kosa said.

Collins wanted nothing more than to hit Kosa hard, to smash him in the face, but he wasn't in Budapest to fight jealous boyfriends, especially when they were members of the secret police. He fought back his anger.

Eva pulled at Kosa's left arm, and he responded by swinging his right hand, cuffing Eva in the face and knocking her to the floor. Collins reacted instinctively, stepping forward and punching Kosa in the face, just below his right eye. Kosa staggered back and yelled in anger.

Ferguson immediately placed himself in front of Collins and Lester Kane and a man from a nearby table did the same with Kosa. Isabelle helped Eva to her feet. Collins could see a red mark on her cheek where Kosa's blow had landed.

"We'll finish this outside," Kosa said.

"Suit yourself," Collins said. Kosa had walked into the Duna bar primed for a fight and Collins decided that he wouldn't disappoint him.

* * *

They left the hotel and filed out into the street. Kosa eagerly removed his leather jacket and Collins shed his jacket coat and handed it to Ferguson. He felt the cobblestones under his feet and hoped he could keep his footing—he didn't want to get into a wrestling match with Kosa who had to outweigh him by ten pounds, most of it muscle.

There wasn't anything to be said, now. Collins glanced over and saw his fellow journalists—Lachlan, Isabelle, and Lester—all with worried faces, watching. Eva stood slightly to the side, also with a look of distress on her face.

Collins kept his balled fists high, ready to defend himself against a sudden attack. He could feel his heart pounding and his mouth had gone dry. It had been a few years since he had sparred in earnest. He could only hope that he wouldn't be too rusty when the time came to exchange punches.

Collins had no doubt that Kosa would be the aggressor, angry over Collins' first punch in the bar, eager to punish him with his fists. He was younger, fitter, but he also would be overconfident. At the Hibernian club in Brooklyn, Digger Callahan had trained Collins to be a counterpuncher, to bob and weave, to keep moving, and to wait for an opening. "Let the fight come to you," Digger had always counseled. "Take what he gives you and hit hard when you do, Denny."

Collins had been successful with that strategy back in his Golden Gloves days, but those bouts were scored on points and not damaging punches, which counted for more in a street fight. Collins wanted a short encounter—he wasn't in great shape and he had to hope that Kosa would make an early mistake and give him an opportunity to finish the fight quickly.

Kosa spit on the ground and began circling to Collins right. Then he advanced rapidly, throwing some awkward jabs with his left hand at Collins' head. Collins blocked them, but he could see that

Kosa had some boxing experience. He quickly retreated a few steps, wary of the other man's right hand—recognizing the danger.

"Stand and fight, you coward," Kosa said angrily.

Collins didn't respond. He didn't care if that angered Kosa more, because an angry drunk was a reckless drunk and he needed the Hungarian to give him an opening.

It was clear that Kosa was trying to set up his right hand. He stepped forward suddenly and launched a one-two combination. Collins only partially blocked the right hand punch and it landed on his left cheekbone, with more than enough power to sting. He stepped back, slightly dazed, trying to get more distance.

Kosa didn't follow up and Collins could hear him breathing heavily—maybe the Hungarian wasn't as fit as Collins had thought. Collins dropped his left fist slightly, hoping to draw another right hand from his adversary. It was a trick Digger Callahan had taught him.

The feint worked; Kosa moved forward and swung eagerly with his right again—a hook—at Collins' slightly exposed face. Collins ducked under the blow and then stepped closer and punched Kosa in the stomach as hard as he could with his own balled right hand. He heard the other man grunt in pain and Collins immediately threw his own combination, a left jab and a right uppercut that caught Kosa square under the chin. The Hungarian keeled over and dropped onto the cobblestones in a heap.

Collins straightened up and stood back slightly, waiting to see if Kosa would try to get to his feet. Collins was prepared to knock him down again—as many times as necessary—and he wasn't going to give him the benefit of a ten count that a sanctioned boxing match would require.

Ferguson bent over Kosa and examined him quickly. "Knocked out cold. He does have a pulse. I wonder if the hotel has smelling salts on the premises."

Before Collins could reply, a tall man in a black leather jacket appeared next to Lachlan. He said something to Eva in Hungarian and she responded. Then the man pushed Ferguson away from Kosa and bent over to attend to him. Collins hadn't seen the man until that moment.

Eva hurried over to Collins' side. "Go back into the hotel," she said. "Now. Before there is worse trouble."

Collins did as she asked, followed by Ferguson and the other journalists.

"Who was that man in the jacket?" Collins asked Eva once they were back in the Duna.

"One of Laszlo's friends from State Security, Istvan Melles," she said. "I explained to him that it was a fair fight. He believed me, thank God. He's one of the better ones. He would not shoot you out of hand like many of them would. But you must be very careful, now. You have humiliated Laszlo and he will not forgive you for that. Or me."

* * *

Hawes was not in his hotel room, and so Collins asked Zoltan at the reception desk to alert him when the Englishman returned.

Collins returned to the lobby twenty minutes later, after Zoltan called him to tell him of Hawes' return. Collins motioned Hawes back out onto the street where they couldn't be heard. They walked down to the Danube embankment to an isolated spot before they spoke. Collins watched as a distant tugboat towed a barge up the river—one Danube pilot wasn't letting the unrest on the streets of the city interrupt his routine.

"How did the meeting with Mr. Pilgrim go?" Hawes asked. "Ready to leave?"

"There are some complications. He insists that Eva come along."

Hawes cursed. "It's a bloody bad idea," he said. "She'll need documents to travel. Even if a passport could be fabricated and smuggled to us through the diplomatic pouch, that will take time we don't have. She can be extracted later."

"He's fallen in love with her. He's adamant about her accompanying him. I don't think he's thinking straight."

"Mr. Pilgrim needs to listen to reason. Our plan depends on keeping it simple. Including her makes it bloody complex."

"Can't we palm her off as a journalist, too? She's dark-haired—she could pass for Greek or Italian. Pilgrim gave me passport photos of her."

"Did he? Cocky bastard, isn't he?"

"He thinks ahead. He always has."

"He looks out for himself, though, doesn't he? In this case the smart thing is to leave her. He's going to jeopardize his defection to say nothing of our safety. I don't care to spend any time in a Hungarian prison and certainly not in a Russian one." Hawes turned from gazing at the Danube and looked directly at Collins. "Zoltan told me you knocked out an AVO man earlier today. Can that be true?"

"Laszlo Kosa. A former boyfriend of Eva. Jealous to a fault. When he struck her in the face, he didn't leave me much of a choice."

Hawes whistled. "I agree, can't let that stand, but it's bad luck. Hardly the way to keep us under the radar, Collins."

"I tried to defuse the situation, but he wasn't going to leave without a confrontation."

Hawes gave him a wry smile. "Zoltan follows the fights. He says you punch like Charles Humez, the French boxer."

"Zoltan saw our fight?"

"From one of the windows in the back. Hungarians are a scrappy lot, you know. I imagine half of the hotel staff must have been watching. Some of them may even have placed bets." Hawes peered at Collins' face. "Looks like Kosa caught you with one just under the eye."

"I'm lucky I blocked most of the punch, or I would have been the one knocked flat. Eva's concerned that Kosa now represents a threat to me."

"Lucky or not, if the trains were running I'd send you out of the country now," Hawes said. "We could follow you later."

"I'd have no objection to that," Collins said. "But that isn't going to work."

"No, it's not."

Collins ran his hand through his hair, a habit when he was under stress. "So what do we do now?"

"It's Wittingham's call, isn't it? I guess it depends on how badly they want Mr. Pilgrim. I'm afraid that Washington will agree to his terms."

"I think we should risk a direct phone call to Vienna," Collins said."

"That's not feasible at the moment," Hawes said. "The hotel switchboard operators say the phone lines to Austria had been cut."

"There's another option," Collins said. "Wittingham suggested using the legation telex in an emergency."

"It means involving the people at your legation and that's something Pilgrim explicitly ruled out." Hawes paused, reflecting on the situation for a moment. "But he can't have it both ways. If he wants his girlfriend to come with us, we need to get approval and papers for her, and our best bet is to go through the legation."

Hawes found his cigarettes and offered one to Collins. He lit Collins' first, and then his own. He took a long drag and exhaled a cloud of smoke before he spoke. "Are you willing to accept the greater risk that bringing her out represents?"

"I'm not happy about it. We won't get him without her, though. If Wittingham can arrange her papers, then we might as well try."

"In for a penny, in for a pound? I'm surprised. I didn't think you cared one way or the other if Pilgrim made it back to the States."

"I agreed to do this. We've come far enough that I'd like to see it through."

"So would I," Hawes said. "On the other hand, they say a prison cell this time of year is quite chilly."

Hawes took another long draw on his cigarette. "By the way, I met one of the Duna girls in the lobby. Zoltan made the introductions. Lovely creature. Her name is Anna Sandor. She does resemble Diana Dors. With all of the confusion in the streets, it appears that State Security has forgotten about her and the other girls. That's according to Zoltan. He says there's usually someone keeping tabs on the girls, a man named Tibor, but he's been missing the last two days."

"Weren't you the one warning me about fraternizing with the girls? Shouldn't you take your own advice?"

Hawes grinned and shook his head. "You're married, I'm not—which makes me a poor candidate for blackmail. If I get the chance, I don't plan to whisper any of the Queen's secrets in Miss Sandor's pretty little ears, either. Just sweet nothings."

Seven

It rained overnight, and in the morning the city streets were still slick and wet leaves plastered Budapest's wide sidewalks. Collins found that the views from his hotel room windows were obscured by a thin fog hanging inertly in the chilly air, making it difficult to see across the Danube to Buda. When he ventured outside, and walked down to the embankment, he found the gray surface of the river matched the overcast sky.

When he looked north to the Chain Bridge, Collins could see Russian tanks and steel-helmeted soldiers carrying submachine guns. He watched as two Soviet officers in long, gray coats stopped to talk to the guards, pointing to the far, Buda side of the graceful suspension bridge. He had heard the distant crackle of rifle fire only occasionally, and wondered if that meant the uprising had been quelled.

Collins checked his wristwatch—it was slightly before six o'clock. Back inside the Duna, he checked at the front desk and learned that the international phone lines were still out.

He took the lift to the second floor and stopped by Hawes' room down the corridor and knocked loudly several times. There was no answer. He wondered where the Englishman could be that early in the morning. When he went back downstairs to the dining room, he didn't spot him among the small group gathered there for breakfast. Collins was halfway through his toast, boiled egg, and tea when Hawes wandered in and sat down across from him. In place of his camera, he had a pair of Ross binoculars hanging from a leather strap around his neck.

"What have you been up to?" Collins asked. "I stopped by your room and you were out."

"That I was. Since first light I've been reconnoitering with our military attaché, Lieutenant-Colonel Cowley. A busman's holiday for me. Noel and I were scoping out the order of battle for the Russians. From what we could tell through the damn fog, they've brought in the 2nd and 17th mechanized divisions. They've retaken the radio building, by the way."

"Isn't that a bit risky? Spying on them?"

"We were quite careful. Made sure not to be part of their morning target practice." Hawes seemed quite pleased with himself and Collins found his cockiness annoying.

"You know that if you get shot up, it jeopardizes the mission?" he asked. "We're here to get Pilgrim out, correct?"

"We'll accomplish that. But I've taken the King's shilling and consequently I have other obligations. Noel asked for my assistance since I'm familiar with the Red Army, and I was glad to help. You needn't worry, we took due care."

"What did you learn?"

"The Russians are positioned at all the strategic intersections. They're controlling access to the bridges. From what we could see, the insurgents are digging in. Barricades all over the place. Overturned buses and trams. Cobblestones piled up. They'll resist if the Soviets challenge them. We listened to Radio Budapest on the car radio. The government is claiming that the so-called counter-revolutionary gangs have been liquidated. They say there are only a few snipers and small armed groups left from what they're calling a foiled coup."

"Do you believe that?"

"I don't. It looks to me like a standoff. Armor alone isn't enough to suppress this—the Russians will need more troops if the plan is to put the uprising down."

"We need to contact Wittingham," Collins said. "The international phone lines are still blocked. We should try the legation telex."

"Why don't you write something up?" Hawes asked.

Collins found his reporter's notebook in his inner coat pocket. He slowly composed the message before ripping the page from his notebook and passing the piece of paper, and a pencil, to Hawes. "Quite good," Hawes said after quickly scanning it. He crossed out one word, and returned it to Collins. "That should do the trick, one way or the other."

* * *

They set out on foot for Liberty Square and the American legation. Nearly all of the buildings they passed were flying Hungarian flags with the Communist emblem cut out. Several residences displayed black flags of mourning. A few buildings had gaping holes in their facades where Soviet tank shells had penetrated and exploded, exposing the rooms inside.

They passed a makeshift barricade of paving stones and piled-up tram rails. Further up the street, a tank had smashed through a similar obstacle, spreading debris in a wide radius around the street. There had been an intense skirmish—glass shards, chunks of masonry, and spent machine gun cartridges were scattered over the surface of the street.

Collins spotted an open-topped Russian armored car that had been destroyed, now a scorched and empty hulk. The lifeless bodies of several Red Army soldiers lay in the back of the vehicle. Two uniformed men sprawled face down in the street, covered with lime. Nearby, those dead insurgents whose bodies hadn't yet been claimed for burial were draped with Hungarian flags and small bunches of flowers.

When they reached Liberty Square, they found a small crowd had gathered by the heavy wrought-iron gate at the entrance to the legation. They pushed their way through, holding up their passports for the armed Marine guard at the entrance. Once inside, a nervous flaxen-haired young man intercepted them and when Collins asked to see Mr. Katona, the man flushed. He muttered something about returning in a moment, and disappeared up the stairwell.

A few minutes later, Brooks Lawrence appeared on the stairway. He was dressed in a well-tailored brown suit and again wore a bow-tie. Lawrence descended the stairs and approached them with a slight frown on his face.

"How can I help you, Mr. Collins?" he asked.

"I'm here to see Gaza Katona," Collins said.

"I'm afraid I don't understand." Lawrence pursed his lips. "Mr. Katona is the political attaché, and I don't have him on the list for your interviews. What does this have to do with your story?"

"It's not about the story. Considering what's happening in the streets, we need to put the interviews on hold. There's something I need to discuss with him. It's urgent. A private matter."

"All of this is quite irregular," Lawrence said.

"I'd appreciate it if you could take us to him."

"I see. Very well, I'll inform him that you're here." Lawrence's tone of voice conveyed a distinct lack of enthusiasm for the idea.

Hawes cleared his throat. "If you could mention that we're here at Mr. Wittingham's recommendation. That might clarify matters for Mr. Katona."

Lawrence nodded in acknowledgment, but the sour look on his face hadn't changed. He was no innocent—he knew Katona's true position at the legation and it was clear that he wasn't pleased that Collins and Hawes wanted to see him. "Please wait here," he said.

They stood in silence while Lawrence disappeared, hurrying up the hall. They didn't have to wait for very long, because Lawrence appeared a few minutes later with a muscular, smaller man in shirtsleeves following him.

"I'm Katona. What the hell is this about?" the man asked Collins.

Collins turned to Lawrence. "Thank you, Mr. Lawrence. We'd like to discuss this with Mr. Katona in private if we might."

Lawrence reddened. "I see," he said. "Very well." He spun on his heel and retreated down the hallway, offended at being excluded from the conversation.

Katona motioned to a door halfway down the hall and they followed him into a small unoccupied office, which had floor-to-ceiling bookshelves. Collins noticed that the shelves held multiple copies of recent American bestsellers like Hemingway's *Old Man and the Sea*, and Steinbeck's *East of Eden*. Katona closed the door firmly behind him. He didn't invite them to sit, so they stood there awkwardly."

"I'll repeat myself," Katona said. "What the hell is this about? What's this about Wittingham?"

"Cliff Wittingham told me to come here and see you if I needed to contact him," Collins said. "I have an urgent message for him. We'd appreciate it if you could please telex it to the embassy in Vienna to Colonel de Silva's attention. "

"Do you mind telling me who you are?"

Collins realized he needed to slow down and provide Katona with a fuller explanation. Wittingham clearly hadn't alerted him. He told Katona his name and explained that he wrote features for the North American Newspaper Alliance and that he was assisting the Agency on a confidential matter at the request of Allen Dulles.

"A confidential matter? In Budapest? Why wasn't I briefed on this? I don't appreciate your showing up on my doorstep without a 'by your leave.'"

"We were asked not to involve legation personnel."

"I don't like this," Katona said grimly. "I don't like being kept in the dark about who you are, and what you're doing here. Especially now, in the middle of a damn revolution." He turned to Hawes. "Who are you? What's your role in this?"

"Felix Winters," Hawes said. "Pleased to meet you. London volunteered my services to help out. I spent some time in Budapest after the war and I can get by in Hungarian. Sorry about all the mystery. Neither Collins nor I had any say over that."

Collins explained that with the phone lines to Vienna out of commission, the legation seemed to be their best option to contact Wittingham with an urgent message.

"The telex is still working," Katona said. "Lord knows if and when they'll dispense with diplomatic courtesy and cut the line."

"We'd appreciate your help in coding and sending the message to Vienna."

"Do you have it with you?" Katona asked.

"I do," Collins said.

"I'll need to read it, you know."

Collins retrieved the note from his inner jacket pocket and handed the paper to Katona. There was no way around letting Katona see the message, but they had crafted it in a way they thought would protect Morris' identity: *Pilgrim demands extraction of girlfriend. If approved, need passport & papers for female journalist (Italy or Greece) soonest. Can send photos by diplomatic pouch. Urgent reply needed. DC.*

The station chief read it quickly and asked only one question. "Who the hell is Pilgrim?"

"Someone Mr. Dulles wants to see on the other side of the border," Collins said.

"Anyone I might know?"

Hawes shook his head. "Can't say. We've been instructed that until he's safe-and-sound in the States we're to refer to him as Mr. Pilgrim and leave it at that."

Sending the telex via the legation presented some risk, but Collins didn't see any way around it. Morris wouldn't leave Hungary without Eva Nemeth, and they needed forged credentials for her to make that happen. Could Katona be trusted? Collins hoped so. If someone within the legation was feeding information to the Hungarian secret police, Collins thought they had adequately protected Morris' identity. By the time anyone could make a connection between Pilgrim and Maxim Rusakov, they would be across the border, safely in Vienna.

"The only people who will see this will be myself and the cipher clerk," Katona said. "I'll watch over him while he sends the message. Do you want to wait here for a reply?"

Collins didn't hesitate. "Considering what's happening in the streets, I think that's best. It may not be easy for us to get back here."

Katona left the room with the message in his hand, closing the door behind him. Hawes looked over at Collins. "The die is cast," he said. "I'd wager that Wittingham says yes to bringing out the woman. How soon he can get us her papers is the problem."

They didn't have to wait for too long for a response to their cable. Within five minutes there was a brief knock on the door and it opened to reveal Katona.

"I have your answer," he said, handing Collins a slip of paper. It read: *Pilgrim's terms acceptable. Send photos by diplomatic courier. Passport ASAP. CW.*

"Our courier leaves for Vienna by car in thirty minutes," Katona said. "He'll have the diplomatic pouch with him. Do you have the photos of the woman?"

Collins again reached into his inner coat pocket and found the envelope that Morris had given him with Eva Nemeth's photos. He handed it to Katona, who left the envelope closed.

"I hope to hell that you know what you're doing," he said. "Whatever it is that you're up to, there's little margin for error. Too many people walking around Budapest with guns."

"We're trying to draw as little attention to ourselves as possible," Collins said. "We're not straying far from the Duna."

Katona nodded his approval. "If and when the documents arrive, we'll get word to you there. But there's no guarantee that they'll let our courier return."

"Understood," Hawes said. "We don't plan to wait much longer. If we have to, we'll leave without waiting for the girlfriend. I prefer the taste of beer to that of vodka, if you follow me. Collins does as well."

"Beer's better," Collins said. "Hands down."

"Ain't that the truth," Katona said with the hint of a smile. "Can't stand vodka, myself. Tastes like bottled machine oil, if you ask me."

★ ★ ★

They pushed and elbowed their way through the crowd of Hungarians still congregated in front of the legation and found the same park bench in Liberty Square they had occupied the other day.

Hawes handed Collins a cigarette and they both lit up. They could hear distant singing and chanting by demonstrators in front of Parliament. Collins glanced over toward the Soviet War Memorial, an obelisk at the northern end of the park commemorating the liberation of Hungary from the Nazis, and saw marchers entering Vecsey Street as they streamed toward Parliament.

Hawes grimaced. "A protest in front of Parliament seems damn provocative with all that's happened. Especially when it's guarded by the Red Army. It's not advisable to poke at bears with a bad temper, even when they're chained."

"You have to admire the courage of these people," Collins said. "They're not backing down."

A sudden burst of machine gun fire in the distance caused Hawes to flinch. When the distinctive "thump" of a T-34 cannon followed, and then the sustained rattle of machine guns firing, Hawes pulled at Collins' arm. "Time to get out of here and back to the hotel."

As they hurried to the southern edge of the square to find better cover, a few stray machine gun rounds from the direction of Parliament Square hit the buildings in the corner closest to Vecsey Street, sending plaster and masonry flying. Some ricocheted off the structures and came whizzing through the square.

They found the shelter of the doorway of a residential building. "We're out of the line of fire here," Hawes said. "As soon as it lets up, we'll head to the Duna."

Moments later a constant stream of people began pouring into Liberty Square, many of them running. Even from a distance it was clear they were in distress. Some in the crowd stopped and peered back toward Parliament Square. Collins spotted an older man carrying a slight woman in his arms—her white shirt was stained with crimson splotches of blood.

When the crowd surged closer, Collins could see the fear and shock on their faces. He saw several women weeping. Then he spotted a familiar face in the mass of fleeing Hungarians, Endre Marton, the Associated Press man they had met in the hotel bar the other day.

Collins called out to him and Marton came over and joined them in the doorway.

"What's happened?" Collins asked.

"It's not completely clear," Marton said. "MacCormac of the *Times* and I followed the demonstrators to Parliament after they marched from Lenin Boulevard. They had persuaded a few of the Soviet tank crews in front of the Astoria Hotel to join the march. But there were snipers on the roof of the Ministry of Agriculture with machine guns. They opened up on the crowd. Most likely AVO. The Russian tanks started firing back with their machine guns and cannons, first at the roofs and then indiscriminately. Lots of people killed and wounded."

"How bad?" Collins asked.

"Very bad. Women, children, students. There are bodies piled up back there."

Hawes cursed. "This will escalate the violence. The tank crews will think the march was a pretext, a way to trap them. The Russians will shoot first now and ask questions later."

"There won't be much trust on either side," Marton said. He looked around at the group of Hungarians who had returned to the entrance of the American legation, now chanting and yelling. "I need to file a story on this as soon as possible. The world needs to know what's happening here."

Marton stepped back into the flow of demonstrators heading away from Liberty Square. Hawes watched him leave and looked over at Collins. "I'm ready to give Mr. Pilgrim an ultimatum. Leave with us tomorrow or we scrub the mission."

* * *

Eva Nemeth intercepted them two blocks from the Hotel Duna. With her beret, scarf, and book bag, she looked to Collins like a Barnard College student you might encounter around Morningside Heights. She glanced quickly behind her to make sure that they were alone.

Collins told her what had happened in front of Parliament.

"We need to see Pilgrim," Hawes said. "Today, if at all possible."

Eva frowned, clearly unhappy with the idea. "That's not possible. It can't be arranged on such short notice."

"There's no time to waste."

"I don't know where Maxim is now. I must contact Viktor and he must make the arrangements. With the Russians everywhere, we must be very careful."

"Tomorrow, then," Collins said. "First thing."

"Did you find out about my papers?" she asked, turning to Collins. "Did the Americans agree? Will they get me a passport?" She saw the look of surprise on his face. "I know all about it. Maxim told me."

"They've agreed to your leaving with Morris," Collins said. "Whether they can get us the papers...." He gave her a shrug. "It depends on what happens now in the streets and at the border."

"I will contact Viktor," she said. "I will return tomorrow to take you to the meeting." She turned abruptly and walked away, moving briskly up the street.

They watched her leave in silence. "I wish you hadn't told her about the passport," Hawes said finally. "It will make Pilgrim dig in his heels. If the conditions worsen, it may become imperative that we make a break for the border. I told you before, I have no intention of spending time in a frigid jail cell this winter."

Eight

It was another night of disrupted sleep for Collins as the intermittent sounds of gunfire kept jolting him awake. Only in the very last hours before dawn did he enjoy a stretch of uninterrupted sleep, and even then he had been bothered by disturbing dreams.

His dreams were filled with ominous, dark images—bodies hanging limply from lampposts, and tanks roaring ominously down long tree-lined boulevards. In the middle of one dream, he somehow he found himself back in Korea with the Marines inside the defensive perimeter at Hagaru—it was brutally cold, stinging cold that made his face ache, and he could hear the shrill whistles of the Chinese officers in the distance as they prepared their men for an assault and the fear he felt was vivid enough to wake him and leave him gasping for breath.

When he abandoned his bed, now too restless to sleep, he felt tired and groggy, and he had a slight headache behind his eyes. Collins made his way to the bathroom sink and dashed cold water on his face. As he shaved, he noticed the dark circles under his eyes. He found his bottle of aspirin and took two tablets.

He had not had the Chosin nightmare in years. Collins wasn't surprised—the sights and sounds of combat had triggered the painful memories that he knew resided permanently somewhere in his subconscious mind.

He found Hawes in the Duna's dining room drinking a cup of tea and studying a pile of leaflets. He gave Collins a curious look when he sat down across from him.

"Tough night?"

"Not much sleep so far this week," Collins said. "I'm bone tired."

"I've got bad news. When I went out to collect these leaflets, to get a sense of the mood of the insurgents, I discovered that the Austin had been destroyed. A total loss. Shellfire hit a building next to where the car was parked. The building collapsed and the Austin's buried under a ton of bricks and mortar." Hawes sighed heavily. "Now I'll have to fill out some bloody forms to satisfy the accountants in London so Caruthers at the legation can get reimbursed for the loss of his car. Forms in triplicate, no doubt."

"What does losing the Austin mean for us getting out today?"

"I don't think that's feasible, now," he said. "With the fighting around the Eastern Station, it's likely they've cancelled the trains to Vienna. So we'll need another vehicle. Not sure I can find one immediately."

"Where will you look?"

"The chaps at the legation say there's a Land Rover we can borrow, but it's parked at a house in Buda. I'll have to talk my way past the Russians at one of the bridges to get across the river. Then I'll have to figure out how to find enough petrol for the drive."

Hawes explained that, under normal circumstances, it would take four or five hours to drive from Budapest to Vienna, but that it might take a day for the trip with the countryside in turmoil. They would have to assume that Highway 1, the main route west through Gyor to the frontier station at Hegyeshalom, would be clogged with roadblocks set up by both the Soviets and the insurgents. That would mean taking side roads whenever possible, slowing them down considerably.

Collins leaned forward, keeping his voice down. "So what do we say to Mr. Pilgrim?" he asked, aware that they were surrounded by Duna guests having breakfast.

"That he must be prepared to leave the moment we have transport," Hawes said.

"He won't go for that."

"We leave without him, then. Neither of us volunteered for arrest by the KGB."

"I didn't exactly volunteer."

"You could have turned Wittingham down."

"I could have," Collins said. "I should have. I regret now that I didn't."

"It's too late for regrets," Hawes said. "We have to make the best of the situation. I'll find a way to secure that Land Rover, and then we'll make our dash for it."

* * *

Collins and Hawes were seated in the hotel bar near the back wall when Eva Nemeth arrived and came over to their table. Collins wondered for a moment if she was staying in the neighborhood, perhaps somewhere near the hotel itself. She seemed always to be close at hand.

When they rose to their feet, she didn't take a chair, but remained standing. Her cheeks were still pink from the cold outside.

"Maxim can meet now," she said quietly, giving Hawes a quick glance. "But just with Dennis."

"Why is that?" Hawes said. His tone wasn't pleasant.

"He doesn't know you," she said.

"I don't know him," Hawes said. "That should make us equally suspicious, shouldn't it?"

"But he and Dennis are friends," she said. "Maxim can trust him. His friends might not take kindly to you showing up. They are very nervous because of what happened with Laszlo Kosa."

Collins thought about Viktor Toth and the small band of insurgents he had assembled. It could be risky for Hawes to force his way into the meeting with Morris.

"She's right," he said to Hawes. "No need for both of us to go. I can handle this by myself. It's simpler that way."

Hawes gave him a curious look, but he nodded, willing for Collins to take the lead.

"We haven't been outside yet," Collins said. "How does it look?"

"The fighting is concentrated in a few spots, mainly in the Eighth and Ninth Districts and in Buda, around Bem Square. The Russian tanks and soldiers are in front of Parliament, at the bridges, the train stations, but it's not that difficult to avoid them. On my way here, I didn't encounter any patrols."

"They've become more cautious," Hawes said. "It only took a few ambushes to put the fear of the Lord in them. Actually, that would be the fear of the Magyars, wouldn't it?"

"Maxim is waiting," Eva said, directing her comment to Collins, her face a mask.

Collins hesitated. It sounded to him that if they avoided the contested areas of the city, they would be relatively safe. Relatively. Yet he was uneasy. After covering Saipan and Okinawa and Inchon and Chosin, had he used up his luck? He told himself that if you were in the wrong place at the wrong time it didn't matter whether you were a novice or a veteran, whether you were out in the open or sheltered in a bunker. He had a Marine officer once tell him that it was simply physics—you didn't want to occupy the same space as a steel-jacketed bullet or a high-explosive shell at the same time. The wrong time.

But it appeared that the fighting was confined to the major boulevards and strategic points, places Eva could steer them around. He would take his chances. "Bicycles again?" he asked.

"Yes. We'll take the back streets. I'd rather not see any Russian faces on the way, if I can help it."

★ ★ ★

It began raining lightly as they left the Duna, leaving a fine mist in the air. Milos again had the bicycles ready for them by the back of the hotel.

"Thank you, Milos," Eva said, handing the boy some coins. "Viktor has arranged for our bicycles," she informed Collins. "And for Milos to guard them."

They mounted their bicycles and began pedaling. There was a slight breeze from the west, and Collins picked up the rich, earthy smell of the river. He figured he would stay dry in his trench coat and wearing his fedora.

The streets glistened from the drizzle and while Collins didn't like the idea of riding a bicycle in the rain, it was better than driving a car with so many trigger-happy young soldiers and insurgents in the streets.

Eva rode at a slower pace than she had the other day, wary of the slippery streets. Collins kept glancing over his shoulder to make sure there were no vehicles following them. There were a few people walking about, most sheltering from the steady rain under black umbrellas.

Eva came to a sudden stop, and when Collins caught up to her he could see the body of a man lying face-up in the gutter, a piece of paper pinned to the lapel of his jacket. His face was covered with grime and blood.

"An AVO officer," Eva said. "They've pinned his pay stub to his body. He made 9,000 forints a month. That's ten times what many of the workers make."

When they resumed their journey, Eva kept them on side streets, as she had promised—it was clear that she knew the city well. They couldn't avoid crossing some of the main thoroughfares, and Eva waved at him frantically to stop when they reached an intersection with Ulloi Boulevard.

A Soviet tank, a T-34, was moving slowly down the street away from them, perhaps three blocks away. The tank's turret swiveled rapidly to the left, firing an explosive round into one of the nearby apartment buildings. When it began to move again, the tank began sliding across the pavement, the treads failing to gain traction, and it rolled toward the curb, finally slamming into a light pole.

"Soap," Eva said. "They've spread soap on the street."

Moments later several boys who couldn't have been more than twelve years old ran into the street and jammed rocks into the treads of the tank. They dashed away and when the tank tried to move forward, there was a grinding sound—it came to a dead stop as one of its tracks slewed out onto the street.

Molotov cocktails—wine and milk bottles filled with gasoline and ignited by a burning cloth wick—began to rain down upon the back end of the tank, where the vulnerable heat vents were located. They were being tossed from either side of the street. Several smashed onto the cobblestones, bursting into flames harmlessly, but one hit the vent of the tank directly and exploded. Heavy smoke started to pour out of the rear of the tank. The turret popped open and one of the Russians appeared, head-first, only to fall back as rifle fire from snipers in the nearby buildings peppered the top of the tank.

Smoke continued to billow forth from the tank and Collins saw the first flames emerge. Even several blocks away Collins could feel the heat and smell the petroleum burning. He turned to Eva and found her face fixed in an emotionless mask. Some of the insurgents emerged from nearby buildings and watched as the tank burned, their submachine guns and carbines at the ready. Collins could see that many of them were teenagers.

"We must go," Eva said. "We'll cross here and then detour two blocks." She flinched at the sudden "thumps" as the flames ignited some of the tank's stored ammunition. Collins tried not to think about the men inside—he hoped they had died quickly.

"How far are we from the meeting place?" Collins asked.

"Another fifteen minutes," she said. "The Russians won't bother with where we are going. It's a place of no importance, not for them."

* * *

This time their destination was located in Erzsebetvaros—Elizabethtown—in the old Jewish quarter. Collins followed Eva to a narrow side street where she stopped in front of a two-story building with a cobbler's shop on the first floor. A hand-painted overhead sign with the word *Csipos* featured a crude illustration of a shoe. Eva left her bicycle next to the front door and motioned for Collins to do the same.

Viktor Toth appeared at the door, his Thompson submachine gun slung over his shoulder. "You're late," he said sharply to Eva.

"Couldn't be helped," she said. "We had to detour around some of the fighting."

"Maxim's waiting for you," Viktor told Collins. "In the back. Straight through the door."

The shop smelled of old leather and shoe polish. Several pairs of women's shoes with tags on them sat on a wooden counter. Eva waited with Viktor in the front as Collins made his way past the counter and through a door with a beaded curtain.

The back room had shelves on three sides, all filled with cheap leather shoes in various states of repair. Morris sat with his back to the cobbler's table, facing Collins and the front of the shop.

"So the word from Washington is good," Morris said. "They've accepted the idea of Eva coming with me."

"They have."

"What about her passport? When can we get our hands on it?"

"When it arrives at the legation. How long that will take them, I can't say."

"They have to understand the urgency. I haven't reported to the Interior Ministry since Tuesday and I'm hoping that they believe that I've been wounded or killed in the fighting. I can't afford to be spotted. Every day now it becomes more dangerous for me to remain here."

"So stay out of sight."

"I will. Eva tells me that you got into a fistfight with Laszlo Kosa after he slapped her. Knocked that son-of-bitch out cold. I appreciate it."

"He was spoiling for a fight," Collins said. "He kept pushing and after he hit Eva I didn't have much choice. He didn't expect that I'd know how to box."

"Nor that you would have an Irish temper."

"I've mellowed, actually. These days I go out of my way to avoid trouble whenever I can. But what about Kosa? How much of a problem?"

"As much as any jealous and bitter man would be. He won't give up. My concern is that he will tail Eva and we don't need that kind of attention." Morris rubbed his eyes. "I had a diversion planned. A rumor fed to Kosa that I had a mistress named Beata, an Austrian agent, in Szeged. Kosa would be eager to investigate, to expose me to Eva and to the authorities. His trip to Szeged would have conveniently placed him 100 miles from Budapest, to the south, at the moment of our departure." He shrugged. "Now, with the turmoil in the city I have no way of planting the rumor. Nor do I know where Kosa might be—if he's smart, he's sought protection from the Russians or he's found a secure hiding place."

"We asked for the meeting with you specifically because we need to leave immediately," Collins said. "While we can."

"Why would I do that? They've agreed to get the papers for Eva."

"There's no guarantee that they'll ever get to the legation. The Russians may not let the courier back into the country. That's why you need to be ready to leave at a moment's notice. Once we have a vehicle and gasoline we'll drive to Hegyeshalom and cross there."

"Out of the question. I won't leave Eva behind."

"Be reasonable. They can get Eva out later."

"If you were in my shoes, would you do that? Abandon her? Count on strangers to get her out later? They'll have no incentive once I'm in the States." He frowned. "What about this Englishman, Winters? Eva doesn't like him. Can we rely on him?"

"I trust him. His father was Polish, an officer, killed by the Russians at Katyn Forest. Feliks is a cool customer. He won't panic."

"There's another reason to wait I haven't told you about. There's something I must recover, something of considerable value. It's stashed where we were going to meet, at the Hill of Three Borders. It will give me some leverage when I'm back in the States."

Collins didn't like the idea. "The Red Army controls the bridges so crossing to Buda would be risky. What is it? It can't be worth the trouble."

"It is worth it." His face was set, determined. "It's scientific information, closely guarded by the Soviets. I'll explain more when the time comes. It's better that you don't know until then." Unwilling to say more, he abruptly changed the subject. "What are you reading these days? It's not been easy getting books in English here."

"I brought Graham Greene's *The Quiet American* with me, not that I've got much reading done."

Morris reached into a valise at his feet and retrieved a slim leather volume; he handed it to Collins. "Add this to your list. It's surprisingly good."

Collins glanced at the title of the book—*The Man Without a Country*. He vaguely remembered the plot and wondered if Morris was trying to elicit his sympathy.

"As soon as you have the papers for Eva, we can leave," Morris said. "I'll make arrangements to recover what I have hidden. It can be done quickly."

"You need to understand something, Morris," Collins said. It was the first time he had called him by his first name. "If it looks like the Russians are going to move into Budapest in force, we won't wait. We're leaving, with or without you."

"I understand. I'll have a clear conscience if that comes to pass. I just wonder whether you will, Denny."

* * *

When Collins left the back room of the shop he found Viktor waiting for him near the front door, a cigarette dangling loosely from his lips. He handed Collins a cigarette and lit it for him. They stepped out into the street together.

"Where's Eva?" Collins asked.

"Fresh air. She'll be back shortly." He studied Collins for a long moment. "Can you get Maxim out of the city?"

"That's the plan," Collins said. He wasn't about to offer Viktor any details.

"It's not safe for him here. My friends and I can only protect him for so long. If he's recognized as KGB he's as good as dead. Do you have what you need to move him? Is there anything I can do?"

"We're set."

"I owe him, you see. Maxim rescued me from the Fo Street prison. I spent ninety unpleasant days there as a guest of State Security. Eva asked him to intercede. Maxim came to the prison and had me released. The AVO didn't like it, but they were afraid of him."

"Eva was your connection to Maxim?" Collins tried not to appear surprised—Viktor didn't seem like he would travel in the same social circles as Eva.

"We were in school together as children and our families have always been close. Then we left for America and I was the only one stupid enough to come back here after the war. I'm the black sheep. My parents are still in the Bronx. I thought that I was homesick for Budapest. Then the Reds took over and I realized that coming back was a big mistake. I stayed out of trouble for a long while, but two years ago I got arrested."

"What for?"

"A buddy borrowed some items from a villa on the Hill of Roses. We call it the Hill of Cadres, you know." He took a puff on his cigarette and blew a delicate smoke ring and watched it float away. "A Party bigwig owned the villa and the police were eager for arrests. They caught my buddy and he claimed that I had masterminded the job. I don't blame him for that. They can make anyone say anything, you know? I was suspect already, having lived in America. I'm just fortunate that I got a message to Eva. I had heard she had friends in high places and Maxim was one of them and he came through for me." He squinted through the cigarette smoke at Collins. "Not all Jews are as book smart as Eva. Take me, I'm street smart. Never wanted to study, but I always was good with people and with my fists." He grinned at Collins. "I hear that you throw a decent punch. You handled that shit Kosa easily after he slapped Eva. Golden Gloves, that true?"

"Golden Gloves was a long time ago. I tried to avoid getting into a scrape with Kosa, but he didn't leave me any choice. I just hope it doesn't cause trouble for Eva."

"I'll make sure it doesn't. He won't bother Eva or you again. Trust me."

Collins heard the drone of an airplane and looked up into the slate-gray sky. A single-engine spotter plane was flying to the north of them and as it banked and turned there was a sudden fusillade of shots. "A Russian observation plane," Viktor said. "The boys have been trying to bring it down for the past two days."

"What about you? Will you leave the city if it gets worse? Maybe back to New York?"

"I wore my welcome out there." He gave Collins a wolfish grin. "Don't think I could get past Immigration. I've got a bit of a record, you see."

"What about London, then?"

"It's an idea. I want to see this through, first. You'd have to live here to understand it. We've been kicked around for too long and it's high time to kick back, to show them that we won't live like slaves."

"There will be consequences to that."

"They'll kill a lot of us. Sure, we know that. But they're taking losses themselves and maybe we'll get lucky and Adenauer and Eisenhower will send in the troops."

"I don't think that's going to happen," Collins said. "Maybe supplies, but sending American soldiers into Hungary would risk another war. Eisenhower won't do that."

"It doesn't matter," Viktor said. "Even if we lose, we win. The bastards from State Security will never walk down the street at night again without worrying that they're going to take a bullet in the back of the head. They'll fear us now, not the other way around. That'd be enough for me."

★ ★ ★

On their return trip to the Duna, Eva kept them from the main streets and boulevards as much as possible, sticking to the side streets and alleys. She left immediately after Milos collected their bicycles, arranging to meet Collins the next afternoon at a nearby cafe. Back inside the Duna, Collins found Hawes in the Englishman's second-floor hotel room. Hawes poured them both small glasses of palinka and located Radio Budapest on the dial of a compact Philips radio set. He turned the volume switch to the maximum, not taking any chances with possible listening devices, and the gay chords of gypsy music filled the room.

"Anna lent the radio to me," he said. "One of her prized possessions. She's a gem."

"I see you've been making friends in my absence," Collins said. "You're already on a first name basis with her?"

"I'm not shy," he said. "But it hasn't all been fun and games. I stopped by our legation to meet with Cowley. It's been a dark day, like something out of Hobbes. Brutish. Vengeance killings of secret police and suspected informers all over the city. The insurgents have been hunting them down and stringing them up by the feet to trees and lamp posts. In some cases, they've soaked them in gasoline and set them on fire."

"My God," Collins said and then stopped. There wasn't anything more he could say.

"Cowley says there are fairly strong rebel contingents in Angelfold, across the river in Moricz Zsigmond Square, and Szena Square. He's not convinced that the Red Army will respect diplomatic privilege if the situation continues to deteriorate. The chaps at the legation are worried by the Wallenberg precedent—the Swedish minister who disappeared after the Soviets took the city in '45. There's strong sentiment to send the legation staff and families out of the country. Leave behind a skeleton crew with Ambassador Fry. No doubt the same discussion at your legation about whether to stay or go." Hawes took a sip from his glass. "So what does Pilgrim say?" he asked.

"I made no headway," Collins said. "He won't go without her."

Hawes raised his eyebrows. "He's a fool. If the fighting intensifies, a lot more people are going to die. I don't care to be one of them." He swirled the brandy in his glass, reflecting. "Too many people dying. What do you think about the last trumpet, then, Collins? What happens afterward?"

"Do you mean, do I think there's an afterlife? Do I think that there's something after we die? I guess that we can hope for it. There are days I think it could be so, and then other days when I don't."

Hawes smiled. "That's not quite 'death, where is thy sting?' I can remember singing that line in Handel's 'Messiah' in the choir at Cambridge and wondering about it. You're not offering much in the way of reassurances about the sting."

"Are you looking for reassurances? You don't strike me as the type. I think we're alike in that. We do what we have to do without banking too much on a heaven or a hell."

Hawes lifted his glass to Collins in a mock toast. "I didn't know you had the makings of a philosopher in you. You could sup at Magdalene College's high table and debate existentialism and the 'great leap of faith.' Camus and Kierkegaard."

"I doubt that. I lean more to Alston and Stengel."

"Sorry?"

"Walter Alston and Casey Stengel. The managers of the Dodgers and the Yankees, respectively. They're philosophers in their own right, but practical philosophers. They believe that you play the game until the last out. No giving up. For my money, they make the most sense."

★ ★ ★

When he got back to his room, Collins washed up and changed into a clean white shirt. He wondered how long he could continue to rely on the hotel's laundry and whether he would end washing his clothes in the sink. He found the slim volume that Morris had given him and lay down on his bed and began to read it.

He was only a few pages into *The Man Without A Country* when he drifted off into a half-sleep. The sudden ringing of the phone awoke him, and he fumbled for the receiver. It was Zoltan, from the front desk, explaining that telegrams for Collins had just been delivered.

"Very unexpected," Zoltan said. "I would not have thought it possible."

Collins hurried to the lift, cursing its slowness, and made his way to the lobby and the reception desk. Zoltan gave him a broad smile and handed him the telegrams.

He ripped open the first envelope and found it was from Maria, a response to his Wednesday telegram. It read: PRAYING FOR YOUR SAFETY. CALL WHEN ARRIVE VIENNA. LOVE ALWAYS. MARIA.

Collins was relieved that his message had reached her—at least she knew that he was safe in Budapest. When he could call her from Vienna was a different question.

The second telegram was from Vienna and the Newspaper Alliance, which meant it was really from Cliff Wittingham. His message was direct: IMPERATIVE WAIT FOR ENTIRE STORY. CABLE VIENNA OFFICE WHEN RETURN TIME CERTAIN. W. Collins understood immediately—Eva's papers were on the way, and Wittingham wanted them to wait until they arrived.

It was an easy request for Wittingham to make, sitting comfortably in the American embassy in Vienna, far removed from the action. It was different in the field, Collins thought, where delay could jeopardize the entire mission. He would have to see what Hawes wanted to do.

"I could use a time certain myself," Collins muttered to himself. He decided that it would be best to ignore that request for notification—what difference did it make whether Vienna knew when they were leaving? De Silva and Wittingham couldn't do anything for them on the Hungarian side of the border, and that was where they might run into trouble.

"All's well?" Zoltan asked.

"All's well," Collins said. "My wife's eager for me to return to Vienna, which is understandable considering what the newspapers are saying about the situation here."

"And when might we expect you to depart?"

"That's a good question," Collins said. "In America, we'd call that the $64,000 question. I have a story my editor wants me to finish, and then Mr. Winters and I will be off."

Collins paused. If Zoltan was reporting to State Security—assuming that anyone was still actively fielding reports at the Ministry of the Interior, which was doubtful—Collins wanted to make sure that his departure from Budapest seemed natural. "If the trains to Vienna aren't running, we may drive," he said. "Soon, I hope."

"That would be wise, sir," Zoltan said gravely. "With all things considered, that would be very wise."

Part Two

At first light, Maxim climbed the rickety fire escape to the flat roof of the tenement, surprising a group of pigeons. The birds took sudden flight, hurriedly flapping their wings as they abandoned their roosting spots. He pulled the collar of his coat up against the wind and walked to the edge of the roof. From his vantage point there he could look north toward central Pest and to the west, he could see Gellert Hill and the Citadel, the nineteenth century stone fortress constructed by the Hapsburgs. Nearby, in a commanding spot, the Soviets had added a massive bronze of a woman holding a palm leaf aloft to commemorate the Red Army's victory over the Nazis—the Liberty Statue, although liberty was hardly what the Russians had brought to Budapest.

Both the fortress and the monument were reminders that the conquerors of the city, dating back to the Romans, had successively shaped its landscape. They had the power to alter the city however they wished, to erect whatever reminders of their vanity pleased them. It had to grate on the Hungarians.

Maxim spotted a few columns of smoke to the northeast, where there had been intense fighting. He figured buildings or vehicles were still burning. The smoke hung suspended in the frigid air. Maxim found himself shivering. He heard the staccato of small arms fire in the distance, but no sounds of heavier guns being deployed.

It gave him a sense of control, of security, to stand on the rooftop and observe the city around him. He was sure that he was safe there. Viktor had found the place, and there was nothing to connect Maxim Rusakov to the neighborhood of run-down streets in the Eighth District. The building was home to two gypsy families and a few elderly Jewish couples, and his room was located in the back, on the top floor.

In some ways, the uprising had come at just the right time. With AVO officers on the run, hiding from possible retribution from the insurgents, it meant Maxim could disappear without drawing the attention of State Security.

The confusion and chaos in the streets had bought them precious time—time for the CIA to fabricate travel documents for Eva. It would also make their cover story more plausible—that they were foreign journalists leaving Hungary after covering the uprising. Their group would be just one of many eager to return to the safety of Vienna.

Maxim had approved of the Agency's plan for his defection. It had the virtue of simplicity, which meant that there was less to go wrong, and it accommodated Eva's addition nicely. And even if some in the Interior Ministry were suspicious about Maxim's absence, he couldn't imagine that they would look for him among the of Western journalists in the country.

* * *

He had once been certain that, however imperfect the Party might be in the here and now, its members were meant to help shape history. He had clung to that faith. It justified all that he had done, the betrayal of his friends and his country, the years he had spent working for Moscow Center.

Then one day he realized that he no longer believed. There was no sudden epiphany, no road-to-Damascus-moment, just a slow, reluctant acceptance on his part that he had been living a lie, that the gap between what the Party said, and what the Party did, had grown too wide. He had lived with that knowledge for almost a year before Khrushchev gave his speech in Moscow detailing Stalin's crimes.

Early that spring he told Eva the truth, that he could no longer consider himself a Marxist, that he could not swallow the falsehoods, could not square the circle that was the reality of Communism. He did not trust the dictatorship of the proletariat; he questioned the humorless rigidity of dialectical materialism. He did not believe a classless society could exist, at least not in this world. Eva had said nothing at first, but then had confessed that she, too, no longer believed.

They knew they had to be careful, even if the new Party line embraced reform and the de-Stalinization of society. He kept his disillusionment secret. He knew that there were no guarantees that the thaw would last. There could be a return to repression at any time and those who had championed reform could contract a bad case of what the Hungarians called bell fever, *esengofrasz*, the fear of the secret police ringing your doorbell and arresting you in the hours after midnight.

He took one calculated risk. When Mikhail Durov—his mentor and protector—visited Budapest in May, Maxim carefully questioned him about the state of affairs in Moscow. He brought Durov to the Hill of Three Borders for an impromptu picnic. He found a spot with a clear view of Budapest in the distance, and they sat under a Norway maple and ate hard-boiled eggs and pickles and black bread, washing their feast down with vodka.

"Comrade Khrushchev's speech came as a shock," he told Durov. "Who could have imagined that the reality was much worse than the rumors?"

"They say that when Stalin was born with the webbed toes the priests warned it was the mark of the Beast." Durov drank directly from the bottle, ignoring the cups in the wicker basket Maxim had brought. "They were right, it seems."

"And the men around him? The men who carried out his orders?"

"The law of the jungle. Stalin called Comrade Khrushchev his Ukrainian bear and made him dance on the table in front of the others. Fat old Malenkov became Malania, a girl, and had to dance with the men. But they did what he ordered, no matter how humiliating, because they feared him."

"And now?"

"I heard a new joke last week. An old couple, Sasha and Irina, live in a flat in Moscow. Irina sends her husband out to buy some meat for supper. He queues at the shop for hours, but when he gets to the counter, the clerk tells him, 'No more meat.' That's too much for Sasha. He starts ranting about how he fought for the Motherland in two wars and he can't believe this shit. A policeman overhears Sasha and lectures him: 'Look, Grandfather, you know you can't talk like this. If Stalin was still alive, you would be shot for saying these things.'"

Durov paused for a sly smile; it was clear that he enjoyed telling the joke. "So Sasha goes home and when Irina sees that he's empty-handed, she says: 'Run out of meat again, have they?' Sasha sighs and says: 'It's worse than that, they've run out of bullets.'"

Maxim laughed politely. "Is it true? Do you believe that they have run out of bullets?"

The question erased the easy smile from Durov's face. "They will never run out of bullets. Who knows whether the wind will blow in a different direction? Comrade Khrushchev may last, but he may not. If Malenkov, Molotov, and Kaganovich—the hardliners—prevail, then we're back to square one. They'll need those bullets again. Plenty of them."

"Could they put the genie back in the bottle? After what's been said and done?"

Durov shrugged. "Perhaps not, but they would kill many, many people in trying to. The first in line would be the reformers. I hope that you have been careful, my American friend. No indiscreet comments."

"I'm careful, Misha."

"You must be. Do you trust this girl, Eva?"

"I do. We are in love."

"That's lovely," he said. "I hope it lasts." Durov drank deeply, smacking his lips when he finished. "She is a Jew?"

"She is."

"Then your sons and daughters will be Jews. With Stalin dead, perhaps not so bad. Comrade Khrushchev may be better—his son married a Jew. Still, they say he has no great love for the Hebrew race and Jews make convenient scapegoats when things go wrong."

"My grandfather was a Jew," Maxim said, surprising himself at his sudden admission. It was not something he told people, even those he considered friends.

Durov grunted in response. "You've kept that quiet. I would keep it so, if I were you. The men at the top don't trust Jews—they think they could all be Zionists, part of some conspiracy against the state. Absurd, but you'd be surprised by who believes that shit. Take my advice, stay here in Budapest, out of sight, and keep clear of the politics at headquarters. A low profile and results, that's best. We'll know in a year or so which way the wind will blow."

"And yourself?"

"Me? Who knows? For now, I'm resolved to do my job and keep my head down and my mouth shut. I was never much for theory. Words." He showed his disdain by pausing to spit on the ground. "The Party was for the worker, and the Fascists and the capitalists weren't, and it always made sense to me to fight them."

"I'll take your advice," Maxim said. "I'll keep my head down." He knew better than to say anything more to Durov. There were limits to their friendship. Even Durov, who as a teenager had fought side-by-side with Lenin and Stalin in the early days of the Revolution, who was famed for his skillfulness as a field agent in Spain and Germany, who had survived the waves of purges in Moscow, even Durov had to careful in his associations. If it became necessary, he would not hesitate to have Maxim arrested and broken, and Maxim knew that.

By the time of their picnic, Maxim had already begun to entertain the idea of leaving, of returning to the U.S. and bringing Eva with him. Only when he could be certain that the plan was sound, that the risks were manageable, would he act. He knew that when he did there would be no turning back.

* * *

Maxim felt for the Makarov in his jacket pocket. He kept the revolver with him at all times now, leaving it next to him on the night table when he slept, ready if he needed it. It was comforting hold the gun in his hand, finger lightly on the trigger, to know that it was a weapon of last resort. If worse came to worse the Makarov could buy him some time, hold off anyone coming up the stairs after him. After all, how long would he need to swallow a cyanide tablet?

Now he had to remain disciplined and patient. He had to stay hidden for a few more days. He worried only about Laszlo Kosa and what he could do if he learned of Maxim's meetings with foreigners. Eva had been cautious when she came and went from their brief meetings, and he trusted her to lose anyone tailing her. If Kosa was smart—and Maxim didn't underestimate his intelligence—he would stay off Budapest's streets, recognizing that if he were recognized as a State Security officer there would be no mercy. He would be lynched and left hanging from a lamp post.

Eva had heard rumors at the Duna that General Serov, the chairman of the KGB, was on his way to Hungary. Soon the city would be flooded with officials from Moscow Center. Maxim wanted to be long gone before that happened.

It all came down to timing. He trusted that the CIA would fabricate a passport for Eva and find a way to get it to Denny. Then, before they left for the West, Maxim had only one task left—he needed to retrieve his life-preserver, the notes from Lukas Nemeth that were hidden in a stone wall in a meadow near the summit of the Hill of Three Borders. That meant a quick detour into the Buda hills before they left for the Austrian border.

Maxim could tell Allen Dulles a great deal about the operations of the KGB in Poland and Hungary, but he wanted to bring him more. Nemeth's notes provided classified details on the Soviet missile program, details that could only come from an insider, and that would raise Maxim's value in the eyes of the Agency.

Maxim had even more, though—there was what he knew about Envoy, the penetration agent hidden somewhere in the CIA. He had learned about Envoy from Durov during his last visit to Moscow. They had been drinking and when the topic of Kim Philby had come up, Durov had mocked the incompetents in British intelligence who hadn't been able to prove that Philby was a spy. Then he had boasted about another agent-in-place that Moscow Center had nurtured over the years—code-named Envoy—who was funneling secret information from CIA headquarters in Washington. Later, Maxim worried that what he knew about Envoy could cost him his life if Durov ever revealed the extent of his indiscretion to anyone else in Moscow Center. But it also meant that he had information that would be worth a great deal to the CIA's counterintelligence officers.

It would be a difficult, but fascinating, conversation when Maxim reached the States. He had seen Dulles once in Washington in 1947—the man looked like an Ivy League professor of Classical Greek with his wire-rimmed glasses, gray hair, and tweed coat. Maxim knew better than to be fooled by that faux academic exterior, or to think that Dulles was in any way soft or sentimental—he was far from it. For the things Maxim would need in the future he had to convince the man of the legitimacy and value of his information. He was convinced that he could—he had too much riding on it to fail.

Nine

Collins had been surprised by Hawes' willingness to follow Cliff Wittingham's advice and stay in the city and wait for Eva's travel documents to arrive. While they were effectively stuck in Budapest until Hawes could requisition the Land Rover, or find another vehicle, Collins suspected his changed attitude had a lot to do with Anna Sandor.

"You're not as eager to make a mad dash for the border as you were yesterday," Collins said to him. "There wouldn't be a blonde involved, would there?"

Hawes raised his hands in mock surrender. "I'm found out. I'll blame you, Collins. You should have tied me to the mast so I wouldn't be seduced by her siren song."

"I'll take no responsibility for that."

"Once you've met her you'll see why I don't mind staying a bit longer. Anna's a delightful girl. Very cultured, very well read. And a true beauty."

Collins raised his eyebrows. "Does she also have that proverbial heart of gold?"

Hawes laughed. "I know how it must seem. I'm not naive about her circumstances, but it's different than I had imagined. During the late '20s, her father had been the military attaché in the Hungarian embassy in Warsaw, where he met her mother. Anna lost them both in 1945, killed by a Russian artillery shell. She was raised by her uncle, along with her younger brother. From what she's told me—and she's been reluctant to talk about it—State Security forced her into working here at the Duna. She was blackmailed. Threats to her family."

Collins didn't say anything. He knew better than to question Anna Sandor's story—he trusted that Hawes would figure out what was true and what wasn't on his own, and there was no need for Collins to alienate him.

Hawes interpreted Collins' silence as an indication of skepticism. "It may actually be so," he said, defensively. "Colonel Cowley says that it was common knowledge that when one of the Party bosses desired a beautiful young girl he would bully and threaten her through her family until he got what he wanted."

"From what I've gathered, with Rakosi in charge, anything was possible," Collins said.

"Cowley had some other things to say. He and the Foreign Office chaps in the legation have a shortwave connection with Whitehall, so they're not as cut off as the rest of us. He hinted to me that something was brewing with the Egyptian situation. An intervention, perhaps, to keep Nasser from closing off the Suez Canal to our ships."

"It's more than rumor?"

"Unfortunately, it is. Very bad for the Hungarians if British or American troops are sent to invade Egypt. Hard to make the case at the United Nations that the Soviets shouldn't be here."

"No question about that," Collins said. "But I'd be very surprised if Eisenhower agreed to any intervention. It smacks too much of colonialism. And with our election in ten days, it's not the best time for a president to start a shooting war."

"Cowley was cagey about the timing. Maybe they'll wait until after your president wins his reelection, but no matter when the balloon goes up, it'll be a bloody mess. Worse, it may embolden the Russians to take harsher steps here."

"More reason to get out," Collins said. "I'm willing to give Wittingham a day or two more. Then, if he doesn't come through, we should leave. Even if it's just the two of us."

"No quarrel with any of that on my part," Hawes said. "I'll concentrate on the Land Rover and Miss Sandor, in that order. We'll be ready to go, trust me."

Collins nodded. He had told Maria that he would be back by Friday, so he was already a day late in returning to New York. If everything fell into place, he might be back in the States by Tuesday or Wednesday, but he had no way of knowing the actual timing.

He decided to send his wife a brief telegram, explaining that his departure from Budapest had been delayed, and that he would call her when he reached Vienna with details of his return flight.

Collins was troubled by the situation. He was annoyed with himself for yielding to Wittingham's pressure tactics and agreeing to the mission, and he was annoyed with Morris for delaying their departure, even if he understood the reasons why. He didn't like feeling so vulnerable, and so powerless to change things.

* * *

It had been four days since the start of the uprising in Budapest and yet Collins did not know quite what to make of it—there was a slightly surreal quality to the conflict. While they could hear the muffled rattle of machine gun fire and the distant sound of tank cannons and self-propelled guns, it was calm in much of the city. Erich Lessing, an Austrian who worked for Magnum Photos, the photographic cooperative, maintained that there were only five or six pockets of resistance in Budapest with active fighting.

The brief street skirmishes were violent and brutal, however, from all accounts. Lester Kane, who had covered insurgencies in Algeria and Vietnam, told Collins there was nothing uglier than irregular warfare. "You can forget the Geneva Convention. This sort of thing degenerates rather quickly into something quite barbaric. The Hungarians are fortunate that the Russians are showing some restraint, at least for now. It's either because they want to patch things up, or because they don't have the troops and armor on hand to finish the job."

Collins knew that Kane—a level-headed veteran correspondent—had it right. Late on Friday Radio Budapest had announced that Erno Gero had been dismissed as first secretary, replaced by Janos Kadar, a Party official who had been imprisoned during the Rakosi years. Kane questioned whether bringing the reformers like Nagy and Kadar into the inner circles of the government would be enough to convince the insurgents to lay down their arms, but it suggested that at least the Russians were willing to wait-and-see if a more conciliatory approach might work.

After interviewing some Hungarian officials at the Parliament building, Kane came away convinced that, despite his title, Nagy and the reformers didn't control the government. A holdover Stalinist faction wanted the Red Army and the secret police to crush the uprising, and they were arguing against any further concessions. Two high-ranking Soviet officials, Anastas Mikoyan and Mikhail Suslov, had arrived in Budapest. What course of action they were advocating wasn't known, nor what role the Soviet ambassador to Hungary, Yuri Andropov, was playing in any closed-door deliberations.

Meanwhile, the revolt had spread to the rest of the country. Rebel groups controlled Gyor and other provincial towns like Debrecen, Esztergom, Sopron, and Tatabanya. The insurgents had begun broadcasting over Free Gyor Radio. There were scattered reports of workers' councils forming in factories in Budapest and other cities. Many of the insurgents called for some form of national Communism, where Hungary would have more independence from the Kremlin.

In the Hotel Duna's island of calm, journalists shared what information they had, trading stories and debating the likely outcome of the uprising. Collins found that he couldn't spend any time in the lobby, restaurant, or bar without hearing wild rumors: West

German tanks poised to advance into Hungary through Austria; United Nations Secretary General Dag Hammarskjold ready to fly to Budapest to broker a truce; Red Army soldiers from the Ukraine switching sides and turning over their weapons to the insurgents. Collins knew better than to place much credence in the stories—they often reflected wishful thinking or someone's over-wrought imagination.

The Duna now was crammed with foreign journalists. Their parked cars clogged Apaczai Csere Janos Street—Mercedes, Citroens, Fiats, a few Chevys and Fords, and a shiny new Austin, a concrete and sad reminder to Hawes of his recent loss.

Collins had found himself stimulated by the presence of so many correspondents—he decided he would try to file at least one story with the Newspaper Alliance about the uprising. He had seen things that he wanted to write about, and he figured he could give readers a sense of what it was like to be in Budapest, the scenes of bravery and horror in the streets that he had witnessed. Norris Jennings would welcome more news commentary datelined from Budapest to send to newspaper clients. Filing a story would also mean Collins wouldn't have to explain later why he hadn't reported on a major news story unfolding around him.

Just before one o'clock, Collins located Milos among the group of children congregated outside the front door of the Duna who pestered foreign visitors for chocolate or other sweets whenever they emerged from the hotel. Collins motioned to the boy to follow him back inside to the hotel lobby. There, he had Zoltan explain that Collins wanted to collect any and all newspapers Milos could find in the next hour and bring them to him at the Cafe Collas, where Collins had arranged to meet Eva. Collins gave Milos a fistful of coins and was rewarded with a shy smile and a bob of the boy's head.

He watched as Milos scurried out of the hotel lobby, through the revolving door, and into the street. He turned to find Zoltan appraising him.

"It will never be the same for them," he said to Collins. "These young boys like Milos. They have seen the true face of the system, and what the men behind it will do to keep power." He paused to look around, making sure they could not be overheard. "Some of them have even learned to strike back. No matter what happens, the past few days can't be erased from their memories. Nor from ours."

* * *

Outside the Duna, Collins found that it had grown slightly warmer. The sky was overcast, threatening rain, and there was a strong wind blowing from the west.

As he walked to his rendezvous with Eva, Collins buttoned his coat against the wind. The leaves drifting down onto the street, many scattered on the sidewalks, served as a reminder that back in Brooklyn it would be time to rake the leaves in his small front yard into piles for burning.

There was extensive damage from the fighting in the nearby neighborhoods. Bricks, mortar, and glass from apartment buildings that had been hit by high explosive shells lay strewn across the sidewalks and street. He spotted a line of women queued up for bread at a small bakery. They waited there stoically, ignoring the danger of a Soviet tank or armored personnel carrier driving by and spraying bystanders with machine gun fire, a nasty tactic that some of the Russians had employed as a way of clearing the streets.

He found the Cafe Collas on a narrow side street with its front plate glass windows intact, no doubt a function of its out-of-the-way location. Inside, one large, well-lit room that smelled of roasted coffee and cigarettes was crowded with tables, most of them occupied by people talking animatedly. A few sat silently, one or two staring blankly into space—Collins figured that they were perhaps struggling with sorrows from the past few days.

In the far corner of the cafe, he found an open table with a clear view of the entrance where they would not be easily overheard. Eva arrived just as Collins' waiter brought him his espresso, and she asked the man to bring her a cup as well.

She waited until she had her coffee before she spoke. "Do you have any messages for Maxim?" she asked. "Any progress to report?"

"Afraid not," he said. "We're lining up transport and waiting for the documents to arrive."

He debated telling her about Wittingham's telegram, but decided against it. If Morris learned that her passport was in transit to Budapest, there would be no hope of persuading him to leave before it arrived.

"Maxim's counting on you, Dennis." She paused. "So I am. We're deeply grateful you agreed to come here and help. I know that you have your own family to consider, and that the uprising has complicated matters greatly. We're thankful that you've stayed to help us. Maxim will be patient."

Collins wanted to remind Eva that Morris wasn't doing him any favors by remaining patient—his insistence that she accompany him out of the country had caused the delay. But what was the point in bringing it up?

So he told her that he wanted to finish what he had started, as did Winters.

"Thank me when we reach Vienna," he said. "For now, I could use your help with a different matter." He explained that he wanted to write a story or two for the Newspaper Alliance, assuming he could get through to the West over the phone or by telex. "If you could translate some of the local newspapers for me, I'd appreciate it."

"Of course," she said, giving him a warm smile. "I am your translator, after all."

As if on cue, Milos entered the cafe and looked around warily until he spotted Collins. The boy walked over to their table carrying a stack of newspapers under his right arm. He smiled shyly at Collins and placed four or five papers on the table.

Collins thanked him, and Eva murmured something to him in Hungarian, producing another smile from the boy.

Eva watched Milos weave his way through the cafe's tables and leave. "His mother drinks," she said, and sighed. "I hope he spends what you gave him on food and doesn't give it to her." She shook her head. "Viktor does what he can for the boy."

She scanned the papers and then showed Collins a one-page broadsheet. "This is *Nepszava*, the paper of the Social Democrats and," she lifted a small tabloid, "this is *Igazsag* or 'Truth.' There are more papers being published every day."

She rummaged through her pocketbook and found a small pad of gray paper and a pencil. As she read the papers she would pause to make notes and then translate for Collins, sentence by sentence. She provided a running commentary, explaining the slant of each newspaper, and how the political parties that disappeared after the Communist takeover in 1947 had quickly resurfaced.

Watching her as she threw herself into translating the newspapers, he better understood her appeal for Morris—Eva's passionate nature surfaced when she was working. He found her enthusiasm infectious—he regretted not being able to read the newspapers on the table and told her so.

"If the reform happens, like in Poland, the government might allow even Western newspapers," she said. "Imagine that. Reading *Le Monde* or *Die Welt* or even the *New York Herald Tribune*. It is hard to imagine. If this lasts, Budapest will be so different, so alive."

"Would you want to stay?"

"Part of me would, but I know better now. I shall not repeat my father's mistake and believe the promises of the politicians. He would have been delighted by what is happening now with these newspapers. Early in his career, he was a journalist, a colleague of Bela Kun. When Admiral Horthy and the Romanians chased Kun out of the country, most of the Party leaders fled to Moscow, and ended up living in the Hotel Lux, where all the exiled European

Communists stayed. My father went West, instead, to teach at the Sorbonne. He took us to Lisbon when the Germans invaded."

"How did he manage to get your family into Portugal? Salazar had no use for Reds."

"My father was a charming man. A saber fencer of some skill as a young man. Skilled enough to fence in some international competitions where he met a Spanish fencer, an aristocrat, Diego Hernandez Santiago. They were polar opposites politically but they were *simpatico* and they became fast friends. Señor Santiago, a monarchist, fought for the Nationalists in the Civil War. When my father had to leave France, Santiago used his influence to arrange for us to live in Lisbon. I'm sure he bribed someone in the Salazar government."

Her face hardened. "The irony is that what saved my father in 1941, this intervention by his Spanish friend, cost him his life in 1950. It was a ready-made indictment for Rakosi's police. My father clearly was a secret rightist—why would a murderous supporter of Franco have helped him otherwise?"

"Why did your father come back to Hungary after the war? Why didn't he stay in Lisbon or Paris?"

"That I understand. It was a mixture of guilt and idealism. He felt that he had sat out the war, made no real sacrifices for the cause. He was a romantic Communist, and when the chance came to build a socialist Hungary he jumped at it. His brother, Lukas Nemeth, a physicist, had gone to work in the Soviet Union. When State Security came for my father, he assumed that his loyalty to the Party would save him. He was wrong."

"Couldn't his brother have run interference for him? Involve the Soviets?"

"It wouldn't have mattered. In fact, it would have harmed him. By then, Stalin believed the Jews were subversives, all part of a Zionist conspiracy. What value would the testimony of my uncle, a Jew, have under such circumstances? Most of the Hungarian Communist leaders were Jews, and I believe that my father, along with Laszlo Rajk and a few others, were sacrificed by Rakosi to prove he wouldn't protect 'Zionists.'"

"Your father was executed."

"He was. Beaten and tortured and made to confess to imaginary crimes."

"And your mother?"

"She died a year later. From heartbreak, I think." She looked over at him. "You have children, Mr. Collins?"

"I do. Two sons."

"How old are they?"

"Caleb is six and Matthew is almost four. We have our hands full."

"We want children. But not here. I've told Maxim I'll not bring a child into the world under these conditions. France or Portugal or the United States, yes. My uncle Lukas says we should go to Israel."

An older man at the table closest to them cleared his throat. He had a trimmed gray beard and deep lines creasing his face. "Excuse me," he said to Collins, carefully appraising him. "Are you English?"

"I'm an American."

"Wonderful," the man said. "Are you a journalist?" He glanced at the pile of newspapers on the table.

"I am."

"You must help us. You must tell America to send us guns. Bazookas to cripple their tanks. Ammunition. Supplies. We don't need your soldiers. We can fight the Russians by ourselves, if you'll give us the tools."

"I understand," Collins said. He could see that the tenor of the conversation had made Eva nervous. She had crossed her arms and she wouldn't look at the man. Collins rose to his feet. "Please excuse us," he told the man. "We must be going, but I will do my best to report what is happening here."

Collins found their waiter and settled the bill before following Eva out of the cafe. Outside, Eva shook her head. "I don't know how much of our conversation that man heard," she said. "I forgot where we were. I should have never talked of the past. I know better. We can only hope that he's not an informer."

She took Collins by the arm and pulled him closer. "I will come to the Duna tomorrow," she said, lowering her voice. "Perhaps you will have better news?"

He told her that he hoped that would be the case, but it depended on Agency officials in Vienna procuring the needed documents and forwarding them.

"They will protect us in America?" she asked. "They'll do what they have promised?"

Collins thought about the one defector he had met in the United States, a Russian diplomat named Vadim Tolstoy. After his debriefing, the CIA had given Tolstoy a new identity and relocated him to Arizona. Tolstoy had been a sad man, homesick, cut off from the life he had known. Collins imagined that he would spend the rest of his life looking over his shoulder. It wasn't an observation he would share with Eva.

"Once you and Morris reach the States, you'll be fine," he told her. "They'll help you start over. They'll keep their word."

Ten

Collins telephoned the American legation early in the morning, identified himself, and asked for Gaza Katona. He waited for several minutes until Katona finally picked up the receiver at his end.

"Anything new to report?" Collins asked, trying to keep his question as vague as possible, aware that the line might be tapped by State Security.

"There's been heavy fighting in the Eighth District, near the Corvin cinema and the Kilian Barracks," Katona said. "An early morning attack led by Soviet armor. From what we can gather, it's been repulsed. The insurgents at the barracks are being led by a Hungarian Army colonel, a man named Maleter." He paused for a long moment. "As to more specific information about Washington's reaction, we haven't heard anything from the embassy in Vienna."

"I see," Collins said. Katona's reference to the embassy in Vienna was clearly meant to signal to Collins that Eva's documents hadn't arrived. In case that the call was being monitored, Collins decided to ask the type of question that a journalist might pose to the American political attaché. "What's the Hungarian government saying about all this?"

"We understand that Prime Minister Nagy will call for a ceasefire and for the dissolution of the AVO. It's still not clear he can control the hardliners in his own government. Can't tell you whether either side will agree to stop shooting, and it's complicated by the fact that the insurgents don't have a well-organized leadership."

"Thanks for the info," Collins said.

"Glad to be of help." Katona cleared his throat. "In the future, why don't you contact Brooks Lawrence about any developments of interest? We ought to keep our press attaché busy, and Brooks can always find me if there's anything of specific interest where I can shed some light."

"That would be fine," Collins said. They said their good-byes and hung up.

He understood immediately why Katona had directed him to Lawrence. The less direct contact that Katona had with Collins, the better. Hungarian and Soviet intelligence officers would know Katona was the CIA station chief, and if they were monitoring the phones and watching the legation they would find any continued connection with Collins suspicious.

★ ★ ★

After returning to the Duna, Collins couldn't find Hawes when he went looking for him. Collins wondered if he was attending to the Land Rover or to Miss Sandor.

After a late lunch, he found Eva Nemeth waiting for him, perched on a couch in the lobby. She greeted him with a smile, but Collins shook his head slightly, signaling to her that he had no progress to report. He was about to invite her to step outside the hotel when Lachlan Ferguson approached them.

"You ought to join us," Ferguson said. "A group of us are having a private party over in the hotel's dance hall. No band, but we'll make do with a phonograph and a few bottles to liven things up."

Eva surprised Collins by clapping her hands together in delight. "I love to dance," she said and then glanced over at Collins. "That is, if you would like to, Dennis."

"Sure," he said. "Why not?" A party with dancing might seem callous to an outsider while fighting continued outside in the city's streets, but Collins had learned that when you covered combat, you had to find ways to relieve the tension. A small light-hearted party was as good a way as any.

The Duna's dance hall featured a high ceiling and an aged crystal chandelier. Its scuffed wooden floor was in need of a waxing. Although the bandstand was empty, sheet music for the dance band still filled the music stands.

Several of the small tables had been pushed together, and a group of journalists, including Lester Kane and Isabelle Lavalle, occupied the improvised table's far end. Bing Crosby and Dixie Lee were singing "The Way You Look Tonight" on a Victrola phonograph that was connected to a wall outlet by a long extension cord.

"I haven't heard that song in years," Collins said. "The last time must have been before the war."

"Not likely there'd be many new American records available after the Reds took over in '47," Ferguson said.

"There was a club, the River Room, which had marvelous jazz," Eva said. "It stayed open when Imre Nagy was premier, but when Rakosi came back in power the government closed it. Decadent music, they said."

One couple left the table and began dancing, and Eva turned expectantly toward Collins.

"Ready, Dennis?" she asked, and then, lowering her voice, she told him that he was the only one there she felt comfortable with as a dance partner. "I don't have to worry about you making a pass at me."

"Fair enough."

He led her onto the floor and quickly discovered that Eva's enthusiasm greatly exceeded her skill. She struggled to follow his lead, but despite her awkwardness, it was clear that she was enjoying herself.

"It's wonderful to hear this music again," she said. "And to dance to it. It's all of the small things they take away. Piece-by-piece until they can control everything."

"You won't have to worry about that," he said. "Not in a few days. You can dance to your heart's content."

Someone put on a slow number on the phonograph and Collins led Eva back to the table. There were bottles of Scotch and brandy on the table, and a few bottles of the local beer with the image of a giraffe on its colorful label. He opened two of the beers and handed one to Eva. He took a sip and found that it had a strong, malty taste. Collins looked up to find Felix Hawes at his elbow, a beautiful blonde young woman at his side.

Hawes introduced her to the group as Miss Anna Sandor and Collins took her hand briefly. "Pleased to meet you, Miss Sandor," he said. "Felix has been singing your praises, as much as a proper Englishman ever could."

"Do you think he is very English?" she asked. "I think of him more as a Polish knight-in-arms. He's medieval."

Collins noticed a thin, white scar ran down the outside of her cheek and stopped at her chin-line. He wondered what had happened to her that would have left such a strange scar. Perhaps sensing his scrutiny, she angled her face slightly away so the mark wasn't as noticeable.

"I'm half-Polish," Hawes said. "But I remain an Englishman. I don't know how proper."

Ferguson overheard them and laughed. "'For in spite of all temptations, to belong to other nations, he remains an Englishman.' Isn't that so, Winters?"

"What are you quoting?" Eva asked.

"It's from a Gilbert and Sullivan song," Ferguson responded. "From 'HMS Pinafore.' Great show. I saw it in London last year."

Hawes and Anna took seats across from Collins and Eva. "Speaking of the stage, tell me, Collins, doesn't Anna look a bit like Diana Dors?" Hawes asked.

"Haven't seen enough of Diana Dors to say," Collins said. "But Miss Sandor would hold her own with the movie stars I've met."

She flushed slightly. "Thank you for the compliment, Mr. Collins. Have you met many of these American movie stars?"

"A few," Collins said. "An occupational hazard of writing a newspaper column in New York. It's strange because you feel you know them, because you've seen them on the screen, but of course you don't. They're completely different from the characters they play in the movies." Rita Hayworth and Grace Kelly were the two most beautiful actresses Collins had met, and either could immediately stop conversation in any room they entered. Anna Sandor had the same striking good looks.

"I'll bet none of your movie stars have read Goethe," Hawes said. "And Anna has."

"She has the advantage over me, then, as well, because I haven't read Goethe," Collins said. "He wrote 'Faust' right? Some German intellectual who sells his soul to the devil? He gets religion at the end?"

Anna began giggling and the rest of the table joined her in laughter. "That's quite a summary of 'Faust,' even it's not quite right," she said.

"Goethe was preoccupied with religion, though," Lachlan Ferguson said. "Never shook off his Lutheran gloom. At least the Catholics have confession so they can sin knowing there's penance. I think that underneath the Marxist veneer, this is a Catholic country." He looked over at two couples who were dancing. "Dancing on a Sunday could never be considered sinful here."

"Where is dancing considered sinful?" Eva was puzzled. "That's quite strange."

"In Scotland nearly everything's considered sinful on Sunday. We're gloomy Protestants, just like the Lutherans. Dancing, singing, whistling—all sins."

"Whistling?"

"We're meant to observe the Fourth Commandment strictly, at least according to the Free Church—what we call the Wee Free. They pursue the venial sins, not the mortal ones, with a vengeance.

There's a joke about it. Should I tell it?" Ferguson waited for nods and smiles around the table before he continued. "On a beautiful sunny Sunday, Hamish Mclare, a fine figure of a man, stopped at a nearby farmhouse. He had quite a thirst and Molly, the farmer's pretty daughter brought him a cool glass of buttermilk. They were young, and it was the spring and one thing led to another and they found themselves rolling around in the hay in the barn."

Ferguson's brogue had deepened. "As Hamish took his clothes off he so pleased with life that he began whistling 'Comin' Thro' the Rye.' Molly glared at him and buttoned her blouse back up. 'Lassie, what are ye doing?' Hamish asked. Molly gave him a frosty look. 'I canna fornicate with a man who whistles on the Sabbath.'"

Ferguson beamed in triumph at the laughter that followed.

"Is this true?" Anna asked Hawes. "What Mr. Ferguson says about Scotland?"

"Some of it," Hawes said. "But I wouldn't put it past him to concoct some tall tales."

Ferguson continued to grin. "I'll need another bottle before the truly tall tales are dusted off."

Eva leaned over and asked Collins if they could talk in private for a moment. They had a brief whispered conversation by the bandstand where he explained that her documents hadn't arrived; they agreed she would stop by the Duna the following morning.

When they returned to the table, Eva thanked Lachlan for including her in the impromptu party before excusing herself. "With all that is going on in the city, my aunt will be worried sick if I'm late," she explained. "I hadn't planned on staying here so long."

After she had left, Isabelle Lavalle slipped into Eva's seat next to Collins. Collins saw Lester Kane glaring at him over her shoulder.

"Lester wants to dance with me," Isabelle explained, keeping her back to Kane. She tilted her head slightly, watching Collins. "I'd rather dance with you."

"That's a bit awkward, isn't it?"

"Only if you don't dance with me, because then I've no excuse for turning him down."

She fixed her eyes on him. Collins wasn't comfortable with the situation, but he nodded. He noticed that Kane got up from the table and left the dance hall when Collins and Isabelle took to the floor.

"Lester's jealous," she said. "Perhaps he thinks you will begin whispering to me, like you were with Eva."

"That was about work," Collins said. "Eva's convinced there are microphones everywhere, so she insists on whispering. Makes me feel like we're in a Hitchcock movie."

"What woman doesn't like having a handsome man whisper to her? You can whisper to me, and it doesn't have to be about work."

Her perfume, Chanel No. 5, was what Penny Steele had worn when Collins had dated her before the war, and it brought back memories of the many times they had danced in New York nightclubs, sometimes until dawn.

The music had changed to one of Collins' favorite Cole Porter songs, "At Long Last Love," and he led Isabelle into a quick foxtrot. She moved smoothly along with him in tempo, her left hand resting easily on his upper arm.

"You're a very good dancer," Collins told her.

"*Merci.* As are you."

"I learned from an Austrian dancing instructor in New York," Collins explained. "She would swear under her breath when I stepped on her toes, so I picked up some German curses as well."

"Do you dance often in New York?"

"Not often enough for my wife," Collins said.

"Is she also a journalist?"

"No, these days Maria has her hands full raising our sons."

"What are their names?"

"Caleb and Matthew."

"I would have guessed that you would have sons," she said. "Will you teach them to box? And to dance?"

"Both boys are crazy about baseball at the moment, so the boxing and dancing will have to wait."

When the song ended, Collins led Isabelle back to the table. He noticed that Hawes and Anna had disappeared, and Ferguson was deep in conversation with a Reuters correspondent.

"You're different," Isabelle said. "Most men ask me about my looks. About my family background. You're not curious?"

"I figured that would be rude," he said. "If you wanted to tell me, you would."

"My father was a French diplomat in China," she said. "He met my mother in Shanghai. She came from a very wealthy family. They fell in love—quite a *scandale* at the time. She died soon after giving birth to me, and my father brought me back to Paris, where I was raised, largely by my grandparents, since he traveled extensively. I did not see him very much as a child."

"How did you become a photographer?"

"It began as a hobby. I spent the war years in Algeria with my father. I had a Coronet Rapide camera, and I took pictures of everything. It became my great passion, *ma passion grande*. After the war I sold some pictures to *Le Monde*, and then *Life*, and the last few years Agence France-Presse has hired me for assignments."

"And what led you to taking photos in war zones?"

"I greatly admired the work of Bob Capa. I wanted to make photos like he did. Combat brings you closer to those moments of pure emotion—fear, terror, sadness, exhilaration, selflessness, courage. It's all there in the faces. There's no pretense. Our masks are dropped."

"Until it becomes unbearable to see," Collins said quietly. "Or you grow a skin so thick that nothing can penetrate. Sorry, but either seems to me a dead end. Capa stopped, didn't he? Then *Life* persuaded him to go back into the field in Indochina, and he got too close. It was a mistake, wasn't it? He should have stayed out."

"His luck ran out," she said. "It was his time. One wrong step, a land-mine, and...." She paused. "If he had turned down *Life*, they would have asked me, and I would have been with that French regiment at Doithan. It might have been my luck running out. And then Capa might have come here. He was from Budapest, you know—changed his name from Endre Friedmann. When he was eighteen, Horthy's secret police beat him badly and threw him in jail for demonstrating against the regime. No surprise that he left Hungary."

She touched him gently on the arm, resting her fingers on his coat sleeve for a long moment. He found her very attractive, which put him on guard, aware of how quickly and easily flirtation could escalate into something more. Collins had seen too many marriages derailed by what started out as a casual fling. He wasn't going to risk what he had with Maria.

"We could continue this conversation in my room, later," she said. "I've a bottle of cognac we could finish."

"That's a tempting offer," Collins said. "But I don't think that'd be very wise on my part. I try to stick to beer."

"I'm sure we can find some beer, and I'm sure we can think of other diversions to pass the time."

"I'm sure we could, but when I was in school Sister Roberta lectured us quite often about the occasion of sin. Being alone with you in your room would fit that bill."

"Do you worry that your Sister Roberta will surprise us by showing up in the lobby and scolding you?" A smile played at the corners of her lips.

"I don't," Collins said. "But I think she was a wise woman, nonetheless."

He was about to say more when the small figure suddenly appeared before them—it was Milos. The boy tugged on Collins' sleeve and said something in Hungarian which Collins didn't understand, but it was clear that he wanted Collins to come with him. Collins turned to Isabelle and excused himself.

"My young friend apparently has something he wants to discuss. If you'll excuse me?"

She nodded, bemused. "The invitation remains open," she said. "If you should change your mind."

* * *

Milos led him down a long, barren back corridor of the Duna. They reached double doors that opened onto an alley behind the hotel. Viktor Toth waited there, his back against the wall, smoking a cigarette. If he had a weapon with him, it was concealed. Viktor said something to Milos and the boy trotted up the alleyway.

"I'm here with a warning," Viktor began. "Since Eva told me about your fight with Kosa, I've had some of my boys keeping watch over the Duna. Kosa was spotted twice yesterday near here. He had a companion with him, a tall man."

"It was probably his colleague in State Security, Istvan Melles. He took care of Kosa after our fight."

"I know Melles," Viktor said. "This isn't good. Maxim agrees. It's quite a risk for Kosa to move about the streets. He's known as AVO and could easily end up hanging from a lamp pole. If he's taking that risk, there must a reason. He may be planning to come after you. Payback for the fight. My boys will continue to watch, but you should arm yourself. Talk to your English friend about it."

"I don't like that idea."

"You must be realistic. If Kosa gets past my boys, you don't want to be defenseless." Viktor frowned. "Have you made any progress on Maxim's departure?"

"We're still waiting for Eva's papers from Vienna," Collins said. "She can't leave the country without them."

"Imre Nagy's been on the radio," Viktor said. He took a long puff from his cigarette. "He says the Soviets will withdraw from the city immediately, and State Security will be dissolved. There's a general amnesty for the rebels and Nagy's ordering a ceasefire." He rubbed his eyes. "I don't know whether to believe any of it. It could be a trick."

"Do you think it will work? Calm things down?"

"If it's on the level, yes." Viktor dropped his cigarette onto the pavement and extinguished it with his shoe. "With Kosa around, we've decided that Eva will no longer come here to the Duna. In the future, I'll be your contact. If you need me, Zoltan will know how to reach me."

"Zoltan?"

"He's been told that helping me—and you—will hurt the Russians. That's all he needed to hear. He's too old to be out in the streets with a Molotov cocktail or a tommy gun, but he wants to do his part. After Parliament Square, everyone does."

Eleven

Monday, October 29

It was bitterly cold in his room when Collins awoke. He checked his watch and saw that it was just before six o'clock. He got out of bed and went over to the radiator and found it was barely producing any heat. He figured that the Duna was conserving its coal.

He tried the hot water faucet in the bathroom and was rewarded by a trickle of ice cold water. He decided against trying to shave just yet—he would ask the hotel kitchen to boil some water for him so that he could attack his two-day-old stubble with some hot lather and a razor.

From the window he could see snowflakes drifting in the air outside, but they were melting by the time they reached the cobblestones below. When he glanced over at the Danube, he couldn't see very far—the Buda side of the river remained shrouded in fog.

A column of Soviet tanks heading across the Chain Bridge disappeared into the fog. By the bridgehead, a line of trucks filled with infantry waited to follow. He wondered whether the Russians were planning to attack the rebels in Buda, either at Szena or Moricz Zsigmond Squares, the pockets of resistance that Erich Lessing, the Magnum photographer, had talked about. Or were they withdrawing as Nagy had announced in his radio address?

When Collins joined Hawes in the dining room for breakfast, the Englishman told him that Colonel Cowley had confirmed a widespread pullback of Soviet forces. "Apparently Nagy has persuaded Suslov and Mikoyan that the heavy boot on the throat will be counterproductive at the moment."

Collins finished buttering his toast before he replied. "I have some news, as well. Pilgrim's friend Viktor stopped by with a warning. Laszlo Kosa has been spotted in the vicinity of the hotel. Viktor says that we should be prepared for Kosa taking a run at us. He thinks both of us should be armed."

Hawes made a face. "So this Viktor chap knows about me?"

Collins shrugged. "Pilgrim and Viktor aren't leaving anything to chance. I'm sure they've debriefed Eva after every meeting with us."

"If Kosa is hanging about, we'll need to be better prepared. I'll see what I can scare up in terms of side arms."

"Do you think that's necessary?"

"Viktor apparently does, and I'm inclined to take his advice. I'll walk over to the legation and see what I can borrow from Colonel Cowley. Lord knows there are enough weapons floating around. I'll also raise the question of transport—if there are other vehicles we might use."

"By the way, Viktor's our contact, now, not Eva."

"Makes sense, with Kosa in the picture."

Collins took a bite of the toast and a quick sip of his coffee. He was hungrier than he had thought—it was probably a function of the cold. "While you're at your legation, I'll touch base at mine. If the courier has gotten through, Wittingham's package should be there."

"Keep your eyes open on the way there," Hawes said. "Any sign of Kosa, head in the opposite direction. There's nothing worse than a sore loser."

★ ★ ★

Collins was spared a trip to the American legation, because when he passed through the Duna's revolving doors, he found Brooks Lawrence stationed outside, waiting for him by the front entrance.

"Thought I'd drop by," Lawrence explained. "Best to stay off the phone lines." He looked up and down the street. "Mr. Katona has asked me to act as liaison. His deputized go-between." Then he winked at Collins. Collins struggled not to laugh out loud at the absurdity of Lawrence—with his uncanny resemblance to the meek Stan Laurel—casting himself in the role of the dashing secret agent.

"Katona mentioned that on the phone. Did the courier from Vienna arrive? Anything in the diplomatic pouch for me?" It was cold enough that Collins' breath hung in the air.

"Afraid not," Lawrence said. "Mr. Katona checked and there wasn't. You're expecting something?"

"I am," Collins said. "From Vienna, something from my editor."

"They gave Evans a bite to eat and then had him promptly turn around for the drive back to Vienna. With any luck, he'll return on Tuesday."

"What about the ceasefire?" Collins asked. "Is it holding?"

"No way of knowing. In fact, there's been talk of evacuating most of our legation staff and their families. The Brits are planning to do the same. Despite Nagy's speech, we're concerned that the fighting may escalate."

"Will you stay at the legation?"

"I've volunteered to do so," Lawrence said proudly. "The least I can do."

"Appreciate your making the trip over here," Collins said. "Could you telephone me immediately if the courier does have something for me tomorrow?" Collins wanted to return to the warmth of the hotel, but the press attaché ignored the hint.

"If Mr. Katona feels the phone line is secure enough, then I'll call. Otherwise, I'll darken your doorstep again. Taking the utmost precautions, of course. Weather eye for the bad guys, of course." He stroked his chin and then lowered his voice. "I owe you an apology about the other day. I hadn't realized that you and Mr. Katona had such a close working relationship. In the future, you can count on my complete cooperation. Just say the word."

"Thank you," Collins said. "I'll stay in touch."

Lawrence nodded, winked again, and after another scrutiny of the street, slowly walked away in the direction of the legation. Collins found himself grinning. The irony was that Brooks Lawrence had the makings of the ideal spy—he was the last person on earth you'd expect to be involved in espionage.

* * *

Feliks Hawes returned to the Duna from his trip to the British legation in a triumphant mood, sporting a wide grin and smoking a thick cigar. He found Collins in the bar and had an invitation for him. "Come outside and see our new chariot."

Collins followed him to the street. There, Hawes pointed proudly to a dark-green Land Rover station wagon parked up the street from the Duna. It had the Union Jack draped across its hood

"Group Captain David, our air attaché, drove us across the Liberty Bridge and we convinced the Russians there to let us pass. Gave the officers cigars." He took a puff on his cigar. "Told them we were picking up a car for the legation, which was technically accurate. David's nickname is 'Hurricane,' by the way—a Battle of Britain ace. As you might imagine, undaunted by a few Red Army soldiers."

"The courier from Vienna did not bring a passport or papers for Eva this morning," Collins said. He described Lawrence's comic visit to the Duna.

"A strange chap, that one," Hawes responded. "Volunteering, is he?"

"Katona's using him as a cut out," Collins said. "To reduce his contact with me and that makes sense. Lawrence's desperate to know what we're up to, but Katona's not about to tell him anything, nor am I."

Collins followed Hawes over to the Land Rover. "Shall we take it for a spin?" Hawes asked. "I think the streets are relatively safe. I drove past several Russian tanks without a problem. We have the flag on the bonnet, as well."

Collins nodded. He was curious to see what Budapest looked like after several days of fighting.

Hawes drove through the center of the city. Although they found street sweepers busy cleaning up the glass, bricks, and debris in the road, they had to slow several times and detour around piles of rubble. When they reached Terez Boulevard, Collins was shocked at the extent of the damage—virtually every intact building showed signs of the fighting on their pitted facades. Several buildings had collapsed, their bricks spilling out into the street.

They passed a burned-out black automobile, turned on its side, a Poboda, the vehicle commonly driven by State Security. Further on, a heavily-damaged Soviet tank and an armored personnel carrier, both badly scorched, sat in an intersection. The tank commander's body was slumped over halfway out of the turret. On the cobblestones around the tank four small bodies were sprawled on the ground and Collins saw that they were teenagers.

Hawes surveyed the scene dispassionately. "David and I have talked about their tactics. The younger fighters run up to the tanks and try to ignite them with Molotov cocktails. Or they jam stones or metal rods into the treads to stop them and then throw the gasoline bombs."

"Where did they learn how to do this?" Collins asked.

"In school, of all places. They were required to study a book, *The Young Guardsman*, about a Soviet guerrilla fighter from the Great Patriotic War. It laid out in detail the tactics the partisans used behind the German lines. Hit and run ambushes. Directions on how to concoct a Molotov cocktail." He cursed under his breath. "I hate to see this. They're children. They should be learning their sums, not killing in the streets."

* * *

Hawes drove west until they reached the river, and then headed south parallel to the Danube. He parked the Land Rover on the street near the embankment, where they could see the Chain Bridge and its famous stone lions.

"I almost forgot my other success of the day," Hawes said. "Colonel Cowley was kind enough to loan us two of these." He reached into his coat pocket and produced a revolver. "An Enfield .38, with the barrel cut down for commando use so it's small enough to carry in a pocket. If we encounter Kosa and his friend at close quarters, I'd like to even the odds." He frowned at the thought. "We'll keep them with us just for the remaining time in Budapest and return them to Cowley before we leave."

Collins explained that he didn't like carrying a weapon. As a rule, journalists only did so as a last resort. It was true that in the fall of 1950 many of the American and British combat correspondents in Korea had armed themselves after the Chinese intervention, but those were desperate times.

"Consider it a necessary evil, Collins," Hawes said, and offered him the butt of the weapon. "It should only be for a few days. The revolver's loaded and the safety is on."

Collins reluctantly took the revolver from Hawes and placed it in his coat pocket. He didn't want to tell Hawes that the last time he had fired a shot he had killed a man. Collins had acted in self-defense—Anatoli Yatov had initiated the exchange of gun-fire–but he had been deeply troubled by what he had done.

Hawes gazed out over the Danube, lost in thought. "So now that we're ready to go, the irony is that I have a strong reason to want to stay. Anna."

Collins didn't say anything.

"She's not like any woman I've been with."

"A romance can be quite intense, when people are dying around you," Collins said.

"I've thought about that. There was this weekend with a girl in London, during the Blitz, where we shagged so frantically I thought we might do harm to each other, or at least break the bed. We had little in common and so when the Jerries stopped bombing us the romance didn't last. It hasn't been like that with Anna. It's more than the physical. We understand each other. She has a marvelous sense of humor, and she's not afraid to laugh at me."

"Not what you expected?"

"Not at all. I've learned more about her past. Her uncle took her and her brother to the family's summer place at Lake Balaton after her parents were killed in '45. They returned to the city two years later and things were fine for a time. Then trouble started. Her brother, Ferenc, was purged from the University as the son of a class enemy. Then Anna caught the attention of a high Party official—with her looks that wasn't surprising."

Hawes kept his eyes on the river, considering his next words. "The bastard, a man named Bela Molnar, had Ferenc arrested and thrown in the Fo street prison. Anna was seventeen years old and loved her brother. When she agreed to become the man's mistress, her brother was released. Then Molnar fell out of favor, and was purged. State Security told her that if she wanted to continue to protect her brother, she would have to entertain selected visitors, businessmen and journalists, from the West. Anna was often clever enough to get them drunk and pry enough information from them to satisfy the AVO without having to go to bed with them. But there were other times…." Hawes shook his head, his face hardening. "She felt lucky, because she spoke English. The girls who spoke only Russian had to sleep with the Soviet officials visiting Budapest, and from what Anna gathered, they were animals."

"An ugly story. I'm sorry for her."

"I've decided to help her get out of Hungary," Hawes said. "It's the least I can do."

"How do you plan to accomplish that?"

"British subjects in Budapest are to be evacuated to Vienna. There will be a convoy, a caravan of sorts, and I want her in it."

"She's not British, though."

"Not officially. An emergency passport made out in her name, however, will get her across the border. The staff at the legation has been very helpful. The passport is good for 30 days. We'll have to find her something more permanent once we're in Vienna.'"

"What about her family?"

"Her uncle died two years ago. Her brother is with the fighters at the Kilian Barracks." Hawes paused, reflecting for a moment. "I thought about using the legation convoy to take Rose and Eva out of the country, but if things went wrong at the border, it would look very bad. The Soviets would seize upon it as evidence that MI6 had masterminded the uprising, along with the CIA. It'd be a propaganda victory for them, and you can imagine the consequences for Rose and Eva."

"We're better off with the original plan," Collins said. "If the documents arrive tomorrow, we may beat the convoy to Vienna."

Twelve

Brooks Lawrence telephoned from the American legation mid-morning with disappointing news. While Evans, the courier, had returned from Vienna without incident, he hadn't brought any mail for Collins.

It was a brief conversation and Lawrence promised to contact Collins as soon as he had more news.

Moments after he hung up, there was a knock on his door; Collins opened it to find Hawes standing there. "Let's take a walk," he said. "Bring along your gift from yesterday, would you?"

Collins put the Enfield in his coat pocket—making sure that the safety was engaged—before following Hawes to the lift.

Outside, it wasn't as cold as the day before and Apaczai Csere Janos Street was bathed in weak sunlight. From across the street, a thin teenager with an acne-scarred face and dirty-blond hair, gave Collins a thumbs-up sign and the older man standing next to him gave him a mock salute. They both wore tricolor armbands and had submachine guns slung over their shoulders.

"Viktor's crew," Collins said. "He told me he would have us shadowed whenever we left the Duna."

"They're here for you, Collins, not me. They ignored me earlier today when I left the hotel."

The men followed them as they walked east, away from the Duna. The blond teenager crossed to the other side of the street, keeping pace with them, and Viktor's other man floated fifteen paces or so behind them.

"A nice show of force," Hawes said. "Is this how the mob bosses in New York are protected?"

"Contrary to common belief, mob bosses aren't found on every corner in New York," Collins said. "Some days you only meet ten or fifteen on the street."

Hawes grinned at the joke. He then related what he'd learned during his visit to the British legation. "The Israelis have attacked in the Sinai. We've issued an ultimatum for both sides to stop fighting. If they don't—and that's likely—it appears that we'll go in along with the French to protect the canal. It's no secret that Eden has been chomping at the bit to go after Nasser."

"And the French think Nasser's stirring up things in Algeria."

"They do. So there's plenty of motivation to intervene." Hawes slowed his pace. "As to the situation in Budapest, Colonel Cowley tells me that it's rumored the Stalinists in the regime flew to Moscow last night—Gero, Istvan Kovacs, Andras Hegedus, and the head of the secret police, Laszlo Piros."

"Clearing the decks so that Nagy can reach out to the insurgents."

"So it appears. By the way, the legation convoy to Vienna left at 8:30 this morning from Vorosmarty Square with Anna safely in one of the lorries." Hawes smiled, satisfied with himself. "Group Captain David is in charge, and Hurricane won't let the Russians rattle him."

"How long should it take them to reach Austria?"

"Half the day? It's likely that they'll be stopped at several checkpoints along the way."

"And Anna? No problems with adding her to the group?"

"Miss Anna Sanderson is carrying a valid emergency British passport on her person. She should be in Vienna by dinner time."

It was obvious that Hawes had fallen for Anna, and had fallen hard. Collins knew the feeling, and he was glad for his friend—it was impossible to think of Hawes as anything other than a friend, now—and hoped that, no matter what happened with their romance, that Anna would start a new life, freed from her past.

They stopped at a side street to watch one of the food deliveries that were keeping the people of Budapest from going hungry. A farmer and his family—his wife and sons—stood in the back of a truck tossing potatoes one-by-one underhanded to a group of city residents. The crowd was well-behaved, and there was no pushing or shoving.

"Looks like the country ridings are voting for the rebels," Hawes said.

Another truck arrived and parked behind the first. A wiry, older man with a mustache hopped out of the truck cab and climbed into the back and began tossing large fish, still alive, to the crowd. A few fish slipped through eager hands and flopped onto the sidewalk or street, jumping around before they were quickly picked up.

They had turned south, on a narrow side street, when Collins spotted two men in leather jackets ahead of them at the next intersection. He immediately realized that it was Laszlo Kosa and his fellow AVO officer, Istvan Melles. Collins grabbed Hawes' forearm.

"It looks like Kosa," he said, and turned around to see if Viktor's recruits, who were slightly behind them, had recognized the threat.

They apparently had because they responded quickly. The teenager sprinted across the street to take up a position on the sidewalk in front of them, his machine gun at the ready. The older man behind them elbowed past Collins to join him. Hawes had his Enfield in his hand. Collins gripped his own revolver, but didn't remove it from his coat pocket.

Kosa spotted the movement of Viktor's men and stopped. He said something to Melles and they turned around and walked briskly away. Kosa looked over his shoulder once, but he and Melles retreated at a brisk pace.

The teenager flashed a smile at Collins and Hawes. "Good," he said. "They go."

"*Koszonom szepen*," Hawes responded. "Thank you."

Collins watched the retreating figures. "I don't think they expected to bump into us," he said.

"I agree," Hawes said. "They seemed surprised. Nevertheless, I'm glad Viktor's friends were Johnny on the spot." He turned back toward the hotel. "Time to get back to work," he said. "I need to scare up some petrol. Once we're on the road to Vienna I don't plan to stop, not for love or money."

* * *

Collins spent the afternoon in his room composing a dispatch for the Newspaper Alliance. He had room service deliver a pot of coffee, and he placed his portable typewriter on a small table and began writing.

Budapest is now eerily quiet after days of bitter fighting between Hungarian insurgents and elements of the hated secret police and Soviet troops. These freedom fighters—students, workers, young boys and girls, bank clerks and bakers, milkmen and professors—have fought the vaunted Red Army to a standstill.

The human cost of the uprising has been high—an estimated 1,000 Hungarians have fallen and perhaps 500 Russians and secret policemen have been killed. The actual casualty numbers may never be known.

The evidence of the ferocity of this struggle is everywhere: rubble in the street, downed power lines, wrecked tanks and armored personnel carriers, makeshift graves in city parks marked by wooden crosses and flowers. Black flags of mourning fly in the October breeze, an unwelcome reminder of the human cost of the fighting.

There are open suitcases on the street filled with Hungarian money, donations for those who have lost family members. There are weapons in some of the phone booths along the city's wide boulevards, left by wounded freedom fighters who hoped others would continue the fight.

Communist propaganda has characterized this uprising as a counterrevolution, led by elements of Admiral Horthy's regime and remnants of the Arrow Cross, the thugs who aided the Nazis in rounding up Jewish Hungarians and sending them to the death camp at Auschwitz. This correspondent can testify that based on everything he has seen and heard that these accusations are lies.

This is a popular revolution, led by students and workers with no connection to Hungary's dark past. The uprising has not been orchestrated by Western intelligence agencies, as the Reds would have you believe. While there have been cases of vigilantism, including the killing of State Security officers by the rebels, the Red Army and the secret police have been guilty of atrocities as well. The charge of anti-Semitism on the part of the insurgents is false, as well. There have been no pogroms, no violence directed at synagogues or Jewish neighborhoods. While it is true that the discredited and despised Communist leaders Rakosi, Gero, and Farkas are Jewish, so are many of the revolutionaries including young insurgent leaders like Istvan Angyal and Joszef Gali.

The Soviets hope to divert world attention from the repudiation of Marxism-Leninism by the very people who have lived under it for ten years. The rebels have taken to the streets with nothing more than bolt-action rifles and Molotov cocktails, dodging machine-gun and cannon fire to destroy the modern Soviet tanks sent against them. Their bravery and courage has been nothing short of amazing.

He wasn't sure how to finish the column. He decided to focus on the Hungarian insurgents and their commitment to freeing their country from Russian control.

How this spontaneous uprising may end remains unclear. Will Nikita Khrushchev and his fellow Soviet party leaders accept the reforms proposed by Prime Minister Imre Nagy? Can the recent peaceful settlement in Poland provide a model for Hungary? Will the United Nations become involved?

There are skeptics here who don't believe that the Soviets will ever allow an independent Hungary. Yet the insurgents vow to keep fighting until Russian forces have left their country and until Hungarians can decide how they will govern themselves in free and fair elections.

"Even if we lose, we win," one proud rebel told me. "No State Security man will ever feel safe walking the streets of Budapest at night."

This correspondent remembers the chant in Parliament Square from the vast crowd—some say there were 200,000 people present—on the night that this uprising began. "We've had enough of darkness," Hungarians called out. "We've had enough of darkness." We can only hope that they accomplish their dream of living in the light.

When he finished the article Collins read it over twice, making a few minor changes with his pencil, until he was pleased with the piece. He called the hotel switchboard and asked to be put on the waiting list for an international call. The operator who answered told him that the earliest he could expect a line would be sometime on Wednesday afternoon. "Beggars can't be choosers," he told her and the operator laughed. He promised to stop by after lunch to place his call.

* * *

Viktor Toth arrived at the Duna just after dinner and met with Collins in the alleyway behind the hotel. Viktor did not come alone—a young man holding a carbine and with a bandolier slung over his shoulder stood guard at the end of the alley.

"So my boys tell me Kosa and Melles showed up today," he began. "At least now they know that my people are watching."

"I don't think they expected to see us," Collins said. "I'm glad your men were there."

"It's nothing. What about Eva's documents?"

"We're still waiting. With the Russians withdrawing, we may have more time."

"Their withdrawal has caused some problems," Viktor said. "They pulled their guards away from the city's Party headquarters in Republic Square, near the Eastern Railway Station. The locals discovered there were AVO men in the building and heavy fighting broke out. Several Hungarian Army tanks started firing at the building, and when it was stormed things got out of hand. Some of the AVO men were lynched."

"Lynched?"

"Shot or beaten to death and strung up. Some of the tough guys from Chicago were involved, and they're not the type to take prisoners." Viktor spat on the ground. "There were news photographers there. It won't look good for the revolution."

"It may also give the Soviets a pretext for intervening."

Viktor laughed bitterly. "If they come, they won't need a pretext." He rubbed his chin nervously. "When will you know? About Eva's papers?"

"The Vienna courier has been arriving at the American legation in the morning," Collins said. "Once I have the papers, I'll alert

Zoltan. Morris and Eva need to be ready to leave at a moment's notice. They should travel light. One bag each. No more clothing than a journalist would bring for a brief visit."

Viktor nodded. "They'll be ready. I'll have them both here within thirty minutes of hearing from Zoltan." He placed his hand on Collins' shoulder. "Did Winters follow my advice?"

"He did." Collins patted his coat pocket. "We're both carrying revolvers now whenever we leave the Duna. Can't say I like that."

"And you are prepared, if the need arises, to use your weapon?"

"If it comes to that," Collins said. "God willing, it won't."

Viktor bared his teeth in a grin. "My experience has been that it's better not to rely on God in such matters. You're a boxer, so you know to keep your guard up. It's always the sucker punch you have to watch out for."

Thirteen

Wednesday, October 31

At nine o'clock in the morning, when Collins hadn't heard from Brooks Lawrence, he telephoned the legation. He was concerned that the courier might have been stopped at the Hungarian border. He waited a long five minutes before Lawrence came on the line.

"Sorry for the delay," Lawrence said. "I've got news for you. We received a telex this morning from your editor, Wittingham. He says there's been a slight delay at his end. He apologizes and promises that the materials will arrive with Evans tomorrow."

"Tomorrow? Thursday?"

Lawrence responded with an annoying, high-pitched laugh. "Tomorrow *is* Thursday."

"When has the courier been showing up at the legation?"

"There's no set time. It depends on whether the border guards are in a bad mood or not. I'll let you know as soon as he arrives." Lawrence paused. "By the way, we may send a convoy of staff and dependents to Vienna in the next few days, like the Brits did. No later than Friday. A few journalists have asked to go along. Mr. Katona wants you to know that you're welcome to join the group."

"Let me think it over," Collins said. "Not sure we'd want to wait until Friday."

"Safety in numbers, though," Lawrence said.

"Tell Mr. Katona we appreciate the invitation."

"Will do."

After they hung up, Collins took a deep breath. He was relieved that the end was in sight—barring any unforeseen problems, they should be in Austria sometime on Thursday. He wondered what lay behind the delay in delivering Eva's documents. If the papers arrived on Thursday, it would have been a full week since he had sent Wittingham the telex with Morris' demand. Had it taken that long to create the forgeries?

He took the lift down to the ground floor and was pleased to find Zoltan alone at the front desk. Collins made sure they couldn't be overheard when he approached him.

"It appears that we'll be checking out tomorrow," he told him. "If you see Mr. Winters before I do, I'd appreciate it if you could let him know. And if you would please pass the word to Viktor that we plan to leave from the Duna sometime in the late morning. We'll send him a message tomorrow once we know."

"Back to Vienna?"

"That's the plan," Collins said. "But as they say, the best laid plans of mice and men often go awry."

"Pardon me," Zoltan said. "I don't understand. Mice and men?"

Collins laughed. "It's an old saying, and I'll confess I don't know why the mice are included. It's a saying I hope won't apply to our plans."

* * *

It was Lester Kane who reminded Collins that it was Halloween. Kane had invited Collins to join him for lunch—perhaps making amends for his behavior at the party over Isabelle.

"Americans will hold costume parties and or take their children trick-or-treating tonight, while the people here will spend the day nursing their wounded and worrying about what the future will bring," Kane said. "We're a strange species, aren't we?" He shook his head. "Are you a father? Will your children be out for Halloween tonight?"

Collins nodded. "My sons would never miss a chance to collect some candy." Maria would take the boys trick-or-treating; Caleb would don his Dodgers uniform, a birthday gift, and Matthew would insist on wearing his Davy Crockett costume, complete with coonskin cap. Maria had finally restricted the playing of "The Legend of Davy Crockett" song to no more than twice a day, and Collins had been grateful.

He could only trust that the boys were keeping Maria occupied enough that she didn't spend all her time worrying about him. She would be reading the papers and watching television and would have known that the fighting in Budapest had been intense.

"My daughter's past that," Kane said. "She's in San Francisco, in college. I don't have much contact with her. Or with her mother, my ex-wife."

"Sorry to hear that."

"I've thought about her these past few days. She's the age of the student fighters in the streets. Never seen anything quite like this before. Twelve-year-olds taking on tanks. Not just boys, girls as well."

"At least the ceasefire seems to be working," Collins said. "With Gero and the hardliners gone, perhaps there's some room for a negotiated settlement."

"There are rumors that the Hungarian Air Force threatened to bomb the Russians if they didn't leave the city," Kane said. "I don't know what to think. They've let the prisoners out of the National Prison, and Cardinal Mindszenty was freed this morning. They held a show trial for him back in '49, and Mindszenty was given a life sentence for treason. He's been under house arrest near Retsag."

"Lachlan Ferguson has it right," Collins said. "It's a revolution. Messy, confused, violent. It's going to take some time for the Hungarians to sort things out. That is, if they're given the time."

★ ★ ★

Collins returned to his room, collected his finished story, and took the lift to the fourth floor where the telephone operators were located. One of the operators, a slight young girl named Panni, managed to connect him to the Newspaper Alliance offices in London on her third try.

The editor who picked up the phone, Ted Dalton, understood that Collins was calling from Budapest and he didn't waste any time. He asked Collins to immediately begin dictating his piece. The line crackled with static, but only once did Dalton stop Collins—to confirm the spelling of "Farkas."

"Well done," Dalton said. "I think that a fair number of papers will carry this."

"I may not file again until I get to Vienna," Collins told him. "The situation is confused, to say the least."

"We'll alert Jennings in New York," Dalton said. "Do take care."

After Collins hung up, Panni told him that the front desk had called—there was a visitor waiting for him in the lobby. He took the lift down and found a new clerk at the front desk who explained, in halting English, that someone was asking for Collins. The clerk gestured to a man sitting on a couch in the lobby.

When Collins walked over, the man introduced himself as Vitali Osin of the Russian embassy. Osin had a long, narrow face, high cheekbones, and dark hair combed back from his forehead.

"A Russian diplomat?" Collins asked. "This isn't the most welcoming place at the moment, I'd imagine." He felt immediately on guard. That Osin had asked for him specifically didn't seem to be a good omen.

"I'm not overly concerned," Osin said. His English was polished, measured. "There's a cease fire, is there not? The hotel is neutral territory. I don't think the counterrevolutionaries or fascists will burst in here and drag me away."

"Haven't seen any counterrevolutionaries or fascists," Collins said. "I don't think there are any in Budapest, despite what you may have heard."

"There you are sadly mistaken," the Russian said. "I hope to convince you of that. I've been providing background to some of your colleagues. Why don't you sit so we can discuss this?" Collins reluctantly sat in a wingback chair facing the couch.

"How long have you been in Budapest, Mr. Osin?" he asked.

"Since the summer. Long enough to become familiar with the political landscape."

"And before Budapest?"

"Most recently Moscow, and before that our London embassy for several years." Osin fumbled in his jacket pocket and retrieved a package of cigarettes. After Collins declined his offer of a cigarette, Osin lit up one and took a long drag.

Osin leaned forward, looking at Collins intently. "Your readers should be made aware what's behind these criminal acts of the past few days. It's a return of the White Terror of 1919, when Horthy and his fascists attacked and killed Communists and Jews. The same reactionary elements are behind this attempted putsch."

"I've seen students and workers in the streets. And some soldiers. No reactionaries."

"Don't be naive. Do you believe that these provocations are spontaneous? Someone is financing them. Guns don't materialize out of thin air."

"The guns are coming from the Hungarian army and police from what I can tell. And I think this uprising was unplanned and spontaneous. Hungarians in the street say they had reached the breaking point."

Osin shook his head vigorously. "That's not believable. This is a conspiracy against the workers of Hungary."

"A conspiracy that includes Imre Nagy? And Janos Kadar? They're Communists."

"Politicians. Easily seduced by promises of money and power. A whisper in the ear. Dollars in Swiss bank accounts. Can you deny that MI6 and the CIA have been at work? It's clear that the British want to divert attention from their adventure in the Suez."

"I think we'll have to agree to disagree," Collins said.

"Tell me, Mr. Collins," Osin said. "Do you think that any of the journalists here are serving two masters? Perhaps, on the side, assisting an intelligence agency?"

"None that I'm aware of," Collins said. "And I'm a journalist, plain and simple. I came to Budapest to write a story about the American diplomats here, and then all hell broke loose."

"A coincidence that you were here? It has nothing to do with your friendship with Allen Dulles?"

"He's not a friend." Collins felt himself tensing. He wondered how much Osin knew about his prior Agency connections. For that matter, how had the Russians become aware that Collins was in Budapest?

"You say Allen Dulles is not a friend. What about Morris Rose? A friend?"

"He's not," Collins said. "The last I heard he was working for you."

"Did you 'hear' that he was working in Budapest?"

"That's news to me." It was obvious that Osin knew a great deal about Collins' relationship with Morris. Why had he approached Collins now? Did he think Collins could lead him to Morris?

"More amazing coincidences. You and Rose are the closest of friends, and then you suddenly arrive in Budapest, where he's living. What should we make of this? It is all coincidence, or something by design."

"Make of it what you will. You're the one telling me that Rose is in Budapest."

"Then you haven't seen him since your arrival?"

"I haven't," Collins said. "Have you?"

"Colonel Rusakov—the name we know him by—has vanished. It's possible, of course, that he was killed by the reactionaries. I don't think so, however. I believe that he is hiding, aiding and abetting the counterrevolutionaries upon orders from the CIA. If that is the case, then, logic suggests that you were sent here, Mr. Collins, to act as his controller, to provide him money and instructions."

"That's absurd."

Osin's eyes narrowed. "A fair warning now, Mr. Collins. We plan to find Rusakov, wherever he may have gone to ground. You would be well served to stay clear of him." The Russian rose to his feet. "We do not leave our account books unbalanced. If you are foolish enough to contact him, you may tell him that. He may believe that you can protect him, but you can't."

"I'm afraid these warnings are wasted on me," Collins said. "I don't know where you're getting your information, but it's way off base."

Osin snorted in disgust. He rose to his feet, glaring at Collins, and strode out of the lobby. He did not look back as he left.

★ ★ ★

Collins found Hawes in his room and suggested that they step outside for some fresh air. It was drizzling slightly, and Collins brought an umbrella with him. They stopped in the alleyway behind the hotel. Collins shielded them from the rain with the umbrella and explained that, according to Wittingham, Eva's papers would arrive tomorrow.

"Finally," Hawes said. "I'll confess I was beginning to question Wittingham's competence. I have news as well. Colonel Cowley says we've begun bombing the Canal Zone. The French are participating, too. Nasser ordered all the ships in the Canal sunk."

"What can they be thinking?" Collins asked. "Why would they initiate this now in the middle of the uprising in Budapest?"

"These things take on a life of their own. They must have been planning this for months, and it looks like it's been coordinated with the Israelis."

"There's another complication for us," Collins said. Hawes

listened intently as Collins recounted his conversation with Osin in the Duna's lobby.

"This is very bad," Hawes said. "Does Osin really believe you're Rose's CIA handler? It's true that Moscow Center sees conspiracies everywhere, but I doubt he thinks you were sent here to direct the uprising. It's more likely that he suspects, or knows, the actual reason that we're here—that Rose wants to make a run for it."

"I'm worried about a leak on our side. How else would Osin know I was here and connect me with Morris? Someone at the American legation? Katona? Lawrence? Or someone we don't know?"

"It could be any of them."

"Why would Osin come to the Duna and warn me?" Collins asked. "Why not just wait and watch for Morris to surface?"

"Simple. Osin wants to rattle you, hoping that you'll panic and head straight to Rose's hiding place. He probably has people watching the Duna as we speak."

"So what should we do?"

"For the moment, nothing. You should know, Collins, that I always preferred Sir Percy Blakeney to Sidney Carton. The Scarlet Pimpernel was no fool. Clever enough to get out of Paris in one piece despite the Jacobins hunting for him. Sidney Carton, on the other hand, did a far, far better thing, made his noble sacrifice, and went to the guillotine. Better literature, but not an example to follow. I'd rather be clever." Hawes gently tapped Collins on the shoulder. "We don't do anything rash. Nothing reckless. Osin's options are fairly limited at the moment. The Soviets have pulled back from the center of the city. He can't move against us quite yet."

"I don't want us to do anything reckless," Collins said. "But I do want to get out of here at the first opportunity."

"We will," Hawes said. "With any luck, the Hungarian military controls the border. We need to procure a *laissez passer* letter from the top brass here in Budapest for our trip. Colonel Cowley should be able to help us with that." Hawes slapped Collin on the back, a gesture of reassurance. "Don't worry too much. We may have to improvise a bit to pull it off, but we will."

Fourteen

Thursday, November 1

Collins reached Liberty Square and the American legation ten minutes after learning that Evans, the diplomatic courier, had arrived from Vienna with mail for him. Viktor's men trailed Collins the entire way there. As far as Collins could tell, there was no sign of Kosa, or of anyone else, shadowing him.

A weary Gaza Katona met him inside the entrance to the legation. Katona's eyes were bloodshot, and his face was puffy from lack of sleep.

"Wittingham finally came through," Katona said. "There was an envelope for you inside the diplomatic pouch from Vienna."

He brought Collins back to the small room with the bookshelves and closed the door before he spoke.

"We've swept this room for microphones," Katona said. "It's clean." He motioned for Collins to sit in one of the wooden chairs. "We've been trying to keep up with developments. Washington's greedy for info. Tom Wailes, the new minister, arrived yesterday and I don't envy him the mess he's inherited."

He handed an envelope to Collins. "If you'll excuse me, I'll get a cup of coffee while you're looking that over. Can I interest you in a cup?"

Collins nodded, not wanting to prolong the conversation. He was eager to examine the documents that Wittingham had sent. As soon as the door closed behind the CIA station chief, Collins emptied the contents of the envelope onto the desktop—a green passport with "Repubblica Italina" on its cover and a cardboard press card, from *Corriere della Sera*, made out to "Luciana Marchetti." He looked closely at the passport; it had Eva's picture and had been stamped for entry into Hungary on October 24. It was well-worn, in the condition you would expect for a well-traveled newspaperwoman.

He found a handwritten note inside the envelope: "*Vital that you cable when and where you're crossing border with Pilgrim. Good luck. C. W.*" Collins was surprised that Wittingham would ask him to send the time and place of their border crossing via diplomatic channels. Even with an encoded message, it meant that Katona, the cipher clerk, and some of the Agency's staff in Vienna would be privy to the information.

The door slowly opened as Katona returned. He had two china mugs of coffee in his hands. He gave one to Collins and glanced over at the passport on the desk.

"Did you get what you needed?"

"We did," Collins said. He paused to drink some coffee from the mug—it was strong and quite good. "The passport for the girl appears to be well done."

"Is State Security after her?"

"Not that we know."

Katona sipped from his mug, reflecting for a moment. "Then the border police won't be looking for her. That's good. And Pilgrim? Is he on their radar?"

"Not on the local radar, but I'm afraid he has attracted the interest of the Soviets. I had a visit at the hotel from a Russian diplomat, Vitali Osin. He's looking for Pilgrim. Do you know Osin?"

"I recognize the name. He's no diplomat. Definitely KGB. It sounds like your cover has been blown."

"Not sure how much Osin knows," Collins said. "Or how he's connected me to Pilgrim. But it's time to leave."

"You shouldn't delay getting out of here. We've had numerous reports of heavy armor and troop transports crossing from the Soviet Union into Hungary at Zahony. The Russians may have decided to end the uprising. In the meantime, the Hungarians have begun forming a National Guard led by a former general, Bela Kiraly. We see it as an attempt to pull together a force that will defend the Nagy government."

"There's nothing the United Nations can do? Or that we can do?"

"I can tell you, off the record, that Spencer Barnes recommended to Washington that we air drop arms and supplies to the freedom fighters. Turned down flat. The United Nations is tied up with Suez." Katona rubbed his eyes and took another sip from his coffee mug. "It's going to take you some time because of all of the checkpoints on the main highway to Vienna."

"We planned on crossing at Hegyeshalom. It seems the logical place for journalists heading back to Vienna from Budapest. We want to make it appear as routine as possible."

"I hope that works for you. We're sending our own convoy tomorrow. And if the Red Army moves to retake the city, we're prepared to shelter any Americans still in Budapest at the legation. That invitation would extend to you, of course, and to anyone else who needs safe haven."

"Thanks," Collins said. "Let's hope it never comes to that."

* * *

The somber strains of Mozart's *Requiem* playing on the radio greeted Collins when he arrived at the lobby of Duna. In a corner of the room, a table covered with the national flag had a framed photograph of a young man with a smiling face and swept-back hair. A lit candle flickered next to the photograph. Zoltan was arranging flowers in a glass vase on the table.

He looked up when Collins walked over. "This is in memory of Tas Szabo," he said quietly. "One of our best waiters, killed Tuesday in the street fighting. Today is All Soul's Day, the Day of the Dead. There are many to mourn for today."

"It's at least relatively quiet outside," Collins said.

Zoltan gazed at him with sad eyes. "My cousin has been bringing us food from his farm in Csemo. He says he has seen many Soviet tanks and troop lorries on the roads. The large tanks, the T–54s."

"Perhaps Nagy can strike a deal with the Russians."

"Who can trust them? They took my brother Janos away in 1949 to work for them in Russia. Construction work on a dam. He was supposed to return here in a year. We never heard from him again." Zoltan coughed. "I fought in the war, so I know that an army needs food and ammunition. I believe that is why they have withdrawn from the city—so they can be resupplied. Once that is done, they will be back."

Collins leaned closer to him and, in a lowered voice, asked Zoltan if he could pass a message to Viktor. "As it happens, we plan to leave today. Can you let Viktor know that our passengers should meet us here at one o'clock?"

"Very good, sir," he said. "That's very good."

* * *

When Hawes returned from the British legation, he wore a broad smile and he told Collins that he had good news to share. They made their way to a secluded spot in the hotel garden, and Hawes gave only a cursory glance around before speaking.

"Anna made it to Vienna, along with the rest of the convoy. Group Captain David says there was no problem at Hegyeshalom, the border guards waved them through and the Austrians couldn't have been more welcoming. The embassy arranged a room for her at the Hotel Bristol. She'll wait for me there, and then we'll get her papers squared away so that she can return to England with me."

"How do you plan to accomplish that? She's still a Hungarian citizen."

"We'll apply for political asylum for her. I can vouch for her, and I think that should be enough. If it's not, I can always make her an honest woman. That is, if she'll have me."

"You're serious?"

"Yes, I am. We've talked about marriage, indirectly. She worries that no matter what I say her past will burden us, that I will be ashamed of what she was."

"I know you well enough that you could care less about what the world thinks," Collins said. "It's how you feel that matters."

"It is. I believe I have my eyes wide open. Would I prefer that Feliks Hawes was the first man she ever slept with? I would, but it's too late for that. And once you're past that hurdle, what difference does it make who she's gone to bed with? In her case, there's never been any emotional attachment involved."

Collins didn't say anything. He could tell that Hawes just wanted someone to listen.

"I can be cynical about it," Hawes said. "Is she in love with me, or with the idea of escaping Hungary and her past? That's unknowable, in one sense, but I believe that her feelings for me are real. There's an undeniable attraction between us. We share interests. She loves art, and has a small collection of books with plates of some of the great artworks. On our way to England, I've promised to take her to the Louvre so she can see 'Mona Lisa' and the Venus de Milo in person. She's thrilled by the idea." Hawes smiled. "As you can imagine, I'm eager to reach Vienna."

Collins silently handed him Eva's documents. Hawes leafed through the pages of the passport quickly. "Wittingham must have contacts in the Italian intelligence agency, the Servizio di Informazioni delle Forze Armate, because this looks like an authentic passport to me. I don't think it's a forgery. The stamps are well done, although they're much easier to fabricate."

"All the better," Collins said. "Her papers should stand up to close scrutiny, then. Not that we expect it. The cover story only has to hold up for a few minutes at the frontier. We'll arrive as a group and Signorina Marchetti will be in the company of other journalists. No reason to single her out."

"One thing left for us to do," Hawes said. "Colonel Cowley gave me a note that should get us in to see Pal Maleter. He's General Maleter, now, the first hero of this revolution. With his signature on a letter we'll breeze through any Hungarian roadblocks."

★ ★ ★

Collins and Hawes showed the armed guards at the Ministry of Defense building their press cards and explained that they had an appointment to interview General Maleter. That was enough to get them into the imposing building, although they had to repeat the process twice before they ended up in the offices occupied by Maleter and his staff.

It was a confused scene—telephones jangling, cigarette smoke hanging in the air, and several officers pounding away at typewriters.

Maleter stood in the center of the room, dressed in a traditional green, Hungarian army tunic, talking with two aides. He had an angular face and with a long forehead and a shock of dark hair that stood up on his head and made him seem even taller. Maleter towered above the other men in the room; Collins figured that he was at least six-foot-six.

One of the aides waved them over, and Hawes handed him the note from Colonel Cowley. Hawes turned to Maleter—and in German so Collins could follow the conversation—explained that they were journalists ready to leave for Austria by automobile, and Colonel Cowley had suggested that Maleter might be willing to provide a letter of safe passage. Maleter fixed his blue-gray eyes on Hawes.

"I would have thought you'd want to stay," he said in German. "To see what happens."

"We need to file our stories," Hawes said. "I need to develop my film, and Vienna is a better place for that."

"And the world needs to know," Maleter said. He called over a junior officer and gave him rapid instructions. The officer looked at them and spoke in English. "General Maleter has asked me to prepare a letter of safe passage." He gave them an apologetic shrug. "The Russians won't honor it, you should know."

"What will they honor?" Collins asked in German. "Will they respect the new government?"

"We know history," Maleter said. "We know what happened in 1848. Only a fool would ignore the parallels—the Russians ended our hopes of an independent and free Hungary. But I know their officers. I fought with them." He touched several medals on his tunic. "I wear these because I'm proud of having earned them fighting against the Nazis. I believe that we can reach an accommodation. A meeting of the minds. They're willing to talk to us about an orderly withdrawal of their troops."

"We wish you well in the days ahead," Hawes said. "I understand one of your poets, Arany, wrote that in dreams and in love there are no impossibilities."

"Janos Arany," Maleter said. "A wonderful poet. Yes, we can dream, can't we? And hope for possibilities."

Hawes switched to Hungarian, and he and Maleter chatted while the letter was typed up. Maleter signed it with a flourish and shook both of their hands before they departed.

In the corridor, Hawes stopped to fold the letter and place it in his inside jacket pocket. "A very impressive man," he said. "Born to lead. If anything should happen to Nagy, I wouldn't be surprised if they turn to Maleter."

"He's very confident," Collins said. "Perhaps he can make a difference. Maleter did serve with the Russians, and you'd think they would trust them."

Hawes had a grim look on his face. "No matter what the Red Army commanders here may think of Maleter, their orders will come from Moscow. And they will obey them to the letter."

★ ★ ★

It was noon before they arrived at the Duna, and Collins immediately stopped at the front desk. Zoltan handed him a folded piece of paper and Collins quickly read it: *1 PM not possible. We'll come later. MR.*

"A delay," he told Hawes. "They say they're coming later."

Hawes shrugged. "Let's get packed and be ready to go."

An hour later Collins returned to the lobby to check with Zoltan, who quickly shook his head when he saw Collins. As he turned to head back to the lift, Lester Kane intercepted him.

"I'm just back from Parliament," Kane said. "I'm not sure I can believe what I've heard. Later today, Nagy will announce that Hungary is leaving the Warsaw Pact, and embracing neutrality. He'll ask for the protection of the United Nations."

"As long as the Russians have their veto in the Security Council he might as well call on Peter Pan and Tinker Belle to come to the rescue," Collins said.

"Actions tell you the true story. The Soviets are planning to evacuate their civilians tomorrow by boat. Most of their embassy staff and their women and children. They've surrounded all of the airports outside the city with tanks—Ferihegy, Budaors, Tokol. They're closing off the exits. Nagy must know that he's in the end game now. There's not much he can do. It will depend on what Comrade Khrushchev and the inner circle in Moscow decide to do."

"You think the Red Army is coming in?" Collins said.

"I do, now. As soon as the balloon goes up, I plan to head for Liberty Square the American legation. It should be safer there, off-limits for casual shelling. I just hope the Reds have it marked well on their maps."

* * *

At three o'clock Zoltan telephoned Collins in his room and told him that he was holding a message for him. Collins found Hawes in the hotel bar, and they walked to the front desk together. There, Zoltan explained that Viktor wanted to meet near the southern corner of Petofi Square at five o'clock.

"Five?" Hawes' face hardened. "That bloody takes it. No way can we leave tonight, then. We don't want to blunder around in the dark."

"Something must have gone wrong," Collins said. "I don't understand why they didn't come here earlier."

It became clear what had gone wrong when they arrived, on foot, at Petofi Square. Viktor and another man waited for them by a Skoda sedan, but there was no sign of Eva. Collins realized that it was Morris standing by Viktor's side.

"My boys are posted nearby," Viktor said when they walked up. "They'll keep watch. For now, it's clear."

Morris wore a winter overcoat and he had pulled the brim of his fedora down, hiding much of his face. He introduced himself to Hawes and turned to Collins and shook his hand.

"Where's Eva?" Collins asked. "What's going on? We've lost the chance to drive out of here before nightfall."

"Eva's why we were delayed," Morris said. "Kosa has her, holding her hostage. When she never turned up for lunch, Viktor went looking for."

"Kosa grabbed her off the street," Viktor said. "The bastard sent his buddy Istvan Melles to approach me about negotiating her release. They want two blank temporary British passports and $1,000 in cash. Melles said that he was sure that our British and American friends could supply these things."

"Kosa would never hurt Eva," Morris said. "He'll hold her as a hostage until we give him what he wants. He probably has figured out that I need to leave Budapest while I still can, so if I plan on taking Eva along, I'll need to agree to his demands."

"It makes sense for Kosa," Hawes said. "British passports and American money. The best of both worlds when he reaches the border. Authentic documents and money for bribing the border guards. If I were in his shoes I'd head directly to Austria"

"So we need your help, Mr. Winters, with the British authorities," Morris said.

"Can you get the blank passports?" Collins asked Hawes.

"I think I can. You'll need to come along with me to the legation. It has to be clear that the CIA supports this."

"And the money?" Collins asked Morris.

"Viktor and I can scare up the cash between us," Morris said. He paused, a pained look on his face. "There's one unpleasant wrinkle. Kosa wants you, Denny, to deliver the passports and the cash. He'll release Eva to you when he has them in his hands. Kosa doesn't want Viktor or me anywhere around during the exchange."

It was hard for Collins to see Morris' face clearly in the dim light of the nearby street lamps, but he could tell how distressed he was. Collins knew something of what Morris was going through—he had once agonized over the woman he loved being held captive and being bargained for. He took no pleasure in seeing Morris struggle with the same feelings of powerlessness mixed with anxiety.

"Is that it?" Hawes was scowling. "How do we know that Kosa isn't asking for Collins so that he can settle old scores?"

"I asked Melles the same question," Viktor said. "He agreed to have you, the Englishman, accompany Dennis. They're even willing

to let you come to the rendezvous armed." Viktor explained that
Melles had given him a phone number to call once they had the
passports and money. Then Melles would give him the location for
the exchange.

"Do you trust him? Kosa? And Melles?" Hawes was clearly
skeptical.

"They're opportunists," Morris said. "They won't want a shoot-
out. They want what we want—a quick exit from Budapest before
the Russians seal off the roads out."

"I don't like the idea of Collins handling the exchange," Hawes
said. "Too risky. Why don't I do it?"

Morris looked at Collins. "It's up to you, Denny. We don't know
whether Kosa is on the level."

"I can go by myself," Hawes said. "They may not like it, but so
what?"

Collins shook his head. "We don't want to give them any reason
for backing out. I'll go." He turned to Morris. "A Russian diplomat
showed up at the hotel yesterday. Vitali Osin. He made it clear that
he knew about our connection and, while he was at it, he accused me
of being a CIA agent, sent here to help you orchestrate the uprising.
Do you know him?"

"I don't. There must have been a leak. Someone has tipped off
Moscow Center."

"That's the conclusion we came to. I think that Osin suspects
that you're planning to defect."

"Osin won't come looking for you until the Russians control the
city," Hawes said. "He'll have additional help from Moscow Center,
then. So you have a reprieve, of sorts, but it's temporary."

"I told you to leave on Monday," Viktor said to Morris. "Eva
could have come later."

"I don't regret waiting," Morris said. "We go together or not at
all."

★ ★ ★

Collins and Hawes walked back to the Duna from Petofi Square. There were lit candles in the windows of most of the buildings along their way. Some small candles had been placed on the sidewalks.

The wind came sweeping down the street, scattering leaves and whistling through the trees. Some of the candles on the sidewalk were extinguished. Collins glanced up at the sky, wondering whether it was going to the snow.

"I half expect a winter snowstorm," he said. "Considering how things are going, it wouldn't be a surprise."

"We've had no luck at all with this operation," Hawes said. "Just when things were looking up—we have transport, Anna's safely in Vienna, and Eva's papers arrive—Kosa gums up the works."

"We'll have to make our own luck, then," Collins said. "My boxing coach, Digger Callahan, always said it was amazing how lucky you could get when you threw a good right hook. We just need to keep punching."

Part Three

Maxim had done intelligence work long enough to know that it was the unexpected and random that often fatally compromised a mission.

He would never have imagined that Laszlo Kosa would turn his back on his comrades in State Security and seek to escape to the West. Nor would he have believed that Kosa would kidnap Eva as a means to that end. And what were the odds that he would take action on the very day that her false travel documents had finally arrived in Budapest?

Maxim had not worried about Kosa as a threat, even when he began hanging around the Duna. Moscow Center had been his chief concern. Vitali Osin's sudden appearance on the scene, however, had made him immediately suspicious. Osin represented the true danger.

"Have you been betrayed?" Viktor had asked. "For this Russian to come to the Duna and seek out Collins, to send that message so directly. He must have been alerted."

"It's someone in the American legation or in the Vienna Embassy," Maxim had replied. By insisting that Denny come to Budapest, Maxim had taken a calculated risk. There were files in Moscow and Washington detailing his history with Collins, and Maxim had gambled that no one would make the connection. But he had been wrong.

He had been properly cautious. Maxim had not stayed in the same hiding spot for more than two nights in a row. He had moved to the next flat in Josephtown or Elizabethtown only after dark, and only after Viktor's small band of fighters had made sure that there were no State Security patrols in the vicinity.

Maxim had communicated with Eva through messages carried to her by teenage couriers. When they needed to meet, the courier would give Eva an address, and she would set off on her bicycle, pedaling down backstreets, keeping an eye out for cyclists or cars that might try to follow her.

They had been so careful, and yet they had missed the now obvious threat—Eva had been an easy target for Kosa and Melles. They had intercepted her when she left her aunt's flat to come to meet with Maxim.

Maxim wasn't surprised by Kosa's demand for blank passports and cash. It made sense. Kosa could not travel without money for bribes, and he needed a passport that could get him out of the country. Kidnapping Eva and trading her for what he needed was, Maxim had to admit, a clever improvisation on Kosa's part. Maxim would recognize, if not fully appreciate, the irony if Kosa's cobbled-together scheme worked as well as in the end as Maxim's more considered plan.

* * *

In July, Maxim had decided to leave Hungary. He made up his mind during a visit by Eva's uncle, Lukas Nemeth, who had stayed with them at Lake Balaton in the cottage Maxim had rented. Lukas had been granted a rare two weeks of vacation from his job at a Special Design Bureau in Kaliningrad, a suburb of Moscow.

Lukas was charming and intelligent and Maxim had warmed to him immediately. Lukas had visited America once, in 1937, consulting with several scientists at Columbia University and later meeting the brilliant physicist and mathematician John von Neumann at the Institute for Advanced Study in Princeton. Lukas loved to talk about New York City and had been delighted to discover that Maxim was a Columbia graduate.

At first, they had avoided politics, Hungarian or Russian. No matter what reassurances Eva might have given Lukas, Maxim was an officer in the KGB, and that alone would have given even the boldest person pause before openly criticizing the status quo. But during their time together, it had become clear to Maxim that Lukas shared his disillusionment with the Party and its leadership. They had talked briefly, elliptically, about the atmosphere of fear that prevailed in both Moscow and Budapest.

The day before Lukas was to return to Moscow, they swam out together to the rectangular wooden swimming platform anchored some fifty yards from the shore in front of the cottage. They sat on the float, enjoying the golden July sunshine and the beauty of the lakefront around them, and had their first frank discussion.

"Eva says I can trust you," Lukas began, keeping his eyes focused on a copse of trees slightly north of the cottage.

"I would never hurt Eva, or her family. You're part of her family."

"Then you are truly in love with her?" Lukas had asked. "Our little Eva, who has grown into such a lovely woman?"

"That I am."

"Then you plan to marry her? And she will bear your children?" Lukas, squinting from the sun, looked directly at Maxim for the first time when he asked the question.

Maxim found himself telling Nemeth the truth. "Eva does not want to have children. At least not under the present conditions."

"You mean under the regime?"

"Yes," Maxim said, reluctantly, because although he didn't believe Lukas would ever inform on them, it still seemed dangerous to admit such a thing.

"Do you feel the same way? About the conditions?" Lukas had sensed Maxim's hesitancy.

"I feel the same. Perhaps even more strongly." Maxim paused, unsure whether to say what he felt. "The constant fear. To know that you could be taken from your children at any moment. To raise them to censor whatever they think and say. Or worse, the idea that your children could embrace it, become part of it. I never imagined it would be like this when I left the United States."

Lukas didn't say anything. He studied Maxim for a long moment.

"There's no future for her, here," he said finally. "For either of you. Can you take her to America? Or to Israel?"

"You do know what you're asking me?"

"I do. It could cost you everything."

"I have thought about it," Maxim said. "I believe that I can get us to the West. I think I can trade what I know for help in getting out of Hungary. It's what happens later that concerns me."

"I don't understand."

"It's quite simple, actually. Moscow Center will send men after us to carry out the automatic death sentence that traitors receive. We'll need protection for the rest of our lives. It's not the first few years I worry about, but what happens five or ten years later. Proper safeguards will be costly. How generous will the American authorities be? Intelligence agencies have budgets, like any other organization. How important will we be to them? To their bureaucrats? Will they live up to their side of the bargain?"

"I see," Lukas said. "Perhaps I can help. My current work focuses on technical matters of great interest to the American military. The information I can give you about advances in the design of a new missile, the R-7, will open many doors in Washington for you. I can provide detailed technical notes because I'm close to Sergei Korolev, the man in charge of our design bureau, and I have worked with Vladimir Glushko on the design of the rocket engines. The short-term goal is to send a satellite into orbit around the Earth, and we are making progress."

"Is that possible?"

"Not yet, but soon. The test flights of the R-7, the Semyorka, have been promising. And when the missile is perfected, it could also reach New York and Washington, just as the Nazis hit London from a great distance with the V-2." His face was grave. "An intercontinental weapon. Imagine a nuclear bomb, a warhead, atop such a missile. There is no defense against it. We can only hope that the Americans can progress at the same pace, can achieve this at the same time, so that Moscow does not achieve superiority."

"If you give me this information, and it's found on me, it will mean your death," Maxim said. He didn't have to say that it would mean his own death as well.

"I have no children. I'm no longer married. Of my family, only Eva remains. I will take that risk if it gives her the chance to escape and allows her to live as she should. As she deserves to. My brother—her father—would have agreed if they had not murdered him." He paused, his eyes focusing on the shoreline. "And if I help the Americans in doing so, all the better."

Maxim knew that once accepted Lukas Nemeth's plan, and took the information from him, they would all be placed in danger.

"I will do this," Maxim said. "For Eva. For both of us."

"Good," Lukas said briskly. "Tonight I will commit to paper what the American aeronautical engineers and physicists need to know about the Semyorka. You must drive a hard bargain with this information, demand the protection that you need."

"If we defect, you will fall under suspicion…." Maxim didn't finish the sentence. Nemeth could be brought in for interrogation, and Maxim doubted that he could hold up under the harsh tactics employed in Lubyanka.

Lukas smiled at him and recited two verses, in Russian: "*I am alone; all round me drowns in falsehood/ Life is not a walk across a field.*"

"What's that from?" Maxim asked.

"A poem by Boris Pasternak, 'Hamlet.' A poem that is presently banned. I would like you to recite those verses for me when you reach freedom."

Maxim repeated the verses twice, memorizing them. "Very striking. I won't forget them."

"Shall we swim back?" Lukas asked with a wistful smile. "I have loved this place, my time here, you know. I'll not soon forget it."

* * *

Maxim knew that his options had dramatically narrowed in the last few days. He had no choice but to give Kosa what he wanted, and as quickly as possible. Viktor had grasped that from the moment Istvan Melles approached him, and Maxim had reluctantly agreed.

"Kosa knows full well how I feel about Eva," Viktor said. "Our connection through our families. And he knows how you feel about her. He's sure that we won't do anything rash. He's right. As long as Eva remains untouched, he can count on that restraint. If we provide the money and the passports, he'll let her go."

"Kosa must be very desperate to attempt this."

"Of course he's desperate. This city is filled with desperate people, Maxim."

"What about Denny? What are the risks for him?"

"I made it clear to Melles that if anything happened to Collins, I would hunt them down. They could only hope that the CIA or MI6 would catch up to them before I did. He gave me his word that Collins would not be harmed."

Maxim was still not at ease with the situation. Things could always go wrong. Kosa would be nervous, as would Melles, and they would be armed when Denny and Winters arrived at the rendezvous.

He told himself that he should not assume the worst. He had been in tight spots before and had always found a way out. He knew how to survive, how to anticipate threats and how to evade them. This was no different.

What he had to do now wasn't complicated. Once Eva had been released, Maxim would retrieve Lukas Nemeth's notes from their hiding place in a meadow at the Hill of Three Borders. Then they could make their run for the border.

Fifteen

Friday, November 2

Feliks Hawes had been a frequent-enough visitor to the British legation that the guards at its front entrance immediately recognized him. They pushed aside some of the Hungarians clustered around the front gate to allow him, and Collins, to quickly enter the building. The legation's imposing granite facade featured four ornamental columns that spanned its third and fourth stories. A large Union Jack hanging from a flagpole above large wooden doors flapped in the stiff breeze.

Collins waited in the main downstairs hall while Hawes the situation to Colonel Cowley and a British official, John Bruce Lockhart, who had arrived in Budapest just after the uprising started.

According to Hawes, Bruce Lockhart was one of MI6's most trusted men and had been sent to Washington after Kim Philby's departure in an attempt to restore American trust in British intelligence. "He tried to recruit me for MI6 a few years ago," Hawes said. "I did a few temporary jobs for him involving Poland, but I told him I was happy at MI5. He understood. John should be squarely in our corner."

Collins read a week-old copy of *The Times* of London while he waited. Hawes returned some fifteen minutes later, slightly exasperated. "They've suggested that I observe protocol and make our request through official channels," he said. "In this case, that means seeing the second secretary, a woman named Blackburn. We must bow to the gods of bureaucracy, it seems."

They were ushered into a second floor conference room where they waited for several minutes before the door opened, and a middle-aged woman appeared. She introduced herself as Clarissa Blackburn and asked how she could help.

"We're here on a sensitive matter," Hawes said. "It's quite urgent. We'd like your assistance in the issuance of some documentation."

Hawes quickly explained that he was in Budapest as part of a joint Anglo-American intelligence operation and that Collins was working for the CIA. Collins winced at that description, but it was accurate—he was in Hungary on behalf of the Agency. Hawes suggested that she contact Gaza Katona at the American legation if she needed to validate Collins' bona fides.

"That won't be necessary," she said. "I'd look to Mr. Bruce Lockhart for any validation. What is it that you're requesting?"

"We have an urgent need for two blank emergency passports."

She pursed her lips. "For you and Mr. Collins?"

"No, they would be used by Hungarians."

She peered at Hawes over her half-glasses. "Hungarians."

"There are quite a few of them here in Budapest," Hawes said with a slight smile.

She didn't return the smile. "Of course I can't very well hand passports over to you without discussing it with the ambassador," she said. "Sensitive matter or not."

"Let me assure you that they will be employed in a very good cause."

"I'm sure they may do *you* good," she said coldly. "Whether the same can be said for the legation is another matter. We will be held accountable by the Hungarians if these passports are misused."

"While I can't discuss the details, this operation doesn't concern the Hungarian government," Hawes said. "And we're in a bit of a hurry. When might you have your discussion with the ambassador?"

"If the ambassador approves, then you could have them in the morning."

"Would it help if I spoke to him myself?" Hawes asked. "We can't wait until tomorrow."

"You should know, Mr. Winters—if that is your name—that I'm aware of the passport you arranged for this Hungarian woman, Anna Sandor—or Anna Sanderson as she was renamed. I objected strongly to this irregularity at the time, but I was overruled. As to your latest request, I shall lodge my objections with Ambassador Fry. The Foreign Office should never kowtow to the Secret Intelligence Service and issue British passports at their command."

"I appreciate your honesty," Hawes said. "We need the passports today. Consult with the ambassador, by all means, but we'll expect that they will be made available this afternoon."

Blackburn stared at Hawes, her face flushed. "We shall see about that," she said and rose from the table. She left without shaking hands.

Hawes waited until they were back in Vorosmarty Square before commenting on the situation. He told Collins that he was sure that they would get the passports that afternoon despite Blackburn's opposition. "Ambassador Fry's a Sandhurst man. He'll understand that the rules must be bent now and then. These are exactly the circumstances under which command discretion is called for, and Bruce Lockhart and Colonel Cowley will be there to help him recognize that reality."

* * *

When Collins and Hawes neared the Hotel Duna, they could hear the sounds of a crowd chanting and whistling coming from the direction of the river. They followed the sound to the Promenade and once there, saw that there were a number of river boats at the quay with a line of men, women, and children with luggage waiting to board them. Several Red Army officers appeared to be directing the effort a dozen or so soldiers stood guard.

"The Russian evacuation," Hawes said. "More than rumor."

A large crowd of Hungarians chanted and whistled at the Soviets waiting in line. Some who stood closer to the docks were throwing clumps of dirt at the departing Russians, and others were spitting at them. Collins and Hawes walked to the edge of the crowd.

"Hardly a dignified exit," Collins said to Hawes.

"Good riddance," a man dressed in overalls and a short coat said to Collins in accented English. "That's what you say, no, in English? Good riddance."

"That's what we say," Collins said.

"We should show restraint," a young woman near them said. Her English was better. She had curly hair and thick eyeglasses. "They will not forgive this. This week has been a humiliation for them. They will not let this stand, and there will be a price to pay."

"She's quite perceptive," someone said in a low tone. When Collins turned to see who it was, he found Vitali Osin standing next to him. Osin wore a long wool coat and a dark homburg. "We have mishandled this," he said to Collins in a conversational tone, as if they had been standing there having a friendly chat. "This hasty withdrawal is a direct consequence of that."

Collins noticed that the Hungarians around them moved away—somehow they had realized that Osin was a Russian official of some sort, and they were giving him a wide berth.

"Are your views widely shared at your embassy?" Collins asked.

"Ambassador Andropov sees things very clearly," Osin said. "If there had to be violence, we should have insisted that Gero employ his own forces, and we should have held our men in reserve. That would have let us seek a negotiated solution, like that in Poland, from a position of power. Even so, we have shown great restraint." He took in the scene around them. "A lovely city. It looked quite different in 1945. It would be a shame to see it in ruins again."

"No one disputes that you can turn Budapest into a pile of rubble," Collins said. "But to what end?" Hawes had remained silent, waiting to see where the conversation would head.

"That would be shortsighted," Osin said. "It's why Chairman Khrushchev has been so patient. There has to be a stable government to negotiate with, however. It does not appear Nagy can offer that. We will not allow Hungary to fall into the hands of the rightists. You can't blame us for that. You won't accept hostile regimes on your borders, in your sphere of influence. Why should we? Don't you have your Monroe Doctrine? Didn't your president authorize your CIA to stage a coup in Guatemala two years ago?"

"The Hungarians don't want you here," Collins said, gesturing toward the docks where the evacuation had continued. "They don't want Communism, either, or at least the brand practiced by Rakosi and Gero."

"Some Hungarians don't want us here," Osin said. "There are others who do. They aren't in the streets rioting."

"You aren't joining the evacuation?" Collins asked.

"No, there is unfinished business for me here." He fixed his gaze on Collins. "You can tell Rusakov that he can come to the embassy when he grows tired of hide-and-seek. He can tell his story, and we won't be unsympathetic. He wouldn't be the first of my colleagues to have doubts. He just must not act on them."

"Even if I knew where he was—which I don't—I don't plan on staying around long enough to pass anyone's messages," Collins said. "This time tomorrow, I'll be in Vienna, eating lunch at the Hotel Bristol."

"I see," Osin said. "That's no doubt quite wise on your part. May you have an uneventful journey." He touched the brim of his hat, turned on his heel, and strode away from them.

★ ★ ★

Just after three o'clock, Hawes left for the British legation to collect the blank passports. Viktor had left word with Zoltan that Collins should meet him at the same spot in Petofi Square at 3:30, and when Collins arrived, he found only Morris waiting for him, again by the parked Skoda.

"Viktor is negotiating the details of the rendezvous with Melles," Morris explained. "It will have to be tomorrow morning. Kosa won't meet after dark. It's taken us all day to collect the money, but we have it. What about the passports?"

"Winters is getting them now." Collins looked around the square. There were only a few pedestrians about. "Viktor's men are watching?"

"They are."

"Osin approached me this morning," Collins said. "He says you'll be welcomed with open arms at the Russian embassy."

"Not in this lifetime," Morris said. He touched his coat pocket lightly. "I don't plan on ever talking baseball with Osin." He paused, reflecting for a moment. "Tell me, Denny, is this kid Mantle on the Yankees as good as they say?"

"He's very good," Collins said. "A switch-hitter with power. He just won the Triple Crown. But I think Willie Mays of the Giants may even be better."

"The Dodgers have anyone promising?"

"Not in the way of hitters. Two young pitchers, Drysdale and Koufax. Drysdale's a big guy who throws hard. Koufax is a lefty with some control problems. He's a Brooklyn kid, so the fans root hard for him."

"Maybe they'll let me see some games at Ebbets in the spring," Morris said. "I'd like that." He looked directly at Collins. "I take it you have our passports?"

"I do," Collins said. "Eva's passport is Italian. I guess that with her looks that was the best match."

"If you have them with you, I'd like mine," Morris said. "You should keep Eva's."

Collins retrieved Morris' American passport from his right inner coat pocket and handed it to him. Morris opened it and studied the page with his photograph. "A happier time," he said. "But what's done is done. I made some mistakes, but I did what I thought was right at the time. There's no point in second guessing myself."

"Maybe you should have done some more second guessing," Collins said.

"I was a true believer, Denny. I thought socialism offered a scientific answer for the injustices and inequities that I saw around me. I knew that the big money guys, the fat cats, the ones with their feet on the throats of the workers, would fight to the death to preserve their privilege and the system that granted it to them. To take power from them was never going to be a bloodless exercise."

"I understand some of it," Collins said. "I've always rooted for the underdog. We were in the same place on Negros getting their civil rights and on unions being a good deal for the workers and for the minimum wage and Social Security. I thought FDR's heart was in the right place. But the Communists always take things to the extreme. And they're ruthless."

"Hindsight is always 20/20. Take Eva and her family. Only the Communists were going to stand up for Hungary's Jews. At the end, even Horthy didn't have the stomach for what Hitler wanted. The Nazis put the Arrow Cross in power here so they could start shipping Jews to the death camps. Who wouldn't welcome the Russians after something like that?"

"But you weren't here," Collins said. "You were in the U.S. It's simple. You don't betray your friends and your country. You don't get into bed with the worst of the worst. My God, Morris, you worked for the KGB."

"Spare me the lecture. It's easy to judge, when you've never had to make the choices I did."

"I don't buy it," Collins said. "I certainly don't look at you and think that 'there, but for the grace of God, go I,' because I would never have done what you did. If I felt that strongly, I would have made a break openly. Quit the State Department, renounced my citizenship. Openly. No secret betrayal."

"And there's the difference between us," Morris said. "I won't let anyone else decide the rules of the game." He glanced at his wristwatch. "After the meeting tomorrow with Kosa, before we leave for Vienna, I have to recover the materials I told you about."

"With Osin watching for you? We shouldn't make any stops."

Morris frowned. "I told you before that I needed to bring the information with me for leverage." He exhaled slowly. "I have detailed notes about the Soviet missile program."

"How the hell did you get them?"

"Through Eva. Her uncle, Lukas Nemeth, works with the Russians. He's a physicist of some note. Lukas gave me the notes in the hope that it would help us get a better deal from the Agency when we got to the States. And he also didn't want the Soviets to have any military advantage." He pulled the collar of his coat up slightly. "I plan to hand the notes over to Dulles."

Collins better understood why Morris wanted to retrieve the information, but he still didn't like the idea. "You're making this harder than it should be, Morris."

"It had to be done this way," Morris said. "I've had to keep my cards close to my chest. It's not paranoia, Denny. Hungarian State Security has a source in the American legation, and Moscow Center has someone at CIA headquarters, a penetration agent. I don't know very much about this agent, only that his code name is Envoy and that Moscow Center is convinced that the CIA has no clue that he is betraying them."

"If we can get you and Eva out of the country, and safely back to the U.S., none of that will matter," Collins said. "Between now and then, we won't share any of our plans with the legation, or with Wittingham in Vienna, so there won't be any leaks. If we're going to worry, let's worry about Vitali Osin and Laszlo Kosa. They're the ones standing in our way, not this Envoy guy."

Sixteen

Saturday, November 3

In the morning, it was chilly and overcast. From his hotel window, Collins could see that a delicate white blanket—the first lasting snow of the season—now covered the Buda hills. Collins ventured outside before breakfast and found the streets around the Duna still and quiet. He turned up his collar against the stiff breeze coming off the Danube.

He hoped it would be his last day in Budapest. If the meeting with Kosa went well—it had been set for 9 AM in Obuda according to a message left by Viktor—they should be leaving the city before noon.

Collins returned to the Duna's lobby, grateful for the sudden warmth once back inside. Zoltan called him over to the front desk. "You have a phone call," he said, handing Collins the receiver.

It was Gaza Katona. "Wanted you to know that our convoy was stopped by the Russians ten miles short of the border yesterday. Our people turned around and drove back and arrived here around midnight. We've lodged a stiff protest with Ambassador Andropov, and he has assured us that it won't happen again. He's given us a safe conduct pass."

"The Russians are in control of the border, then?"

"Looks like it. We're going to give it another go with the safe conduct pass. The offer for you to hitch a ride is still open, but the convoy leaves from Liberty Square in fifteen minutes. Sorry for the late notice. I've been trying to reach you all morning."

Collins cursed out loud. The timing wouldn't work for them. It would be an hour before their rendezvous with Laszlo Kosa. And then there was Morris' detour to the Hill of Three Borders.

"I'm sorry but that won't work. We can't leave just yet."

One other thing," Katona said. "We've heard that Janos Kadar and Ferenc Munnich have disappeared. Nagy's people can't find them. Kadar's not only the Minister of State, but he's also the general secretary of the Hungarian Socialist Workers' Party, the new party the Reds formed. There are some rumors that he's switched sides."

"What does that mean for negotiations between Nagy and the Russians?"

"We don't know," Katona said. "If the Russians make a move and you're still here, come over to the legation. You're welcome to hole up there with us for the duration, however long that may be."

In the dining room, Collins joined a table of journalists that included Lachlan Ferguson, Isabelle Lavalle, Abe Kaufer, and Lester Kane. He ordered coffee and toast after the waiter informed him that food supplies were limited, and the kitchen had run out of eggs, milk, and bacon.

He wondered how long a city the size of Budapest could last without food deliveries. If the Red Army blocked the farmers from supplying the city with food, it wouldn't be long before people ran through whatever they had on hand. Then it would be survival of the fittest with the sick, the old, the weak starving first. Collins had heard the horror stories of what it was like in Stalingrad and Warsaw and Berlin when they were besieged. It would be a tragedy if Budapest joined that list.

"From all that we can gather, the city is completely surrounded," Lachlan said. "At the same time, General Maleter is supposed to be negotiating with General Malinin about an orderly withdrawal of the Russian troops."

"Time to get out," Kaufer said flatly. "I hear the trains to Gyor are running again."

"No flights out," Isabelle said. "The Russians control all three airports."

"I'm staying." It was Lester Kane. "Remember, the same thing happened last month in Warsaw. The Red Army ringed the city and then Khrushchev flew in and struck a deal with Gomulka. No bloodbath."

"There was no fighting in Warsaw beforehand," Collins said. "And the Poles didn't try to leave the Warsaw Pact or hold free elections."

Isabelle nodded in agreement. "Dennis is right. The Hungarians have fought them to a standstill. The Russians won't let such an insult to the honor of the Red Army go unpunished."

"Perhaps that's so," Kane said. "But I think there's room for compromise. Radio Moscow is accepting the Nagy government as legitimate. Khrushchev can look like a world statesman if he settles this peacefully while the Brits and French are tangled up in Suez."

"What will you do?" Isabelle asked Collins. "I thought you were quite eager to leave. Yet you're still here."

Collins shrugged. "I had planned to be gone by now," he said. "Winters finally found us a vehicle, so we'll take off today."

"Do you think the Russians will attack?"

"I do," Collins said. He had been convinced by what Gaza Katona had told him about the Soviet forces entering Hungary from the Ukraine. Why dramatically increase troop levels if they were ready to withdraw? "I believe they're going through the motions with the negotiations, buying time to get their tanks and troops in place. I wish it weren't so."

He was interrupted by the arrival of Hawes. "Sorry to barge in," he said to Collins. "We have that errand to run."

Collins checked his wristwatch—it was almost eight o'clock, time to drive to the rendezvous. He made his good-byes and followed Hawes out of the dining room.

"I brought the blank passports," Hawes said. "Miss Blackburn looked like she had been sucking on a lemon when I picked them up yesterday at the legation." He handed the passports to Collins, who put them in his inner coat pocket. "Zoltan says we're to meet Viktor in Bem Square. We'll head to the meeting with Kosa from there. I settled the bill for both of us. Bring your luggage to the Land Rover. Once we cross the river, we won't be returning."

* * *

Isabelle Lavalle stopped Collins as he crossed the lobby to take his canvas bag and typewriter to the Land Rover.

"Can we have a word?" she asked, motioning to the same couch that Vitali Osin had occupied a few days before.

"I don't mean to be rude, but it'll have to be quick."

They sat on the couch, side-by-side, and Isabelle studied his face for a moment before she spoke.

"Did you know that Eva Nemeth reports on her clients to State Security?"

"That may be so," Collins said. "But I have nothing to hide, and the new government has disbanded the AVO. So for the moment, there's no one for her to report to, is there?"

"Perhaps she's not the only one with more than one employer."

"I'm not sure what you mean."

"I think you do. Your photographer, Winters, works for British intelligence. He's been in and out of the British legation all week."

"Feliks has friends at the legation. That doesn't make him a spy."

"Do you also have another employer?"

"Don't be absurd."

"Am I being absurd? I had never heard of Winters, and neither had any of the other photographers here. So I asked a favor of a friend at the French legation, to check with the proper authorities in Paris about Felix Winters and Dennis Collins."

"And what did you learn?"

"They had nothing on Winters. But there was a file on you, Dennis, detailing a visit you made to Paris in 1951. You came to brief General Eisenhower on the situation in Korea, and were accompanied by a CIA official named Matthew Steele. There was an incident with Czech agents, an attempted shooting."

"Their file is accurate, up to a point," Collins said. "I agreed to tell General Eisenhower what I had seen in Korea, to give him an unvarnished report in the hopes that if he got the chance to change our strategy there, he would. I'd like to think that it helped influence him to push for the armistice. But that doesn't make me a spy."

"The file said you were a brave man," she said. "Calm under fire. There's a thin line between courage and foolhardiness. Whatever you are doing here, whatever scheme the British may have enlisted you for, please reconsider. Don't think you can come to Hungary and assist an officer of British intelligence without attracting the attention of the AVO and the KGB."

"They have much greater worries at the moment," he said. "Besides, I'm just doing my job as a correspondent. Nothing more."

"Why did Vitali Osin stop by the hotel to talk to you? He pretends to be a diplomat, but he's KGB."

"Osin wanted to set me straight on the origins of the uprising. How it was engineered by Arrow Cross. I laughed him out of the lobby." He smiled at her. "I appreciate your concern, but you need not worry about me."

"I'm only trying to help." She placed her hand on top of his and looked into his eyes, moving closer to him so that her leg touched his. He gently removed his hand from hers.

"A man far from home should be careful," he said. "Ulysses learned that with Calypso, didn't he?"

"I'm no nymph," she said lightly. "And I've never imprisoned a lover on my island. You're in no danger."

"Winters and I are leaving the city. What are you planning to do?"

"I have arranged to stay at the French legation on Lendvay Street. The Red Army will not dare cross the legation's threshold. Moscow would not want to be seen violating French sovereignty—that would not look good for Thorez and Duclos and our Communists. I will take what photos I can, and then I will get out. Agence France-Presse has already asked me to go to the Suez."

"Good luck," he said and, before he could say anything more, she had leaned into him and kissed him softly on the lips.

"Something for you to remember me by," she said.

* * *

Hawes parked the Land Rover next to the Skoda on a side street near Bem Square.

Viktor greeted them with a brief nod and a smile. He explained that they were to meet Kosa outside the ruins of the Roman amphitheater in Obuda, the oldest part of the city, to the north of where they stood. He showed them the rendezvous location on a bedraggled map. "It's a good spot for an exchange. They can see anyone coming from a distance."

He handed Collins a thick leather billfold. "Some of the cash is counterfeit," he said with a grin. "It'd be fitting if Kosa got pinched for passing phony bills once he reaches the West."

Collins found himself grinning as he placed the wallet in his inner coat pocket.

"When you come back with Eva, Maxim will be waiting for you on Kapucinus Street," Viktor said. "One of my boys will be with him. Maxim has a brief side trip he must make once he knows Eva is safe."

"A side trip?" Hawes shook his head, his jaw tightening. "We've never discussed this before. The moment we have Eva, we should go."

Viktor didn't respond; he glanced over at Collins, clearly expecting him to take the lead in defending the idea.

"Morris told me about it," Collins said. "He needs to collect some documents that he thinks will be of great interest to the Agency. He couldn't risk keeping them in his flat where they might be discovered."

"How far does he have to go?"

"The Hill of Three Borders."

Hawes didn't like the idea. "Too far. I think this side trip is a mistake."

"He feels very strongly about it," Collins said and hesitated, not sure how much he should reveal to Hawes. "It's information about Russian weaponry. Stuff that the U.S. military doesn't have."

"Is it worth the risk?"

"It is."

Hawes shrugged. "I hope you're right."

Viktor checked his wristwatch. "You should leave now," he said. "You don't want to be late." He shook hands with Collins and Hawes. "I'm heading back across the river, so I won't see you again. Best of luck."

"If you ever do make it to New York again, look me up," Collins said.

"I'm more likely to head to Tel Aviv than New York," he said. "I hear they need tough Jews willing to fight. I think I fit the bill."

★ ★ ★

On the drive north to Obuda, Collins admitted to Hawes that he was feeling anxious.

"I was involved in another meeting like this," he told him. "An exchange. It didn't end well. Some very bad memories. It's hard for me not to think about what could go wrong."

"Don't worry," Hawes said. "I'll have you covered the entire time."

"You should stay in the vehicle," Collins said. "That will give you a fighting chance if it's an ambush."

"I don't think they'd try that," Hawes said. "They're looking for a quiet exit. Just like us."

They passed a queue of women in front of a bakery and then saw a small group clustered around a cart where a man was selling chestnuts in paper cones.

"It looks like a normal day," Collins said. "If you ignore the Sword of Damocles in the form of several hundred Russian tanks waiting just outside the city."

They drove through Obuda's Main Square and then followed Szentendrei Street north and passed the Aquincum Museum. The rendezvous spot was further up the road, outside the ruins of the Roman amphitheater. Hawes parked the Land Rover on a grassy spot just off the road.

Collins left the vehicle and walked toward the amphitheater's circular gray walls. He stood there for a few minutes, feeling exposed and vulnerable. He wondered how long he would have to wait. Just then Laszlo Kosa emerged from around a corner. He was unshaven, with dark circles under his eyes.

"Do you have what we asked for?" Kosa asked

"We do," Collins said. He was relieved that Kosa didn't feel it necessary to point a weapon at him. "But Eva, first. Once she's in the Land Rover, I'll hand you the passports and the money. I'll wait here with you until you're satisfied that we've kept our side of the bargain."

"Good," he said. "We don't want trouble." He stepped back and motioned with his right hand. A minute or so later, Istvan Melles appeared, grasping Eva's right arm. They walked over to where Kosa and Collins were standing.

"Hello, Dennis," Eva said. "I'm sorry you have been caught up in this."

"Are you all right?"

"I'm fine."

"We've agreed that you can walk over to the Land Rover," Collins said. "Winters is there. Once you're in the vehicle, I'll give Kosa what he's asked for."

Eva pulled her arm free from Melles and gave Kosa a look of contempt. "Are you taking money?" she asked him. "You kidnapped me for money? You're nothing more than an opportunist."

"We need American dollars to get out of Hungary," he said. "Is it any different for you and Rusakov? You're running away, too."

Eva started to say something, but stopped herself. She spun on her heel and walked over to the Land Rover and climbed into the back seat. Hawes watched intently from the driver's seat. Collins found it reassuring to know that he was ready to intervene if Kosa tried anything.

Collins pulled the passports and the billfold out of his inner coat pocket and handed them to Kosa. He studied the blank passports for a moment and grunted in satisfaction. Kosa tossed the billfold to Melles, who quickly counted the cash and then grunted.

"Satisfied?" Collins asked.

"Yes. We need for you to stay here, in the open, until we are gone." Kosa gave Collins a look of appraisal. "Eva says you're a decent man. I give you credit for courage, too. Not like that shit that she's with now. I wish I could have fought Rusakov instead of you."

"I wasn't looking for trouble," Collins said.

"I know that," Kosa said. He looked over at Melles. "Istvan tells me that when I'm drunk, I'm a lousy boxer. But you have no need to worry about me. I have no quarrel with you."

Melles said something to Kosa in a lowered voice. "We'll be on our way, then," Kosa said. He gave Collins a sly smile. "Tell Rusakov that I hope his former comrades catch up to him. They should be here very soon. Then he'll get what he deserves."

Seventeen

Hawes drove them south toward Bem Square, smoothly shifting the gears of the Land Rover as they passed through Obuda. The Danube remained within constant sight to their left, and Collins caught a glimpse or two of Margaret Island. Hawes began whistling, cheerfully, a tune Collins recognized as "For He is an Englishman" from Gilbert and Sullivan.

When Hawes finished whistling the chorus, he grinned at Collins. "Well done," he said. "On to Vienna, post haste."

"Have you had any luck with my papers?" Eva asked from the back seat. "Will I be able to leave?"

"Your passport and press card arrived Thursday," Collins said, turning his shoulders so he could face her. He reached into his outside coat pocket and retrieved the small envelope he had kept them in and handed it to Eva.

She quickly scanned the documents. "Luciana Marchetti, *Corriere della Sera*," she read out loud. "You know that I don't speak Italian?"

"We'll all stick to English at the border," Hawes said. "No Hungarian and no Russian."

"Will we be able to get out of the city?" she asked. "Laszlo kept saying that the Russians are about to attack."

"We think that the Russians will be happy to let foreign journalists pass through their lines," Collins said. "Fewer witnesses around when the time comes."

"Laszlo and Melles planned to leave today as well," she said. "I overheard them talking. Their plan is to cross the border into Austria and then try for asylum in Germany. Melles has relatives in Hamburg who moved there after 1947."

"Asylum?" Collins asked, surprised at the idea. "They're State Security officers, responsible in the past for God knows what actions. They're partly the reason the uprising started. Why would the Germans give them asylum?"

Hawes laughed. "By the time they're interviewed by the immigration authorities, they'll have transformed themselves into freedom fighters. Heroes of the Kilian Barracks. Sorry to be cynical about it, but their type finds it very easy to turn coat. They say the AVO recruited some of their best operatives from the Arrow Cross."

"So what's their answer if they're exposed as AVO?" Collins asked.

"They were only following orders," Hawes said. "They didn't like it, but they had no choice."

"You're right," Eva said in a quiet voice. "So few are innocent. Most of us made compromises in order to survive. Under Rakosi and Gero, only the thieves and pickpockets and whores in the Eighth District had clean hands. The first were last, and the last were first."

* * *

They found Morris waiting on Kapucinus Street, leaning on the hood of the Skoda. Standing nearby was a thin young blond man, the same man who Viktor had assigned to watch Collins outside the Duna, holding a submachine gun. He acknowledged them with a grin.

After Hawes parked the Land Rover, Eva immediately ran over to Morris. They embraced and then exchanged several passionate kisses.

"Any problems with the handover?" Morris asked Collins.

"They were quite professional about it," Collins said. "Although Kosa had some less than flattering things to say about you."

"The feeling's mutual," Morris said. He motioned toward the parked Skoda. "Why don't you come along with me when I run this final errand? Mr. Winters and Eva can stay here."

"What about road blocks on the way?" Hawes asked. "You may run into the insurgents or the National Guard."

"We're American reporters," Morris said. "We have the press cards and passports to prove it. They should let us through."

Hawes looked at his watch. "It's almost one o'clock," he said. "The day is slipping away on us. We don't want to drive after dark if we can help it. How long is this going to take?"

"No more than a couple of hours," Morris said. "Assuming it all goes smoothly."

On the way to the Hill of Three Borders, Morris drove slowly through the streets of Buda. He explained to Collins that it would be easier to spot anyone tailing them.

"There's no one behind us," Collin said after glancing back.

As they began climbing into the hills, there were fewer and fewer residences around. When they reached Szepvolgyi Street, which led to the Hill of Three Borders, there was little traffic. Collins saw one black sedan by the side of the road with a man in a winter coat and fur hat standing next to it, smoking a cigarette. He didn't recognize the make of the car.

"That's a Zim," Morris said. "Russian."

They followed the winding road until they reached Harmashatarhegyi Street, which took them higher into the hills. A boxy building came into view. "The restaurant," Morris said. "We have to go on foot from here."

He parked the Skoda at some distance from the restaurant and then motioned for Collins to follow him. Morris walked several hundred feet back toward the building. When they got closer a man stepped into view—it was Viktor Toth.

"All clear, Maxim," Viktor said. "The restaurant's closed. I've checked the trail. It's empty."

"Good," Morris said. He looked over at Collins. "I didn't want to say anything in front of Winters about Viktor being here. After Philby, you can understand why I'd be wary of British intelligence."

Collins nodded. While he trusted Feliks Hawes, he could understand why Morris might have reservations. Whether there were still Soviet penetration agents in Britain's intelligence agencies remained an open question.

"We saw a man next to a Zim on the way here," Morris said to Viktor. "It's probably nothing."

"I'll keep an eye out," Viktor said.

Collins followed Morris as he strode away toward a small stand of trees. There was a trail there that Morris took and they walked for perhaps ten minutes, until they reached an opening and a small meadow with patches of light snow. Morris led Collins toward a low stone wall near the edge of a clearing. Their shoes left tracks in the snow.

Morris squatted down on his haunches as he examined the stone wall. Collins heard him counting under his breath. "The fifth stone in the middle row," Morris said out loud. He pushed one of the stones aside, opening up a wider space. Then he reached his right hand into the space and pulled out a thin oilcloth package. He shoved it into the outside pocket of his overcoat.

"I've got what I came for," he said. "The notes are in this package."

They retraced their steps through the meadow and reentered the woods. They walked along the trail single file. It was silent on the trail. Morris suddenly came to a stop, so abruptly that Collins almost bumped into him. Collins looked up and saw the reason. Vitali Osin stood blocking their way. He held a revolver in his right hand, pointing it directly at Morris.

"Hands to the side, away from your bodies," Osin said.

"What are you doing here?" Collins asked. "Is this your idea of diplomacy?"

"No movements," he said, ignoring Collins. "I have a few questions. Then we'll take you both to Durov."

"Durov's here?" Morris asked.

"Many are here from Moscow, including Durov and General Serov. And now we have proof that this uprising has been orchestrated by CIA agents."

"Neither of us work for the CIA," Morris said.

"Who is the case officer?" Osin asked. He shifted the revolver and pointed it at Collins. "Is it you? Or is Colonel de Silva in Vienna in charge?"

"I told you before, I'm a journalist," Collins said.

"You told me that before, and you also said you were ignorant of Rusakov's location. Yet here you are, together. Rather than continuing to lie, you should answer my question. Are you the case officer?"

"How did you find us?" Morris interrupted him. "How did you know we would be here?"

"We had a man waiting on the road, watching for your Skoda," Osin said. "Your fondness for this place is noted in your dossier, and Durov thought that eventually you might come here. We stationed another man by your flat on Castle Hill in the event you stopped by there."

Over Osin's shoulder Collins caught a flash of movement further up the trail.

"I'm not the case officer," Collins said, hoping to keep Osin's attention focused in front of him. "He's in Vienna."

Moments later, Osin suddenly flinched and then stiffened.

"Yes, that's the muzzle of my submachine gun in your back," a voice said. "Drop your gun and put your hands up. Slowly, of course." It was Viktor; he had come up the trail without alerting Osin.

Osin did as he was told, carefully placing his revolver on the ground and raising his hands over his head.

"Is he alone?" Morris asked Viktor.

"Another man drove him here in the Zim. He waited down below. I took care of him before I followed this one."

Morris said something to Osin in Russian and the man stared back at him, never losing eye contact.

"*Nyet*," he said. "But you'll never get out of the country."

"Department Thirteen?" Morris asked. "Are they looking for me?"

"What does it matter? Do you think that General Serov will allow you to defect? Can you imagine that Durov will?"

"How long have you known?"

"We were not sure until after Collins was in the country," Osin said. "We planned to arrest both of you at your first meeting, but then the fascist uprising began and made following Collins impossible."

"Who first alerted you? Someone in the CIA? The American legation?"

Osin laughed. "How would I know? Ask Durov. Maybe he'll feel like answering your questions."

"Don't waste any more time with him," Viktor said. "You should go. I'll keep him here."

Morris carefully stepped around Osin and Viktor and continued up the trail. Collins followed suit. As he walked away, Collins heard Viktor say something to Osin in Russian, and the diplomat laughed.

There was a black Zim sedan parked closer to the entrance to the woods than the Skoda. As Collins passed the vehicle, he saw that there was a man slumped over the steering wheel. He kept walking.

Morris put the Skoda in reverse and backed out until they faced the road. Collins glanced at his watch—it was 3:20. Even if they weren't delayed on their return to Bem Square, they would be hard-pressed to reach the Red Army lines before sunset.

He was about to say something to Morris about it when there was a sudden, short burst of machine gun fire in the distance. Morris did not look at Collins, and neither man spoke. He put the Skoda into gear and drove away.

* * *

Morris waited until they reached Szepvolgyi Street before he broke the silence.

"We couldn't risk letting Osin go," he said. "Viktor will make sure that the Zim disappears, along with Osin and the driver. That should give them pause."

"It's a lousy business," Collins said.

"If our roles were reversed, Osin wouldn't hesitate to do the same thing."

"Who is Durov?"

"He's one of the top men at Moscow Center. He's the logical choice to oversee my return to the fold." He gripped the steering wheel tightly. "If Durov catches up to me, I won't last very long. I'll confess that I hate the idea of dying here, so far from home. I know it's irrational—why should it matter where? If the worse happens, I'll be beyond caring, won't I?"

"I wouldn't worry about it," Collins said. "I like our chances of making it to Vienna."

"You've always been a fatalist, Denny. I'm not. I want to take things in my own hands, shape my own destiny."

Collins laughed. "You make me sound like I'm taking a dive for destiny, like a fighter who's reluctant to throw any punches. That's not the case. I think you do your best in whatever situation you find yourself in, but in the meantime, there's no point worrying about the outcome."

"And that hasn't changed for you? Now that you're married? Eva told me you have children."

"I know how much I have to live for, but I try to put that out of my mind. If I didn't, I'd go crazy. I focus on getting through the next five minutes and then the next five. You hope things will work out, and you do your best."

"What was Matthew Steele like?" Morris asked. "As a man, I mean."

"Why do you ask?"

"Curiosity. Steele's the reason I'm here, in a way. I've had a lot of time to think about it. I studied his Moscow Center file and on paper he didn't seem particularly interesting. Ruling class. Yalie. OSS." Morris looked at Collins. "He married Penny, didn't he? That made it into his file, a clipping from the *Washington Star*."

"He did marry her," Collins said. "They were in the same social circles in Washington."

"What was he like?"

"Steele changed in the time I knew him. Karina's death bothered him more than I would have imagined. He had used her as a pawn—hell, he manipulated all of us. Then Steele came down with cancer in 1950. He spent his remaining time trying to make amends."

"What happened to Karina was wrong. A crime." Morris' tone softened. "The two of you had something. I could see that just by looking at your faces. It's one of the mysteries of life, how that happens. I never loved a woman, truly loved her, until Eva." Morris glanced over at Collins. "And you? You've found the right one?"

Collins nodded, but didn't say anything. He didn't want to talk about Maria. He wanted to keep her, and his sons, and that part of his life walled off from Morris Rose and Cliff Wittingham and their shadowy world.

"What happened after that night in New York?" Collins asked. "After I gave you the microfilm."

"Yatov had an escape route prepared. I traveled to Mexico City under the name of Roger Egan, an importer of Aztec antiquities. I took a DC-6 to Mexico City. American Airlines, stopping at National in Washington and Love Field in Dallas."

"And from Mexico City?"

"A Polish passport until I reached Warsaw, and from there, to Moscow. Yatov remained in the States. He had another legend, another identity that he could assume. Then he disappeared two years later, sometime in the spring or summer of 1951. There were lots of theories in Moscow about what happened. They had their people poke around in New York and Washington and found nothing."

"What do you think happened to him?"

"I think he's dead. I hope that he died slowly and painfully from an incurable disease, but if I had to guess it was a car accident or a heart attack." He paused, reflecting for a moment. "But who knows? Maybe he got tired and decided to go AWOL. Maybe he's living under an assumed identity in Buenos Aires, along with all the Nazis, playing chess with ex-Gestapo men. I figure they would enjoy comparing notes about the old days."

Eighteen

They abandoned the Skoda on a side street in Buda and walked several blocks to the rendezvous location on Kapucinus Street. Hawes and Eva were waiting there in the Land Rover and Eva jumped out of the vehicle and rushed over to Morris when they arrived.

"Did you get it?" she asked in a low tone of voice.

"I did," he said. "We had some trouble, though. The Russian diplomat, Osin, followed us. Viktor had to handle it." He saw the look of dismay on her face. "It had to be done. We had no other choice. Viktor has bought us the time we need."

Eva didn't respond, but it was clear that she was troubled by what she had heard.

Hawes glanced at his wristwatch. "It's almost four o'clock. No time for high tea, and I doubt we could find scones and jam. Shall we finally leave?"

"By all means," Morris said. "When we reach the first Red Army checkpoint outside the city on the road to Gyor, let me talk us through."

"Be my guest," Hawes said. "Then we'll need to stop and wait until dawn before we start driving again. Driving in the dark will get us killed. These Russian peasants they've dressed up in uniforms shoot first and ask questions later."

Morris took the front passenger seat, next to Hawes, and Collins and Eva sat in the back seat. Hawes drove the Land Rover carefully, taking the somewhat indirect route out of the city that he and Morris had agreed upon.

It was nearing dusk when Morris asked Hawes to stop by the side of the road. He left the vehicle with his suitcase and disappeared behind a nearby oak tree. He emerged a few minutes later in the uniform of a KGB officer, complete with visored cap, medals, and polished leather boots.

"Is this your plan?" Hawes asked. "To talk us through the checkpoint as a KGB officer? How are you going to explain why we're driving a British vehicle?"

"You'll see," Morris said. "I'll turn that to our advantage."

They arrived at the first Red Army roadblock just before sunset. Collins counted fifteen massive M-54 tanks parked by the side of the road and tents set up in an open field. The scene was illuminated by two large bonfires. A tank had been parked so that it blocked the road.

"Flash the headlamps," Morris said. "Quickly now. Let them know we see them. Then come to a very slow stop."

Hawes did as Morris had asked, and moments after the Land Rover had stopped Morris jumped out of the vehicle. They watched as he strode purposefully up to the Red Army soldiers standing in front of the tank.

Through the open windows, Collins could hear Morris speaking to the soldiers in rapid Russian, his tone commanding. A moment later an officer appeared and Morris immediately began hectoring him.

"He's as bold as brass," Hawes said, smiling. "I'll grant him that. He's informed the captain that he's on the staff of General Serov, head of the KGB, and should face no interference. Morris has the captain on his back foot. Count on the Russians to grovel before the man wielding the whip."

"How did he explain the Land Rover?"

"Rose told them that we're a special unit in search of British secret agents, the ones behind the uprising. General Serov has ordered us to Gyor. The Land Rover and Union Jack are tricks to help us flush out the imperialist spies."

"A bit far-fetched?"

"That's why it should work. Russians love conspiracies. It's such an outlandish story that it would have to be true."

Morris returned and opened the back passenger door. He rummaged through his luggage and produced a bottle. "Captain

Krupin will appreciate the gift," he said. "I'll have the first vodka with him, and then we'll get the hell out of here."

* * *

Once the Russian checkpoint was ten minutes behind them, Hawes briefly consulted the map by flashlight. He turned the Land Rover onto a dirt road and drove for five minutes before pulling over by the side of the road into a small clearing.

"We'll stay the night here," he said. "I don't want to chance any more driving in the dark." Hawes turned to Morris. "Get rid of the uniform. From here on, you're an American journalist. Once we're back on the road, we can't risk running into some rebels with you in that outfit."

Collins waited for Morris outside the Land Rover. He offered Morris a cigarette when he returned, once again dressed in civilian clothes.

"I can tell you what happened to Yatov," Collins said quietly. "Why and how he disappeared."

"How would you know that?"

"Because I helped Matthew Steele find Yatov in the spring of 1951. Steele had figured out that he was Kim Philby's controller."

Morris exhaled. "He was. Yatov ran the most important cells in Washington."

"Steele convinced Philby that we were about to expose him as a Soviet agent. This was in May. Philby panicked and we followed him to his rendezvous with Yatov at the Great Potomac Falls. There was a brief confrontation. Yatov tried to shoot his way out and was killed."

"You witnessed this?"

"It was my shot that killed him," Collins said. "Yatov made a run for it. I was blocking the way and we exchanged fire. I acted in self-

defense. I can't say I rest easy about it. To kill another human being."
He paused. "It's one thing to see men die, like I did in the Pacific and
in Korea. It's another thing when you're the one pulling the trigger,
and the person dies right there in front of you."

"And Philby?"

"Steele let him go, convinced that we had enough evidence for
the British to prosecute him and put him in prison. Later, Steele
convinced the head of the CIA at the time, General Smith, to demand
that the British remove Philby from his role as liaison to American
intelligence in Washington. They did."

"The authorities didn't become involved in the Yatov shooting?
No police reports?"

"No. His body went into the Potomac. Steele kept the episode
out of the Agency's files in order to protect me. Philby has kept silent
for his own reasons, I imagine. It's been more than five years, now."

Morris gave him a weary smile. "You did me a good turn. Yatov
never cared for me. I feared that they might recall him to Moscow
and that he might blame any failures in the States on me. I certainly
won't shed any tears for him."

* * *

They had an uncomfortable night. As the temperature started to
drop, Hawes started up the Land Rover's engine and turned on the
heater, running the engine for fifteen minutes until the inside of
the vehicle was warm. He was to repeat that process throughout the
night.

They raided their luggage and put on several layers of clothes,
hoping to stay warm. Collins took the front passenger seat, dozing in
stretches, while Morris and Eva huddled in the back seat.

Collins was jolted out of a light sleep when he heard what at
first he thought was the sound of thunder. Then he realized that it

was artillery firing. His watch read four o'clock. He cursed softly and turned to Hawes, who had also been stirred awake.

"Feliks? Did you hear that?"

"I did. It sounds like heavy artillery, M-46s, and perhaps some Katusha rockets. The Red Army must be hitting Budapest. They want to soften up any resistance before they go in."

"Do you think that they have specific targets or is it just indiscriminate shelling?"

"A bit of both. They have the coordinates of the Kilian Barracks and Szena Square and Csepel and some other strongholds, but they're also going to lob in some random shells. It serves to terrorize the population."

"It's very Russian," Morris said quietly from the back seat. "The casual brutality. The indifference to suffering. Afterward, they'll drink themselves senseless with vodka and some of them will weep about what they've done. They're sentimental that way."

"You'd be the expert on that," Hawes said.

"I would, I imagine. I won't apologize for believing that the Russians were building a better world, a more just world. I won't apologize for attempting to help them. It just turned out that I was wrong."

Nineteen

Hawes put them back on the highway at first light. They made fairly good time for the next thirty minutes. Collins occupied the time watching for roadblocks ahead. He certainly wasn't going to be distracted by the unchanging scenery—mile after mile of treeless fields, dusted lightly with snow, on either side of the highway.

Collins turned on the radio and located Radio Budapest on the dial. There was a burst of Hungarian and Eva responded immediately to what she was hearing.

"Pull over," she said.

Hawes steered the Land Rover to the side of the highway. He pulled up under a copse of trees and switched off the headlamps.

"It's Radio Budapest," Eva said. "It's about the Russians." They listened for a few minutes and then an announcer spoke in English, explaining that he was reading Prime Minister Nagy's message to the people: "Today at daybreak Soviet troops attacked our capital with the obvious intent of overthrowing the legal democratic Hungarian government. Our troops are in combat. The government is at its post. I notify the people of our country and the entire world of this fact."

It was silent inside the Land Rover. Finally Eva spoke. "The bastards were lying when they said they would negotiate the exit of the Red Army from the country. They never intended to leave."

"I'm sorry that it's come to this," Collins said.

"They have a very primitive view of the world," Morris said. "They don't hesitate to use massive force, when they feel threatened.

They learned that from fighting their civil war and from beating back Hitler from the gates of Moscow."

Hawes didn't say anything, but he pulled back onto the highway and gunned the Land Rover's engine. When Collins looked over at the speedometer he saw that they were moving at 50 miles per hour.

★ ★ ★

Ten miles further west on the highway, Collins spotted a makeshift barricade in the distance. He checked the map—they were between Komarom and Gyor from what he could tell. Hawes slowed the vehicle and when they got closer they could see that the road was blocked by a long piece of wood suspended over two steel cans sitting on either side of the road. A small group of men in overcoats stood next to the road and Collins could see that they were all armed. Hawes brought the Land Rover to a complete halt.

"Why don't you and I reconnoiter?" Hawes asked Collins.

"Sure. I'd like to stretch my legs anyway."

"No sudden moves on our part," Hawes said. "Keep your hand near your revolver, though."

Collins nodded—he reached into his right coat pocket and felt the butt of the Enfield.

A stocky man emerged from behind the barricade and strutted up the road toward them. He wore a long overcoat, a wool scarf, and a visored officer's hat that was missing its red star badge.

"I am Colonel Bela," he said in heavily accented English. "Freedom fighters. *Ruszkik haza.*" He took in the Union Jack on the hood of the Land Rover. "English?"

"Quite right," Hawes said. "English and American. Journalists. Here to tell the story of the revolution to the world."

Colonel Bela looked over Hawes's shoulder, eyeing Morris and Eva. He turned away and signaled the men at the barricade with a quick wave. Collins wasn't sure how to interpret the signal, but he slowly moved his hand into his coat pocket and gripped the Enfield.

Hawes stepped closer, trying to establish a bond with the man. "Can we interview you, then, Colonel? Chance to tell your story to the world. Encourage our governments to send arms and ammunition. Support the revolution."

"We kill all AVO," the man said. "The Russian colonel I kill." He touched the officer's cap and grinned at them.

"Has a workers' council been formed?" Hawes asked.

"No council. Fighters, not politicians." Now the smile had turned sly. "We make our own law."

Two of the men at the barricade had moved closer to them. Colonel Bela glanced at Eva and said something in Hungarian to the man nearest to him and they both laughed. Collins didn't like the predatory way the men looked at Eva, and he could tell from Hawes' stiffened shoulders that he didn't like it either.

"Where you drive?" Colonel Bela asked. "Very dangerous to drive."

"We're headed to Vienna," Hawes said. "The Russians are moving on Budapest in force, and we decided to get out. We'll file our stories from Vienna."

"Russians come back?" The man spit on the ground. He looked over at his two compatriots. "Russian tanks bad." He grimaced. "We need money. Buy more guns."

"We don't have much money," Hawes said quickly, "but we'd be glad to help out. Your bravery deserves it." He reached into his pockets with both hands, and produced a wad of bills in his left hand, but at the same time he also pulled out his Enfield.

Collins didn't hesitate—he trained his own revolver on the man next to Colonel Bela. Out of the corner of his eye, he could see that Morris had left the Land Rover and had his Makarov drawn, pointing toward the insurgents.

Hawes slowly offered the cash to the man, without lowering his revolver or taking his eyes off him. Colonel Bela took the bills and stuffed them into the outside of his overcoat.

"Thank you," he said.

"You're welcome," Hawes said. "We'll be on our way now." He kept his attention focused on the Hungarian. "Rose, if you could join us," he said loudly enough that Morris could hear him. When Morris reached them, Hawes spoke rapidly. He wanted Collins to get Eva in the Land Rover and drive up the road a few hundred yards once the barrier had been removed. He and Morris would disarm Colonel Bela and his men and then join them further up the road. Hawes handed the car keys to Collins, who slowly retreated to the Land Rover.

Hawes turned to Colonel Bela and addressed him in a matter-of-fact way. "We'll need to have the barrier lifted." He stepped next to Bela and placed the muzzle of the Enfield so it was no more than an inch away from the man's chest. "Tell your men to place their rifles and weapons on the ground."

Collins got into the driver's seat of the Land Rover and Eva took the front passenger seat. The engine started immediately when Collins turned the key in the ignition and he put the vehicle in gear. Two of the insurgents moved the wood plank away, and Collins slowly drove the vehicle past the steel barrels. Eva kept watch out the back window.

"Maxim has collected some of the guns," she reported. "Hawes has his gun in the leader's back and they're coming our way."

Collins braked and stopped the vehicle. In the rear-view mirror, he saw Hawes, Morris, and Colonel Bela moving toward them. Morris carried several rifles under his left arm.

When they reached the Land Rover, Morris threw the rifles into an irrigation ditch by the side of the road. He got into the back seat of the vehicle behind Eva.

Hawes opened the back door on the other side. He said something to Colonel Bela and then, without warning, hit him hard in the side of the face with his revolver. The man clutched his face, staggered away, and fell onto the road.

Hawes entered the Land Rover. "Drive," he said to Collins. "Be quick about it."

Collins responded by hitting the gas pedal and soon the vehicle was back up to 50 miles per hour.

"I know they were talking about Eva," Morris said to Hawes. He was upset. "I didn't hear all of what they were saying, but I didn't like the drift of it."

"You were right not to like it," Hawes said.

"What did they say?" Eva asked from the front seat.

Hawes hesitated. It was clear he didn't want to answer her.

"Tell me," Eva said.

"They were considering shooting us, and then taking turns with you," Hawes said. "Sorry. Quite ugly, I'm afraid."

"I'm glad that you hit the man," she said. "You could have shot him dead for all I care. They never would have had me. I would have died first. I would have grabbed Maxim's gun and made sure some of the bastards went with me."

"At least you gave Colonel Bela something to think about," Collins said to Hawes. "Perhaps he'll see the error of his ways."

"He's no more a colonel than I'm the Archbishop of Canterbury," Hawes said. "He's a cutthroat, a common thief. Lenin once said that revolutions attract the best and the worst."

"Lenin said that?" Collins asked.

"That he did."

"Lenin was right," Eva said. "Not about much else, but he was right about that."

* * *

Five miles down the highway, Collins noticed that the gas gauge was indicating that only a quarter of a tank remained. He asked Hawes whether they should stop and refuel.

"Stop," Hawes said. "And I'll take over as driver."

Collins waited until he found a relatively flat spot by the side of the road, and pulled off and parked. Hawes went to the back of the Land Rover and moved the luggage around until he exposed the jerricans of fuel. He took one of the cans and, using a funnel, began refilling the gas tank.

"While he's refueling, I'd like a word with you," Eva said to Morris. "In private."

Morris shrugged. "Sure."

He followed Eva as she moved away from the vehicle, out of earshot. They stood facing each other and Eva began talking. Although Collins couldn't make out the words, it was clear that they were having some sort of dispute.

Hawes had finished filling the tank by the time Eva and Morris returned. Eva spoke first. "Maxim must tell you both about Durov. You need to know about him."

"Durov?" Collins asked. "I thought he wasn't a concern."

"I was mistaken," Morris said defensively. "Eva has persuaded me that I'm not being realistic. He does represent a danger. Durov was my mentor, my protector, at Moscow Center. He's been with the secret police since the 1920s. I believe he was sent to Budapest to find me."

Hawes frowned. "So he was working with Osin?"

"It would seem so. Durov may be at the border, now, waiting to intercept us."

"Why weren't you concerned earlier?" Collins asked.

"When Osin said that he was going to take us to Durov, I assumed that meant Durov was in Budapest. I thought Durov would wait until the Red Army controlled the city before searching for me. Eva has convinced me that's wishful thinking. Durov knows me, knows how I think. If Durov learned about Eva's travel documents, he would not wait around in Budapest."

"We must assume that someone at the American legation has told the Russians everything," Eva said. "We have to assume the worst."

"Durov won't waste time trying to locate us in Budapest," Morris said. "He knows that if I'm defecting there are only a few places where I'm likely to try to cross the border."

"So you think he may already be at the border?" Hawes asked.

"Circulating my photo. And Eva's." Morris' features softened. "Durov knows that I wouldn't leave her behind."

Hawes arched his eyebrows. "I see. Then we can't use our press credentials or passports."

Morris had a grim look on his face. "Durov will have them stop all foreigners arriving at the border. Anyone who matches my or Eva's description will be held for questioning, and Durov will handle the interrogation personally. They will hold him accountable if I defect, so he won't leave anything to chance."

"All this certainly clarifies matters," Hawes said. "We have the Land Rover. It can handle bad roads and a meadow or two. We'll need to find a place where we can cross without bothering with credentials."

Collins interrupted. "Aren't there border patrols? Barbed wire, minefields?"

"There are," Hawes said. "But they removed some of the mines and fences in the months after Khrushchev's speech. My colleagues in Vienna have been looking for soft spots ever since. We've identified a few. With enough forints or pounds sterling we should be able to scare up a local to guide us to a gap."

"Where would this be?" It was Eva, not hiding her skepticism.

Hawes produced a compass and placed their road map on the hood of the Land Rover. He checked the compass and then studied the map.

"Near Sopron," he said. "That's the spot for us. There's open farmland at the border. We'll have to find a back road and hope there are gaps in the barbed wire. There are a number of Austrian villages on the other side."

"What other options do we have?" Collins asked. "Could we drive further south? Cross in a place that's not as close to Vienna?"

"We could try Szombathley," Hawes said. "The roads there won't be the best."

"The further we drive, the more checkpoints we'll run into," Eva said. "Or criminals like Colonel Bela. We should try Sopron."

"I agree," Morris said. "Sopron's our best bet."

"We'll need a guide, won't we?" Collins asked. "Where are we going to find a one? I don't imagine they advertise in the local newspaper."

"We'll need to find a priest," Hawes said. "It's less likely that he'd betray us to the Reds, and he'll know who can help us get across. There's always a local lad who earns his keep by smuggling. No border is ever completely secure and this one is no exception."

Twenty

After they had passed through the small village of Kophaza and were nearing Sopron, Eva suggested that they delay their entrance into the city.

"If we approach a priest it should be later in the morning," she said. "It's Sunday, so they'll be saying mass. We want to call as little attention to ourselves as possible."

"That's true," Hawes said. "And I could use some sleep."

Hawes turned off on a rutted dirt road and—fields on either side of them—drove until they were out of sight of the main road. Collins and Morris stood watch as Hawes napped in the driver's seat and Eva stretched across the back seat and slept.

They had parked near a vineyard bordered by thick, silent woods. Morris motioned for Collins to move away from the Land Rover so they could talk without disturbing Hawes or Eva.

"I have another favor to ask," Morris said. "There's no way I can ever thank you enough for what you've done already, and I understand why you might not want to help on this."

"What's the favor?"

"I'd like you to hold the material from Eva's uncle for me. What I brought from the Hill of Three Borders. Not now, though. Not until we're on the other side of the border. If you take it now, and we're caught, it would incriminate you beyond the shadow of a doubt." He shook his head. "You'd be charged with espionage anyway, but I should take responsibility for Nemeth's material if something goes wrong."

"What's the point of my holding the notes for you *after* we're out of Hungary? I don't understand."

"Once we're in Austria I'll come under the control of whoever from the CIA is waiting there for us. I assume you know who that is."

"I do. A man named Cliff Wittingham. Dulles sent him from Washington. He's been our contact in Vienna."

"Once Eva and I are under his protection, Wittingham's unlikely to respect my privacy, although he'll be very polite about it. He'll want to look over any papers I have. That's a problem. There's no way for me to know if any of my initial interrogators are working for the Russians. I know I sound like a broken record, but I want this material to be seen by Dulles, and Dulles only."

"And if I'm holding it, the idea is that it's out of their reach?"

"Exactly. You keep it until I'm sure of the situation. I'll ask you to return it when I know I can give it directly to Dulles."

"You do remember the last time you asked me to hold something for you?"

"Of course I do. This is different. You know everything this time. You can say 'no' and I'll understand, but I think it's important that the top people in Washington get this information, Denny. Lukas Nemeth was willing to risk his life to get it to the West."

Collins understood why Morris wanted him to hold the papers, and as long as he didn't take possession until they were in Austria he was willing to help out. "All right," he said. "I'll do it. Maybe the second time is the charm, and holding this won't prove to be a mistake."

"It won't be a mistake. You'll help me make up for some of the wrong that I've done."

* * *

They let Hawes and Eva sleep for two hours. In that time, Collins spotted only one ancient truck on the main road, and there was no traffic on the dirt road.

Eva had been in Sopron once for a wedding, and she directed Hawes to drive to the center of the city. It was an attractive place—Baroque, Renaissance, and more recent buildings filled the general vicinity. The Firewatch Tower, built in the thirteenth century, stood guard over the oldest section of the city.

They parked near the Church of St. Michael, an impressive neo-Gothic structure. Eva and Hawes left Collins and Morris in the vehicle while they went to make inquiries at a nearby coffeehouse.

Collins and Morris waited an anxious thirty minutes for their return, keeping an eye out for the police or for Russian soldiers. Collins was relieved to finally see Hawes striding up the street toward them, Eva a half-step behind.

"We'll wait here," Hawes told them when he reached the Land Rover. "We've discovered an ally, the manager of the coffeehouse. As a young man, before the war he lived in Liverpool and liked the English. He knows we're looking to cross the border."

"What reason did you give him?" Collins asked.

"We told him we have photographs of the fighting in Budapest that we thought the border police would confiscate. We want the world to see them. We also told him that we'd trust any guide vouched for by one of the local priests."

"He was sympathetic," Eva said. "A patriot. He will help us."

They had purchased bread, cheese, and some cheap wine and the four of them had a makeshift late breakfast. They had just finished eating when two men and a priest in a black cassock came up the street. Hawes left the Land Rover to greet them. Collins watched as they conferred for a few minutes, and then Hawes shook hands with one of the men and the priest. He turned and signaled to them with a thumbs-up sign.

Hawes and the shorter of the two men walked back toward to the Land Rover. The priest and the other man set off in the other direction. Collins, Eva, and Morris got out of the vehicle and waited for Hawes.

"Our guide," Hawes said when he reached them. "His name is Tibor."

Tibor, a middle-aged man with a weather-beaten face and thinning gray hair, tugged at his chin nervously. He spoke to Hawes in rapid Hungarian, waving his arms vigorously. Eva interrupted him and responded sharply and the man shook his head.

She turned to Collins to explain. "Tibor says we should drive close to the border, but then he thinks we should go on foot. He's worried that the Land Rover's engine is too loud. He's also not sure it can make it through the fields where we'll cross into Austria. The ground is very rough."

"I'm not concerned about that," Hawes said. "The vehicle was built to go off road. It's land mines we need to worry about." He said something quickly to the guide.

Tibor pointed to the west and launched into a long speech.

"He says some Russians showed up yesterday in an armored car, but they didn't stay," Eva said. "He worries that they'll be back. The Hungarian border guards are waiting to see what happens. They haven't been patrolling as actively, so parts of the border should be relatively open."

"And he can show us the way?" Collins asked.

"For what we've agreed to pay him, I should hope so."

★ ★ ★

Tibor sat in the passenger seat and directed Hawes while Eva squeezed in between Morris and Collins in the back seat. They drove along one-lane roads for twenty minutes before Tibor told Hawes to pull over.

"He says Austria is on the other side of this field," Hawes said. Tibor pointed wordlessly to the northwest.

"What about land mines?" Morris asked.

"He says this field has never been mined. There was a barbed wire fence, but they removed it in the spring."

"If that's the case, he can join us for the ride," Morris said. "We'll quickly learn how confident he is about the land mines. After we're in Austria, we'll pay him and he can walk back."

There was a sharp argument, conducted in Hungarian, between Hawes and the guide, with Eva adding a few comments.

"In for a penny, in for a pound," Hawes said. "He comes along or he doesn't get paid. If we do hit a mine, Tibor can guide us to Kingdom Come."

Collins tried not to think about the damage a land mine could do to the Land Rover. In Korea, he had seen a Marine two-and-half-ton truck destroyed when its driver veered off the road into a mine field and triggered an explosion. Everyone aboard had been killed.

Tibor said something to Hawes and the Englishman turned to Collins. "He's agreed," Hawes said. "I had to offer him a tad more. Not too jolly about it, but he's along for the ride."

Hawes turned off the road onto the field and began driving in the direction of the border. Collins found that he was clenching his fists. He looked over and saw that Eva had closed her eyes. Morris was gazing out the window. In the front, Tibor was muttering something under his breath.

They were jolted when, for a moment, the vehicle dipped into a depression in the hard ground underneath. Hawes gunned the engine and the tires spun and slipped and finally they lurched forward.

Then, more quickly than Collins could have ever imagined, they were across the field. Hawes drove out of the field onto a dirt road and brought the vehicle to a stop. "Which way?" he asked over his shoulder.

Morris studied their map. "It appears that we're near a small village, Klingenbach, and if we head to the right, we'll run into the road to Siegendorf," he said. "If I'm reading the map correctly, we're definitely in Austria."

"Are you sure?" Eva asked.

"Winters' compass says we're heading northwest, and Siegendorf looks like the closest town."

"I think we can bid farewell to our friend from Sopron," Hawes said. "Eva, why don't you pay him?"

Eva counted out the bills silently and handed them to Tibor, who glared at her in response. He exited the Land Rover quickly and they could hear him cursing in Hungarian as he stalked back toward the field.

"He'll cheer up," Hawes said. "He has proof positive that there's a safe escape route. In the next few days he should have plenty of customers looking to get out."

Collins moved to the front passenger seat and Hawes put the vehicle in gear and drove northwest. In five minutes they came to a crossroads where there was a road sign for Siegendorf. "We're in Austria," Collins said, exhaling in relief. "No question of that."

"Thank God," Eva said and laughed. "After all that worry about the border guards, we never saw even one of them. Nor the Russians."

"That's how it is, sometimes," Hawes said. "An operation goes so smoothly at the crucial moment that you wonder why you worried. Other times it's the exact opposite. What should be easy gets all bollixed up. We were lucky today."

"I'll drink to that," Morris said. "Lady Luck took her sweet time in showing up. She's a bit fickle."

"We should be sitting in the bar of the Hotel Bristol within an hour or so," Hawes said. "Since Dennis is the one with the healthy expense account, perhaps he can stand us to the first round."

"Count on it," Collins said. "Courtesy of the North American Newspaper Alliance."

Part Four

He didn't truly accept that they were in Austria, that they were free, until he saw the first road sign in German. Then he felt an overwhelming sense of relief, a feeling of lightness and of release. They had escaped.

The sunlight seemed stronger, the autumn colors more vivid, and the countryside more inviting—irrational, he knew, because there was very little difference between the scenery on the Austrian side of the border and that found in Hungary.

He squeezed Eva's hand and when he turned to look at her in the seat next to him, he saw that tears were streaming down her face. She made no attempt to wipe them away. He found a clean handkerchief in his coat pocket and gave it to her.

"No need to cry," he whispered to her. "We're safe, now."

She dabbed at her cheeks with the handkerchief and he held her hand tightly, wanting through his touch to communicate to her the depth of his feeling.

He leaned forward to address the occupants of the front seat of the Land Rover.

"Thank you, Denny," he said. "And you as well, Mr. Winters."

"Glad to help out," the Englishman said. "Trust me. I'm happy to be miles from the nearest Russian. You'll never find a Pole who's comfortable when he's surrounded by Russians."

"Or a Hungarian," Eva said.

"There's something we can agree on," he said. "We can drink to that thought in Vienna."

"It's been ten years," Eva said. "Ten years since I was last in Vienna. We must stop by the Hotel Sacher for coffee and sachertorte, Maxim. It must be the best chocolate cake in the world."

He smiled at her. "Why not? And when we visit Brooklyn you'll have to try an egg cream."

"Which has neither eggs or cream," Collins said. "But in Brooklyn, they claim it's the best chocolate drink in the world."

* * *

He knew that there were still dangers ahead. He remembered his final conversation with Durov before his friend flew back to Moscow. They had sat in Morris' Skoda in the parking lot outside the Ferihegy Airport terminal and talked quietly while waiting for Durov's flight.

Durov was in a reflective mood. "They're concerned at the Center about our agents in the West. After Comrade Khrushchev's speech, it was decided that there would be much greater vigilance at our embassies."

"Concerned about their loyalty? About defections?"

Durov nodded solemnly. "The temptations can be considerable. As you know, you can live well in New York or London if you are part of the ruling class. Moscow wants to be sure that the consequences of deviation, of treachery, are fully understood." He glanced out the windshield at an Aeroflot Ilyushin aircraft taxiing for takeoff. "Beria and Abakumov are dead and gone, but General Serov has long teeth and Department Thirteen will hunt down any traitors. There will be no safe havens."

"And I would imagine that our adversaries will seek to take advantage of the situation."

"They will, of course, probe for any weaknesses. Not only our men, but diplomats. Anyone traveling in the West." Durov sighed. "The CIA has a program called Redcap that seeks to recruit our diplomats. There have been several defections already. Vladimir Petrov from our embassy in Australia, Peter Derabian in Vienna, Nikolai Khokhlov in Frankfort. Do you know the story of Khokhlov?"

Maxim shook his head.

"A brave man. A hero of the Great Patriotic War. Two years ago Moscow Center ordered him and a mobile group to Frankfurt to eliminate a counterrevolutionary emigre, Georgiy Okolovich. Khokhlov told his wife about the assignment before he left Moscow. She was religious, and she convinced him that to kill Okolovich would be a great evil. She dissuaded him from his duty and when Khokhlov reached Frankfurt, he alerted Okolovich and then defected. At first, the Americans did not believe his story, but the other two men in the mobile group corroborated it."

"And his wife?"

"Sent to the camps." Durov rubbed his eyes and Maxim noticed how old and tired he looked. "Sometimes I think that it would have been better if Comrade Khrushchev had kept his mouth shut," he said. "It has caused many problems. I always thought that Khrushchev was a Menshevik at heart."

"You will let me know about developments in Moscow, Mikhail?" Maxim had asked, aware that his question betrayed a certain level of anxiety on his part.

"I will," Durov said. "And you must not worry too much, Maxim. You know what we say: 'He who is afraid of bad luck will never know good.' Look at me, still in harness after all these years, outliving more bastards than I care to admit. I've had good luck, that's all."

★ ★ ★

He could not expect mercy from Durov. By defecting, Colonel Maxim Rusakov became an outcast, a traitor, a deserter. Durov would not rest until he had seen justice rendered—which in this case would mean administering a sentence of death.

As a couple, they would be easier to find. They became vulnerable when they settled down, established roots, had children. *So when did Mr. and Mrs. White first arrive in town? Does she have an accent? Does he ever talk about having lived back East? New York?*

Brooklyn? He knew they would be thorough and patient, waiting for them to make a mistake.

That's why he had to prove his value to Dulles. They would need money—lots of it—if they wanted to stay hidden. Money so that they didn't need to expose themselves by working in any job with public contact. Money for a house in a neighborhood where private guards were common and strangers stood out. Money to buy them protection.

He had resolved that he would give Dulles everything, every scrap of information, every detail he could dredge up from his memory of past Moscow Center operations.

He had two assets of great value: Laszlo Nemeth's notes and what he knew about Envoy. They could tip the balance in his favor. He would not hesitate to bargain with Dulles, to offer the notes in exchange for enough money to give them a fighting chance against Department Thirteen.

Dulles was a man of the world. He would understand that Morris arrived with mixed motives—that he wanted to help the Agency against Moscow Center, but that he also had personal needs that had to be met. Morris had been on the other side of the table, negotiating the terms of betrayal, weighing the value of proffered information, and he knew Dulles would not look down on him as a mercenary when he asked for the funds.

In a few days he would shed the persona of Colonel Maxim Rusakov and again, for a time, become Morris Rose, American, graduate of Columbia College and Columbia Law School, Dodgers fan, the prodigal son returned. He knew that there would be another identity he would soon assume, one the CIA would fashion.

A new name meant starting over, it meant he could leave behind Morris Rose and Maxim Rusakov and their mistakes. He had always envied his Catholic friends who could turn to confession and penance and the promise of a clean slate. He could have something like that now, a chance to begin again with Eva, and he would do whatever he needed to keep it.

Twenty-one

On the drive from Siegendorf to Vienna, Hawes kept the Land Rover at a constant 60 miles per hour. Collins fully relaxed for the first time in days as they sped through the peaceful Austrian countryside.

Morris produced a bottle of palinka from his bag and tapped Collins on his shoulder. "I was saving this for our border crossing," he said. "I hoped I wouldn't have to give it away at a checkpoint."

They passed it around, each taking a sip or two of the apricot-flavored brandy. "They say that in small amounts palinka's a medicine, in large amounts it's a remedy," Eva said.

"It's going to put me to sleep," Collins said, suddenly aware of how tired he was. He wondered if Hawes was feeling the same and needed to pull over and rest. When he asked him, the Englishman smiled in response.

"Anna's waiting for me in Vienna," he said. "I'm eager to get there. Ulysses and Penelope, you know."

"But no group of suitors to outwit."

"You're right. It's just been a bunch of nasty KGB chaps."

The drive took only an hour, and they reached the First District of Vienna in the early afternoon. Collins found the city as he left it—fashionable women in elegant clothing strolling down the street, Viennese families enjoying Sunday dinner after church, cafes filled with young people—and the contrast with Budapest was stark.

Hawes maneuvered expertly through the traffic brought them to the front entrance to the Hotel Bristol. He jumped out of the vehicle and patted the hood. "A damn fine machine," he said.

Morris tapped Collins on the shoulder and silently handed him an envelope—the notes from Lukas Nemeth. Collins placed them in his inside pocket of his overcoat. It was remarkable, he thought, how many sensitive documents he had kept in his coat over the past week. He was fortunate that he had never been stopped and searched.

Hawes volunteered to call Wittingham and suggested Collins take Morris and Eva to the dining room and wait there.

"I'll arrange for a room for them," he said. "And I'll let Anna know we're here." He paused. "And Wittingham, too."

* * *

It took Cliff Wittingham twenty minutes to join them in the Hotel Bristol's dining room. Collins made the introductions and Wittingham shook Morris' hand and nodded to Eva.

"We're back where we started," Collins said. "It just took us a little longer than we'd planned."

"We had our people waiting across the border from Hegyeshalom," Wittingham said. He wore a new tweed jacket, a freshly-starched buttoned-down shirt, and a club tie. "Why didn't you cross there?"

"We had to improvise," Collins said. "Didn't want to have to show any papers. Moscow Center had sent a man named Durov to hunt down Morris, and we figured he would have alerted the border guards at Hegyeshalom and the other official crossing."

Hawes took a sip of the tea he had ordered. "We found a local guide in Sopron who knew where the soft spots in security. A smuggler, no doubt."

"Clever," Wittingham said. "Quite clever."

"Do you know whether the convoy from our legation made it through?" Collins asked.

Wittingham shook his head. "They didn't. Stopped 200 yards from the border at Hegyeshalom by the Russians."

Collins was surprised. "They had a safe conduct pass from the Soviet ambassador in Budapest, Andropov. It wasn't honored at the border?"

"Apparently not. The Swiss Red Cross has told us that the Russians took their passports and detained them in a school building in Magyarovar. The State Department is raising holy hell."

Collins turned to Morris. "Do you think Durov ordered this?"

"Undoubtedly. He wouldn't take any chances. Stop the convoy and question all of the passengers to make sure that we couldn't sneak out hidden in a group of Americans."

"We were lucky, then, that the convoy left on Saturday morning before we did," Collins said. "We might have joined it if the timing were better. That would have been a less than happy ending."

"What can you tell us about the situation in Budapest?" Eva asked Wittingham.

He explained that information about the Russian assault was limited, and what he knew came from radio reports that had been monitored at the embassy and one telex from the legation. "It's been rough. The Soviets are responding to any resistance by blasting away. The insurgents are holding out at the Kilian Barracks from what we can gather. There are reports that the workers on Csepel Island are dug in and are prepared to fight for as long as they can."

"What about Imre Nagy?" Eva asked.

"He's taken refuge in the Yugoslav embassy, along with a number of his cabinet members. We're hosting Cardinal Mindszenty in the legation. There's a puppet government led by Kadar and Munnich that's been recognized by the Soviets."

"So Kadar betrayed Nagy." It was Morris. "Strange. I never thought that Kadar would support the hardliners. Under Rakosi, he was imprisoned and tortured. Kadar was only recently rehabilitated. I wonder what pressure the Russians brought to bear on him."

"Or maybe they didn't need to pressure him very much," Collins said. "Maybe he's ambitious and wanted to be the top dog and he saw his chance and took it."

"This new government of Kadar's will never be seen as legitimate," Eva said. "The Russians will need to keep their tanks and their troops in place. They'll have to occupy the country."

"What of General Maleter?" Hawes asked.

Wittingham frowned. "The reports are sketchy. We believe the Russians invited him to their base at Tokol for negotiations, and then arrested him just before they moved against the city."

"No action by the United Nations?" Collins asked. "Hasn't there been an uproar over what the Soviets are doing?"

"Suez is the preoccupation at the moment," Wittingham said. He glanced over at Hawes. "Washington is peeved over what the British and French have done. They say Ike is quite upset. The election's in two days, and the timing couldn't have been worse. It's stirred up Labor in Britain. There was a massive rally in Trafalgar Square yesterday. Bevan spoke and said the government had besmirched the name of Britain, offended against every principle of decency, and it was time to get out."

Hawes shrugged. "You won't find me defending Suez. A sorry idea from the start."

"They're going to be very happy in Washington when I report that you've made it out safely," Wittingham said. "All of you."

"How soon can you arrange a flight to the States?" Morris asked. "How soon can I meet with Allen Dulles?"

"We'll uphold our end of the bargain," Wittingham said. "You'll see Mr. Dulles. We're planning to fly you back in a day or so. I'm trying to arrange a military flight out of Tulln."

"I'd like Denny to accompany us," Morris said.

"That's up to Dennis," Wittingham said. "We asked him to help you get out and he's done that. He's held up his side of the bargain."

"Denny? How about it?" Morris asked.

Collins hesitated. He didn't want to fly to Washington and delay his return to New York. He wanted to get home to Maria and the boys. Yet, there was something about seeing the mission to its conclusion—to make sure that Morris and Eva reached the U.S. safely.

"We would appreciate it," Eva said.

"Fair enough," Collins said. "I have a few things I'd like to say to Mr. Dulles myself."

"So now what?" Morris asked Wittingham.

"We have a safe house in Rudolfsplatz, close to the river, where you can stay the night. You'll be safe there. We want you to stay there, out of sight, until your flight."

"Moscow Center has agents in Vienna," Morris said. "By now, Durov will have realized that I made it to the West. He won't give up, and they'll be looking for me."

"If they are, they won't find you. In a few days, you'll be on a flight to London and then on to the States. Even if they've been alerted to look for you, it will take the KGB some time to sort things out."

"I'd rather remain here, in the hotel," Morris said. "I have reason to believe that they know where all of your safe houses are located."

"There's no way to control access to the Bristol," Wittingham said. He tapped his class ring on the table impatiently. "It's risky to leave you in such a vulnerable spot."

"The Russians won't be looking for me here," Morris said. "We'll stay in our room. Our only exposure will be from the time we leave the hotel until we reach the airport."

"We could put someone in the lobby," Wittingham said.

Morris gave him a skeptical look. "If they recognize your men, they'll conclude that something's up. I'd rather that you keep your distance."

"I'm armed," Hawes said. "I've had a room arranged for Morris and Eva on the fourth floor—the same floor where Collins and I have rooms. We can keep an eye on them."

It was clear from the grim set of his mouth that Wittingham didn't like the idea, but he reluctantly agreed. "You win," he said to Morris. "Just please stay in your room. No wandering around Vienna tonight where someone might recognize you."

"Don't worry," Morris said. "All we want to do is sleep."

Wittingham rose to his feet. "I'll start in on the arrangements for the trip," he said. "Call the embassy if I'm needed."

They watched him leave the dining room. Morris spoke first. "I can't say I care for him. Headquarters all the way."

"Someone has to push the paper," Hawes said. "I'm thankful it's not me."

"It doesn't matter," Collins said. "We'll all be done with him a day or so. I sincerely hope that he will never darken my doorstep again."

"Nor ours." It was Eva. "I don't like his eyes."

"Don't they say that the eyes are the window to the soul?" Hawes asked. "But Wittingham's a bureaucrat from Headquarters, and they aren't issued souls. Don't need them."

"As long as he gets us on a flight out, I won't worry about his soul," Morris said. "I'll happily leave that to others."

Twenty-two

Collins was pleased that their informal debriefing with Wittingham had been relatively quick. He hurried to the Bristol's front desk where the ornate wall clock showed that it was slightly after four o'clock—just after ten o'clock in the morning back in New York.

"We have held your room for you, Mr. Collins," the clerk at the front desk said. He was a thin, gray-haired man with a narrow nose and thin lips. "A Mr. Wittingham from the American embassy called and asked us to keep it reserved until you returned. I understand you've been in Budapest. A tragic situation. They say the Russians have returned, in force."

"They have," Collins said. "A shame."

"That it is."

"I have a favor to ask, *bitte.*" Collins reached into his canvas bag and found the envelope Morris had entrusted to him. "Could you place this in your safe?"

"Of course," the man said, taking the envelope from Collins. "And if there is anything else I can do, please don't hesitate to ask."

"Can I get an international line?" Collins asked. "I'd like to call the United States."

The man directed him to a nearby table with a phone. After the hotel switchboard operator had placed the call, Collins was pleased when Maria picked up on the third ring.

"I'm calling from Vienna," he told her. "We just arrived from Hungary, and I wanted you to know. In one piece and ready to come home."

"Thank God!"

"How are you? How are the boys?"

"We're fine."

"Sorry I missed Halloween."

"That doesn't matter," she said. "I've been so worried."

"All's well. I'm eager to get home."

"When will that be?"

"My return flight will be through Washington, and so I'm not sure about the connecting flight. I'll call or send a telegram as soon as I know. Most likely I'll be home by Wednesday."

"Was it as bad in Hungary as it looked on television?"

"I'm afraid so. We can talk about it once I'm back."

"I can't wait," she said. "I've missed you so."

"I love you, Maria. I'll tell you that face-to-face soon enough."

★ ★ ★

The five of them—Collins, Morris, Eva, Hawes and Anna—gathered in Hawes' suite for a celebratory dinner. They feasted on Tafelspitz—a tasty boiled beef dish with applesauce-horseradish sauce—and Wienerschnitzel along with Vienna rolls, pickled gherkins, a lettuce salad, and pan-fried potatoes. Collins and Hawes drank Ottakringer beer while the others drank a local wine. For dessert, there were sachertortes—Hawes had called the Hotel Sacher and persuaded them to send over several of their famous cakes by messenger—and coffee.

After they had finished their meal, Hawes opened the champagne and poured it into fluted glasses. Morris lifted his glass and proposed a toast.

"To freedom."

They touched glasses, and Collins saw Anna tearing up. Hawes had his arm around her shoulder, and he whispered something to her.

"I thought our dash across the border might be a bit of a suicide squeeze," Morris said.

"A what?" Eva was puzzled.

"It's from American baseball," Collins said. "It's when a runner starts to steal home as soon as the pitcher delivers a pitch. If the batter doesn't get a good bunt down, the runner's easily tagged out at the plate."

"I have no idea what you're talking about," Hawes said.

"Nor do I," Eva said.

"It's a high risk play," Collins said.

"Is baseball complicated?" Eva asked. "Morris keeps telling me I'm going to love it."

"You're a quick study," Morris said to her. "You'll be screaming that the ump is blind in no time."

"I can't believe we're here talking about baseball," Anna said. "Free to talk about it, or about anything we want to. I could not have imagined this a week ago."

"We were on the road near Sopron this morning, worrying about border police," Eva said. "I didn't imagine I would be in a Vienna hotel room sipping champagne hours later."

"Champagne is the favorite drink of class enemies," Anna said. "I've always liked the way it tickles your throat."

"Even English and American class enemies can't afford champagne very often," Hawes said. He smiled at Anna. "Collins asked me to order beer. He's no spendthrift."

"I've seen Denny order a Rheingold in the most exclusive nightclubs in New York," Morris said. "The Stork Club. El Morocco. Even when they've offered him a complimentary glass of champagne."

"I'd like to see the Stork Club," Eva said. She looked at Morris. "Can we?"

"We can, but Denny will need to put in a word with Sherm Billingsley, so we get a decent table."

"I haven't been to the Stork for a while," Collins said. "But I'll see what I can do."

"I'd like to see New York," Hawes said. "Haven't made it to the States, yet." He turned to Anna. "It's Paris first, and then London, but I'm due for a vacation. New York?"

Anna began to cry. "I'm sorry," she said. "It's all too much. I worry that it's a dream, and I'm going to wake up and find this has been an illusion."

Eva took her hand. "It's not a dream."

Morris struggled to his feet, unsteadily, and began speaking in Russian. Hawes, Anna, and Eva listened intently. Hawes nodded when Morris finished.

"I'm odd man out, since I don't speak any Russian," Collins said. "What were you saying, Morris?"

"It was the last two verses of a poem," Morris said. "Written by Boris Pasternak, a poem entitled 'Hamlet' that still may not be recited in public in Moscow. *I am alone; all round me drowns in falsehood/ Life is not a walk across a field.*" I promised someone that I would recite it when we reached freedom. And now I've kept my promise."

★ ★ ★

After dinner, Collins returned to the front desk of the hotel. He had composed a brief telegram that he wanted to send to Norris Jennings: IN VIENNA. FILE STORY TOMORROW. THEN BACK TO US. DC. He left the telegram with the concierge; he would write the story in the morning when he was rested and had a clear head.

When Collins stepped into the lift on his way back to his room, two men followed him into the cage. They looked Slavic—both had dark hair and brown eyes, and the shorter of the two bore an angry scar on his right cheek. Collins hit the button for the fourth floor and neither of the men moved toward the control panel. They let Collins leave the lift first.

Collins walked up the corridor toward his room. He heard the sound of someone knocking on a door, and then the voice of one of the men saying "*Etagendienst*" and then in English, "Room service."

Collins turned back, troubled, and watched as the door to Room 401 opened, and there was a brief exchange in German with the occupant of the room—who Collins couldn't see—with the shorter of the two. Collins heard the man apologizing and then the door to the room slammed shut.

The two men moved up the corridor to the next room, 402, and the larger man knocked on the door, this time without making any announcement, and again when the door opened there was a brief conversation. Collins was troubled by the scene. The men didn't seem to be hotel employees; they weren't dressed as waiters, and they had arrived empty-handed, without trays of food or bottles. They were only one room away from 405, where Morris and Eva were staying.

Collins turned the corner and walked past his own room, 408, and knocked on the door to 410, Hawes' suite, calling out the Englishman's first name. Hawes appeared at the door.

"There's something going on," Collins said. "Two men are working their way up the hallway, knocking on doors. They're looking for someone."

Hawes cursed and ducked back into the room. He appeared a moment later with the Enfield revolver in his hand.

Collins followed him around the corner and saw the men were at Morris' door. One of them was hunched over the lock, fiddling with it.

"What are you doing?" Hawes called out loudly, but as he did, the man working on the lock pushed the door open.

The other man, the shorter one, turned toward them and Collins saw that he had a revolver in his hand.

Hawes didn't hesitate. He raised the Enfield and squeezed off two shots. The man at the door recoiled as if he had been punched, and then collapsed to the floor. Hawes sprinted down the corridor, and Collins followed him.

Collins heard two quick gunshots and then a scream from inside the room. Hawes stepped over the man outside the door, and Collins did the same. Once inside, Collins saw the first man standing near the bed. The man spun around to confront Hawes and Collins caught a glimpse of Morris collapsed face up on the bed, blood on his shirt, and Eva next to him, shock on her face.

Without thinking Collins pushed past Hawes and lunged for the man, hoping to tackle him. There was a sudden deafening report, and Collins felt a hard blow strike him in the chest, spinning him back. A split second later he heard another loud report from behind him and the man clutched at his throat and then collapsed heavily to the floor.

Collins managed to stay on his feet. Eva was talking to Morris rapidly, softly, in Hungarian, and Collins could see that Morris wasn't responding, and he knew that it was a very bad sign.

"We need to get you to a doctor," Hawes said. "You've been hit."

"Not too bad," Collins said. His chest burned with a strange, sharp pain, and he started feeling dizzy. He tried to say more, but words didn't come.

"Are you sure?" Hawes asked.

Collins was about to respond, but his legs suddenly wouldn't support him. The last thing he remembered was the look of concern on Hawes' face, and then everything around him went completely dark.

Twenty-three

When Collins came to, the first thing he saw was sunlight across white sheets and he realized he was lying in bed. When, disoriented, he looked around and saw the walls were institutional gray he knew he wasn't in the Hotel Bristol.

He heard someone cough and turned his head to find that Feliks Hawes was occupying a chair at the edge of the bed. That movement cost Collins—he felt a sharp pain in his chest. The memory of the confrontation in Morris' hotel room came flooding back.

"How do you feel?" Hawes asked.

"Not very good," Collins said. His mouth was dry, and, under the tightly-wrapped bandages on his chest, the wound ached.

"You were hit once, just under the collarbone. They had to operate to extract the bullet. You're in the U.S. Army hospital on Peter Jordan Strasse, by the way. We brought you here last night, and it's Monday afternoon, the fifth." Hawes looked at his watch. "Two o'clock."

"Monday?"

"How much do you remember?"

"Enough. It's a bit fuzzy. Morris? Eva?"

"Eva is fine, but we were too late for Rose." He got up from the chair and walked over to the window and looked out, his face drawn and worn. "He shielded Eva with his body, and that saved her."

Collins tried to prop himself up with his right elbow and quickly became dizzy. He lay back.

"Easy does it," Hawes said. "The doctor said you should take it slow. It will be a few days before you're back to full strength."

"What the hell happened?"

"You were properly heroic. You beat me through the door and charged the man inside. That distracted him enough that he never got a chance to aim. In the confusion, I was able to catch him with a shot to the throat. He did hit you, however."

"Who were they?"

"The one in the corridor was a Pole, living in Vienna and working for the Russians. The man who winged you was a Russian. He had Austrian papers, but they were forged. The Pole had American dollars in his wallet, and we know that Moscow Center prefers to pay in dollars. I'm sure that they weren't Department Thirteen because it was a slapdash operation."

"If I were feeling better I'd fully appreciate the irony," Collins said. "The Russians pay their killers with greenbacks."

"They're quite practical," Hawes said. "It's rumored that they have a set of plates in the basement of the Kremlin where they print their own counterfeit dollars." He studied Collins for a moment. "How much do you remember after he winged you?"

"After I was hit, I blacked out."

"That you did. Eva began applying pressure to your wound. We got an ambulance to the hotel as quickly as we could. Eva kept the blood loss to a minimum. Ruined her night gown. If the bullet had been another few inches to the right, we wouldn't be having this conversation."

"My wife," Collins said. "I told her I would be back in New York in a few days."

"Your embassy sent a nice chap by. He wanted to contact your wife, but I persuaded him that I would take care of it."

"And you have?"

"I had a nice chat with Norris Jennings. I asked him to call your wife and tell her that you're safe and sound in Vienna but somewhat under the weather. A touch of the flu." Hawes paused. "I didn't see the need to alarm her. The official story is that just as we were leaving Budapest you were hit by a shot that had ricocheted off the masonry of a building. Bloody but nothing serious. You understand?"

"I understand."

"As soon as you feel up to it, you should call home."

"How did they find us? What does Wittingham think?"

"I haven't had much time with him. He and de Silva have been busy explaining to Washington about how we managed to blot our copybook."

"How did the Russians know Morris and Eva were in the Bristol?"

"I'm afraid that someone must have alerted them."

"We were betrayed. That's what you're saying."

"That's the long and the short of it."

"Morris was convinced that the Agency had been penetrated. A double agent named Envoy. That's why he wanted the legation staff left out of the equation, why he wanted to deal directly with Dulles, why he wanted me along on the flight on Washington."

"It could have been bad luck," Hawes said. "Durov could have alerted their people in Vienna to look for Morris and Eva. Perhaps the Russians had a spotter at the hotel."

"That seems unlikely," Collins said.

"I agree. That would narrow the field to those who knew about Morris' defection. That's a short list."

"A leak from Washington?"

"Dubious. The timing doesn't work. How could a penetration agent in Washington alert Moscow Center in time to arrange a hunting party in Vienna? And how would they know about the Hotel Bristol? I don't see that."

"That leaves Wittingham, and whoever he might have told."

"That's the conclusion I've reached," Hawes said. "I'll need to have a cup of tea with Wittingham and Colonel de Silva. Perhaps Wittingham has been careless. He may have bragged to a local girl, or shared too much at the embassy."

"Wittingham? A lover?" Collins was skeptical. "He strikes me as all business."

"All the more reason to check. He may have met a pretty fraulein who shared their pillow talk with the Russians. We know that when the Reds left Austria last year they left several networks behind. You know what Orwell said about keeping secrets—you must also hide them from yourself." Hawes moved toward the door. "I must be off," he said. "Anna and I have an appointment at the embassy to review the paperwork for her asylum request. Tomorrow I'll have that chat with Colonel de Silva and Wittingham."

"I'd like to know what it is that you learn from them."

"You may count on it," Hawes said. "By the way, the convoy from the American legation finally showed up. The Russians let them cross the border this morning.

★ ★ ★

Collins called home that night from the hospital. Maria answered immediately, and Collins quickly told her the truth about his health.

"I know Norris Jennings said I was under the weather. It's not the flu. After I talked to you on Saturday, there was an incident later that night."

"An incident?" Collins could hear the alarm in his wife's voice.

"I can't talk about it on the phone, but I'll tell you everything when I get home. I was slightly wounded in the chest, but I'm fine. It's a scratch. You don't need to worry."

"Dennis," she said. "Of course I'm going to worry when you tell me something like that."

"I'm fine. I would tell you if I wasn't."

"I'll worry until I see you."

"If anyone asks, I got hit when I was leaving Budapest—a ricochet off a building."

"I wish I knew what was going on. Not knowing is very hard."

"I promise that I'll clear up everything when I get back to New York."

"I love you. Please hurry back."

"I love you, too. I'll call once my flight is booked."

* * *

Collins mended quickly. His surgeon, a taciturn captain from Punta Gorda, Florida, named Gary McQueen examined the stitches in Collins' chest on Tuesday morning and pronounced himself pleased with how the wound was healing. He wouldn't agree, however, to immediately release Collins from the hospital.

"One more night here," McQueen said. "Your body needs a chance to recuperate."

"I feel fine," Collins said.

"That's what they all say just before they keel over," McQueen responded. "Trust me on this. All things being equal, we'll have you out of here tomorrow morning."

Hawes returned for a visit that evening, right before dinner, and Collins abandoned the *Herald Tribune* he had been reading when the Englishman arrived. He was feeling better—while his chest still hurt, he had marched up and down the hospital corridors, ready to prove that he was well enough to check out.

"I have news," Hawes said, sitting down in the chair closest to the door. Collins took the other. "Disturbing news."

"From your meeting with Wittingham?"

"In a way. In fact, Wittingham didn't show up at the American embassy for the meeting I had scheduled this morning at eleven o'clock. Colonel de Silva and I went to his flat, and had the landlord let us in with a passkey. We found his body in his bed, a bullet through his temple. There was a typed note on the night table."

"What did it say?" Collins managed to ask, stunned by the news.

"Just 'I'm sorry.'"

"That's all?"

Hawes nodded. "A suicide."

"Are you sure it was suicide? Could it have been the Russians?"

"Anything is possible, of course. Colonel de Silva will consider all angles. There will be an official inquiry. A number of officials are flying in from Washington."

"Somehow he didn't seem the type to take his own life," Collins said. "Too arrogant."

"There's more to it," Hawes said. "I found some documents in his room that cast a different light on matters." He opened the manila envelope and spilled out a passport and some papers onto the hospital bed. "A Polish passport in the name of Cezar Novak, with Wittingham's photo, a recent photo. And an airline ticket to Warsaw from Schwechat, leaving tomorrow on LOT Airlines, and a prepaid train ticket from Warsaw to Moscow."

"These were in his flat? Could they have planted by the KGB? To make us think he was a traitor?"

Hawes shook his head. "I don't think so. It looks like he was Envoy, the penetration agent that Rose told you about."

"He betrayed us? Why?"

"Perhaps he was another true believer, like Philby or Donald Maclean. Or perhaps the Russians had something on him. Or they were paying him. Whatever the motive, it appears that he went bad."

"What did de Silva say about this?"

"I haven't said anything to him, and he hasn't seen the passport or tickets."

"But weren't you there together at Wittingham's flat? Wasn't he there when you found them?"

Hawes looked away. He remained silent for what seemed to Collins an unusually long period of time before finally speaking. "I obtained these somewhat earlier in the day."

"How could that be?"

"I'll leave that to your imagination." Hawes walked across the room and stared out the window, turning his back on Collins so that his face was hidden. "Wittingham never would have talked. Even if Washington believed that he was Envoy, they'd let him quietly resign. It's better that it ended here in Vienna. At least he paid a price for his crimes, unlike Burgess and Maclean and Philby. A high price, but a commensurate one."

Collins realized then what Hawes was telling him, that the Englishman had visited Wittingham's flat alone, earlier in the morning, and had either discovered his suicide or—and Collins was reluctant to accept this—had somehow played a role in his death. Could Hawes have done it? Collins remembered how Hawes looked when he hit Colonel Bela in the face with his revolver. He was a man who didn't shy away from doing hard things—his friend was, indeed, capable of killing Wittingham and making it appear to be suicide.

"Wittingham never planned to return to Washington," Hawes said. "The Russians would have insisted on his defection. They would have to assume that Rose might know about Envoy." He turned back from the window. "Please keep Wittingham's false passport and the tickets. You can decide whether to give them to Dulles or not. They shouldn't come from me."

"Is that how you want it?"

"That's how I want it. Under the circumstances, it's the best we can do. The Soviets don't get to trot out Wittingham in front of the press in Moscow as the American Maclean. Envoy is done. Dulles will want to take a very hard look at Wittingham's history with the Agency. Any colleagues he seemed close to. Missions that failed where he was privy to the details. That sort of thing."

"All right," Collins said. "But if I give them to Dulles, he'll figure it out. You could come under scrutiny."

"I doubt that highly," Hawes said. "Dulles won't want to advertise the Agency's failure to detect an enemy penetration agent. Too many failures all around. I include the sorry decisions by our leaders in London and Washington about Hungary."

"I agree," Collins said. "And for what it's worth, I plan to tell Dulles that when I see him."

★ ★ ★

In the morning, Collins left the Army hospital after being cleared by Dr. McQueen. He took a cab to the Hotel Bristol. The concierge called Pan Am and arranged a seat on a Friday flight to London, connecting to New York. Collins eagerly called Maria with the details of his return.

When he reached his hotel room, he set up his typewriter on the desk and sat down to write his impressions of his last days in Budapest.

> *For twelve days the brave residents of Budapest sought to banish the darkness from their city, to live in the light as free men and women.*

> *I saw the crowd gathered in front of Parliament on the Tuesday night their revolution began, lighting newspapers and leaflets, illuminating the square as they chanted: "We've had enough of darkness."*

> *Then I saw Hungarians light candles and place them in windows and on cobblestoned streets on the Friday of All Soul's Night, the Day of the Dead, as a memorial for those who had died resisting any reimposition of tyranny by Soviet tanks.*

> *I saw the joy and elation when, for a few tantalizing days, Hungarians tasted freedom. For the first time in years, they could hear church bells ringing freely and read uncensored newspapers and not fear the scrutiny of the secret police. Sadly, those days were to come to an end.*

He paused to think about what he had experienced, and then wrote more about what he had seen. The courage of teenagers—boys and girls—armed with Molotov cocktails and rifles standing against modern tanks and artillery; and the resolve of the people fighting against long odds. The concluding paragraphs flowed naturally.

I have made a promise to myself: every October 23rd until the people of Budapest are free I will find a church and light a candle. It is a small, symbolic gesture, and I know may strike some as sentimental or futile or maudlin. I don't see it that way. For me, it will be a matter of keeping faith with the freedom fighters of October 1956. I believe the day will come when all that they fought and died for will become immanent, a reality.

On that day, I hope to return to a free Budapest and light another candle. I will not lose faith. In the Book of Numbers, we are told that at the sound of the trumpets, God will save the oppressed from their oppressors. May that day arrive—in God's time—but without earthly delay.

Collins unrolled the last sheet of paper from the typewriter. He'd take the article over to the Associated Press office in the morning so that it could be telexed to the Newspaper Alliance in London.

* * *

On Thursday, Collins called on Eva Nemeth at the American embassy on Boltzmanngasse. He found her occupying a cramped second-floor office that had been converted into a makeshift bedroom. Colonel de Silva had insisted that Eva stay in the embassy where he was sure he could protect her.

"How are you?" she asked Collins. "Your wound?"

"I'll be fine in a few weeks. It's healing. Thank you for what you did. Winters told me you stopped the bleeding."

"It was nothing. You risked your life for us. Both of you."

"I'm sorry we didn't arrive soon enough."

She looked down at the floor. "You were there in time for me. Not for Morris."

"He loved you," Collins said, and then stopped. What more could he say? There were no words of comfort that he could offer that would alter what had happened.

"And I loved him."

Collins looked around the room, taking in the Army cot and Eva's battered suitcase on the floor. "How long will you stay here? Is there anything I can do to help? When you get to the States, can we show you around New York?"

"I'm not sure about the States, now. Without Morris?" She blinked away tears. "We were meant to do that together. I asked them about Lisbon. They don't think it would be safe for me there. We've talked about Israel. Colonel de Silva says that I could be protected there, and he has approached a friend in the Israeli embassy about it. I will see his friend tomorrow to discuss it. I believe I could make a fresh start there."

"Viktor talked about going to Israel."

"I know he did," she said. "I think I could be of use there. They need young people."

"So I've heard."

"It's sunny and warm in Haifa," she said. "You can see the bay from Mount Carmel. They say that you can pick oranges right from the trees."

"You're making me envious. We can't pick oranges in Brooklyn."

"I would have liked to see Brooklyn," she said. "To see where he grew up. To drink an egg cream." She sighed. "He loved you, Dennis. He so regretted what happened. I think if he could change anything in his past, it would have been that."

"He told me that, more or less. And while he couldn't change the past, he made the most of his second chance. Morris wouldn't leave without you. He didn't take the easy path."

"I wish he had," she said.

Collins rose to his feet. "My flight is tomorrow. Call me at the hotel if you think of anything I can do before then. If you ever do get to New York, we can show you the old neighborhood, where Morris and I grew up."

"I would like that," she said. She kissed him on the cheek. "Good-bye, Dennis."

* * *

On Friday morning, Collins retrieved the envelope with Lukas Nemeth's notes from the hotel safe, gladly paid his large bill, and checked out of the Bristol. Feliks Hawes waited outside with Anna in a Mercedes-Benz sedan, ready to drive Collins to Schwechat Airport. Anna wore a fashionable two-piece wool suit with a string of pearls, and she attracted admiring looks from several of the men who passed by the car.

At the airport, they sat in the British Airways waiting area and talked about the tour of Paris and London that Hawes had planned for Anna until Collins' flight to London was announced.

"We'll see you in New York," Hawes said. "I believe you owe us lunch in an automat."

"You're on," Collins said. "Maria will also insist that we hit all the night spots, so I can promise you won't get much sleep."

Hawes surprised him by wrapping him in an embrace. He and Anna stood by the door and watched as Collins and the other passengers walked out on the tarmac to board the aircraft. Collins turned to give them a final wave before he climbed the steps to the cabin.

Twenty-four

Saturday, November 10

Collins saw only ugly, gray clouds through the windows of the Pan Am Stratocruiser as they made their final descent into Idlewild. He peered down, hoping to catch sight of New York below, but there was no break in the thick cloud cover.

He had read the London newspapers on the flight—they were filled with stories about Hungary and the Suez. Britain and France had reluctantly agreed to a ceasefire called for by the United Nations. President Eisenhower had publicly expressed his displeasure with the Anglo-French incursion, and had supported the creation of a United Nations Emergency Force to secure the peace in Egypt.

The news from Budapest was uniformly grim. The Soviets had crushed resistance in the city, and Hungarian refugees continued to stream across the Austrian border. The temporary camps set up outside Vienna were overflowing. In Budapest, Imre Nagy and members of his cabinet remained holed up in the Yugoslav embassy; Cardinal Mindszenty was being sheltered in the American legation.

Collins was relieved to be home. He was exhausted, and when he left the aircraft and walked the short distance across the tarmac to the terminal his chest wound, still healing, ached from the sudden cold.

As he entered the building, a Pan Am steward took him aside and told him that someone from Washington was waiting for him in a private suite. Collins was annoyed; he wanted to see Maria, Caleb, and Matthew, and he didn't want to waste any time with some officious functionary from the Agency trying to debrief him.

But when he followed the steward to the room, he didn't find a low-level bureaucrat waiting for him, but instead, Allen Dulles, the director of the CIA. His hair had thinned, his face was more creased, and when Dulles rose from his chair—pipe in hand—to greet Collins he moved with more care than Collins remembered from their meetings in Washington in 1951. He wore a tweed jacket with elbow patches and a dark blue tie.

"You asked to see me, Mr. Collins?" he began. "Alone? That's the message that you sent from Vienna."

"I had planned to come to Washington next week. Didn't Colonel de Silva pass that along?"

"He did. I didn't think you would have made the request unless it was important. That's why I'm here."

"There are things I need to give you," Collins said. "And something I want to say."

Dulles motioned for Collins to sit across from him. "It's been nothing but bad news from Hungary," he said. "And the operation to extract Rose came to a sad end."

"Morris Rose and Cliff Wittingham, dead," Collins said. "I'd consider that a sad end, yes."

"A shock about Wittingham," Dulles said. "A very promising young man. Very capable. Some thought he was a bit of a cold fish, but he had handled a number of difficult assignments with aplomb. Then again, what drives a man to suicide is often a mystery, is it not? The psychoanalysts I've talked to say that's a very complex question. Dr. Jung's notion of the shadow, the hidden and repressed, the dark side of our personality, may hold the key."

"I don't think it was particularly complex in his case," Collins said. He opened his travel canvas bag and located the envelope with Wittingham's false Polish passport and the airplane ticket from Vienna to Warsaw. He handed it to Dulles silently. Through the suite's large picture windows, Collins watched a TWA Super Constellation taxi up the runway and then slowly rise into the air. When he looked back, Dulles met his gaze.

"Where did these come from?" Dulles asked in a subdued voice. He peered at Collins through his wire-rimmed glasses, his blue eyes alert and penetrating.

"They were removed from Wittingham's flat before Colonel de Silva arrived."

"I see," Dulles said. "They certainly put things in a different light. What does this suggest about Wittingham, then? That he had been turned? That he was working for the Soviets? An agent-in-place?"

"It would explain why he had a Polish passport and tickets to Warsaw. It would explain how the KGB tracked down Morris Rose to the fourth floor of the Hotel Bristol in Vienna—Wittingham tipped them off."

"And his suicide? Caused by guilt? There was a typed note, I believe. 'I'm sorry.' So he killed himself out of remorse? That was his motivation?"

"What other explanation fits?" Collins wouldn't directly lie to Dulles, but he wasn't going to implicate Hawes in Wittingham's death.

"His suicide could have been staged by Russians. They could have planted the passport and tickets to incriminate him."

"To what end?"

Dulles took a quick puff on his pipe and hesitated before he spoke. "I'm not sure. To confuse us? To distract us? To destroy trust within the Agency? What you have handed me will certainly require a full investigation. We'll need to look closely at everything Wittingham touched over the past several years. I'll ask Jim Angleton and his group to get to the bottom of this."

"Whose idea was it for Wittingham to review Matthew Steele's files in 1952? To come and see me in Key West?"

"I approved it," Dulles said, frowning. "My recollection is that Wittingham volunteered to examine the Trojan Horse operation. He concluded that Matthew had overstepped the bounds on a few occasions, but he didn't find anything that required further action on our part."

"Moscow Center was trying to find out what happened to Anatoli Yatov, Philby's controller," Collins said. "I think Wittingham was asked to learn what he could. I remember he was most curious about Yatov when he interviewed me." He paused—it was time to deliver more bad news to Dulles. "Morris had learned of a double agent in the Agency. Code name of Envoy. That's why he used Reisinger to communicate with you, and why he insisted that I bring him in. He didn't trust anyone else. He was convinced that he would be a target until he could get back to the States and talk to you face-to-face."

"And Wittingham was Envoy?"

"It would seem so. I think that he had tipped the Soviets about Rose's plans to defect, even before we arrived in Hungary. Had the uprising not occurred, we would have been arrested in Budapest. Then Wittingham delayed getting the travel documents for Rose's lover, Eva Nemeth, to buy time for the Russians to hunt him down."

Dulles slowly shook his head. "Wittingham was somewhat opaque. We missed whatever signs there might have been of his involvement with the Soviets. I'm sorry."

Collins looked directly at Dulles. "There's much more for you to be sorry about. The Hungarians fighting and dying in the streets expected us to do something. Parachute supplies in, send weapons. That's all they wanted. If we weren't willing to do that, then at least we should have pressed the issue in the United Nations. Rallied our European allies to do something. Instead, we stood back and let the Soviets roll over them."

Dulles remained silent, but Collins could see he was biting down on his pipe stem in anger. Collins didn't care.

"When they asked me why America wasn't helping, I didn't know what to say."

"I can make no excuses for that," Dulles said. "Some of us argued for making drops of arms and supplies from the air. I certainly did. I thought they deserved that. President Eisenhower said no. I understood his thinking. We had an uphill climb because of Suez. The Russians were threatening to intervene, and we wanted to keep them out of the Mideast."

"Was that the deal? Stand aside in Hungary and let the Red Army do their dirty work as long as the Russians agreed not to interfere in the Middle East? Is that what you're saying?"

"There was no explicit deal. We signaled that we had no desire for a confrontation over Hungary, that we had no intention of including it in NATO, and we could live with a Tito-like regime in power. The President didn't feel he had any options. If Hungary had a port, access to the sea, or if Austria wasn't neutral, we might have had ways to counter the Soviets. We didn't. We weren't about to start another world war over it."

"I'm not suggesting that we should have fought a world war over Hungary," Collins said. "But it didn't seem like we put in the effort. We didn't push in the United Nations. We haven't made the Russians pay for what they've done in any significant way, from what I can see."

Dulles removed the pipe stem from his mouth. "I'm afraid the die was cast. Khrushchev felt he had no choice but to suppress the revolution. His enemies, the hardliners in Moscow, have been arguing that his February speech exposing Stalin's crimes opened Pandora's box. In Hungary he had to prove he wasn't soft, that he wouldn't hesitate to wield power over the satellite nations. At least the world has seen the true ugliness of their system, now. That's one consolation."

"Cold comfort for the Hungarians. Does anyone in Washington take responsibility for what we did? Preaching rollback and liberation to the East Germans and Poles and Hungarians when we had no intention of intervening if they acted on our propaganda and revolted?"

"We misjudged the situation," Dulles said. "I don't dispute that. We missed the potential for a true uprising. There were some excesses at Radio Free Europe, some of the Hungarian emigres there got carried away with what they broadcast. Nonetheless, the President made it crystal clear publicly all along that we weren't going to intercede."

"A quite convenient position to take in the last weeks of a presidential campaign," Collins said. "No need to worry voters."

"That had nothing to do with it. The President didn't make his decision based on politics. That's not the way he thinks."

"I'd like to believe that. All of you will have to live with your own consciences." Collins paused for a long moment. "One other thing. Wittingham had agreed that the Agency would pay me one thousand dollars for every day of the mission. The money was to be paid to the International Rescue Committee in honor of Karina Lazda."

"I understand. We will make good on the debt. How many days?"

"Twelve," Collins said. "Twelve days."

"Is there anything else? Anything I can do for you?"

"As it happens, I have a gift from Morris Rose for you. I promised him I would give it to you in the event he couldn't." He reopened his canvas bag and found the envelope with Lukas Nemeth's notes. "These notes outline Soviet progress on their R–7 missile. An intercontinental ballistic missile."

"Where does this information come from?"

"A scientist working on the project, a man named Nemeth. Hungarian. He had two purposes in passing this information along. He worried about the Russians achieving superiority with their missiles. He had another, more personal, reason. His niece, Eva, was Morris' lover. He wanted her to defect to the West along with Morris, and he believed this information would smooth their reception." Collins handed the notes to Dulles. "The Russians plan to use the R–7 to launch a satellite into orbit. It's meant to be a major propaganda victory."

Dulles emptied his pipe into an ashtray. "We've been tracking their program. Colonel White and our Office of Scientific Intelligence. We've been monitoring their test flights from Kapustin Yar. We didn't know that they were that far along."

"Are we working on anything similar?"

"Plenty of activity. We have our own missile programs. Jupiter. Thor. Vanguard. Perhaps too many programs—it's what you'd expect from the Pentagon. The Naval Research Laboratory has been working on launching an Earth-orbiting satellite. It sounds as if the Russians have jumped ahead of us." He quickly scanned the notes. "I'll need to get these analyzed. If the information holds up, we'll brief the President about these developments."

"For what it's worth, Morris would have been pleased to know it'll be of help. He thought it could matter."

"It matters," Dulles said. "It most decidedly matters."

Collins rose to his feet. "My family is waiting for me," he said. "I don't have anything more to report."

Dulles stood up, slowly, and shook Collins' hand. "Thank you again for what you've done. Colonel de Silva specifically noted in his report your bravery in confronting the Russian agents at the hotel. I wanted to commend you for your courage."

Collins hesitated before he responded, picking his words carefully. "It was instinct more than courage. And we failed to protect Morris."

"Will we see you in Washington?" Dulles asked. "You're more than welcome to stop by E Street."

"I don't think so," Collins said. "Unless the Senators somehow make it to the World Series, I don't expect to be in Washington any time soon."

"If it depends on the Senators, then I'm afraid we won't see you. But the offer still stands. By the way, I asked Pan Am for another room where you could meet your family in private. It's just up the hallway."

* * *

Collins found his eyes filling with tears when he saw them waiting for him: Maria with a son holding each hand, and his brother Frank standing behind them, a crooked grin on his face. Maria was in her Sunday best, wearing one of her nicest dresses, and she smiled when he caught her eye.

Collins dropped his bag, and his sons ran to him to hug him. He picked up Caleb first, and then Matthew. After he had put them down, Maria came into his arms, and she kissed him on the lips, hard. She touched his cheek gently.

"I've been so worried," she said. "Are you all right?"

"My chest's still a bit sore, but I'm fine."

"We missed you for Halloween," Caleb said. "I got lots of candy."

"So did I," Matthew said. "But the tail came off my Davy Crockett cap."

"I wish I could have been there," Collins said. "Next year. And we'll see if we can fix your cap, Matthew, when we get home."

"Mommy already did."

Maria laughed. "I had to. Otherwise, I would have never heard the last of it."

Collins motioned for his brother to come closer. Frank had been hanging back, not wanting to intrude on their reunion.

"Glad to see you're back in one piece," Frank said. "Aren't you getting too old for this sort of thing? You ought to stick to covering the World Series and the Kentucky Derby—where bullets ain't flying around."

"That's good advice. I'm going to take it."

"I read your articles from Budapest," Maria said. "They were in the *Daily News*. It must have been quite hard. Those poor people."

"It was," he said. "And I have more to tell you, but it can wait. I couldn't say anything on the phone. It involves Morris Rose, and why I was in Hungary."

"Morris Rose," she said, her face darkening. "I thought that all of that was done and behind us."

"It's done. Not how I would have wished, but it's done."

She sighed, and then hugged him again. "You're home," she said. "Home for Christmas, just like the song says. That's more than enough."

Epilogue

Saturday, August 19, 1989

They waited in a rented Volkswagen van on the Austrian side of the border. A few other journalists and photographers had parked by the side of the road from St. Margarethen, curious about whether the Pan-European peace festival, being held in a nearby field in Hungary that afternoon, would produce anything newsworthy.

Caleb Collins had grown used to the waiting part of his job. Much of journalism involved sitting around waiting for news conferences to start, or for government officials to show up for an interview, or for an event to get underway.

The organizers of the festival had been touting it as a symbolic opening of the Iron Curtain. The posters for the picnic featured a dove and barbed wire and the authorities in Austria and Hungary had agreed that for a few hours border controls would be relaxed.

The picnic would feature a brass band and folk dancing and sausages and beer—all meant to encourage Hungarians and Austrians to mingle and enjoy a momentary thaw in East-West relations.

Caleb was there because one of the foreign editors at *The Christian Science Monitor* had heard from a friend in Vienna that disaffected East Germans camping out at the West German embassy in Budapest might try to cross the border during the picnic. Caleb, in London to write a profile of the Labor leader, Neil Kinnock, had been asked to cover the story. Would the Hungarian border guards allow such an exodus? Or would there be an "incident," perhaps violent?

The cynics among the journalists at the Hotel Sacher bar in Vienna had suggested that a deal had been struck between Miklos

Nemeth, Hungary's prime minister, and West German Chancellor Helmut Kohl. Kohl would underwrite Hungary's faltering economy and Nemeth would allow East Germans an escape route to the West. It was true Nemeth had instructed his Ministry of the Interior to remove the barbed-wire fence separating Hungary and Austria. This "green border" move didn't seem targeted at Hungarians—who had been allowed to travel to Western Europe for years under Janos Kadar's "Goulash Communism"—but rather at the thousands of East Germans in Hungary eager to escape the neo-Stalinist regime of Erich Honecker.

"I hope we're not wasting our time here." It was Derek Pryce, a freelance photographer who had hitched a ride with Caleb. Caleb had worked with him in the past. "It won't be much of a story if the East Germans don't make a dash for it. Who knows if the Hungarians will let them cross. They may not want to offend Honecker. Or Gorbachev."

"We'll know soon enough," Caleb said. He checked his wristwatch: it was 2:45. "They're going to let the Austrians cross into Hungary in fifteen minutes."

His interpreter, Bettina Lindner, couldn't have been more than twenty-five years old. She seemed incredibly young, in her blue jeans and peasant blouse.

"I'm going to take a look-see," Caleb told them. He stepped out of the van and trained his binoculars on the fields beyond the border gate. Nothing. No sign of East German tourists looking to make a dash for freedom. He got back into the van.

"Are you ready, Derek?"

"Ready as ever," he responded. "The border guards looked relaxed, so this should be nice and easy. No shooting. Shooting makes me nervous."

"Didn't you tell me once that if you weren't nervous, you weren't close enough to the action?"

"Probably. But I say all sorts of stupid things."

"My father covered the uprising in Budapest in '56," Caleb found himself telling Derek and Bettina. "He always talked about the incredible courage of the young men and women in the streets, how they ignored the long odds against them and kept fighting. I wish he could be here and see that there are some holes opening in the Iron Curtain."

He had always wondered whether it had been an accident that Dennis Collins had arrived in Budapest when he did. There were things his father hadn't shared with him, but what father didn't edit his personal history, elide over some of the messiness, the mistakes, the regrets of the past?

Caleb knew that the owners of the North American Newspaper Alliance had ties to the CIA. Matthew Steele, the man who had married his mother when she was pregnant with Caleb, had been a senior official of the Agency. Did his father have some connection with the CIA? Was he in Budapest solely as a journalist?

In 1984, after his father died, Caleb had filed a Freedom of Information request with the CIA, asking for any files relating to Matthew Steele and Dennis Collins. He received a form letter informing him that the Agency did not release operational files. That did not mean, the letter continued, that there were any files associated with the names he had submitted. Caleb tried pursuing it further, calling around in the hopes of finding some retired CIA official who might be able to enlighten him, but he came up empty.

In some ways, he didn't want to know. While it was a simpler time, and many newsmen (and they were predominately male, then) had helped the Agency out of a sense of patriotism, Caleb would have been disappointed to learn that his father was one of them. The Church Committee had exposed the ugly, dark side of Langley, and Caleb hoped Dennis Collins had been able to stay clear of any entanglement.

* * *

Caleb positioned himself where he could see the wooden border gate and the line of Austrians waiting to cross. Several uniformed Hungarian border police had begun processing paperwork and allowing some of the Austrian visitors through the barrier.

Bettina came and stood next to him. "There's a group approaching from the Hungarian side of the border," she said, excited.

Moments later, Caleb saw a small cluster of people nearing the gate. Suddenly, they began running, perhaps fearful that the crossing would suddenly be closed. The Hungarian border guards studiously ignored them, focusing instead on the Austrians waiting to enter Hungary.

Someone unlatched the gate and a group of East Germans surged past it, rapidly moving up the road toward Caleb.

"*Wir sind frei!*" It was a young blonde woman with a rucksack over her shoulder, dressed in running shorts and a t-shirt. "*Frei.*"

Derek shot photographs of the East German refugees as quickly as he could, the automatic motor on his camera whirring.

Bettina asked a young couple with a small child, a boy, if they would stop and talk. When they agreed, Caleb asked them several questions and Bettina interpreted. The father, whose name was Erik, explained that they had been vacationing at Lake Balaton when they heard about the festival. They had driven to Sopron in the hopes of somehow making their way to Austria.

"He says there was no life for them or his son," Bettina said. "They abandoned their Trabant on the side of the road and walked here. He says that when they saw the gate was open, he didn't hesitate."

With Bettina interpreting, Caleb interviewed five more refugees, most of them in the late twenties or early thirties. Several of them had been staying at the West German embassy in Budapest, and saw the Pan-European festival as a possible opportunity to escape.

"I've got what I need," Derek told him. "Don't feel you have to stay any longer for me."

Caleb led the way back to the Volkswagen. He looked up at the dark clouds forming on the horizon, signs of a summer thunderstorm on the way. He hoped it would hold off until they returned to Vienna.

He wondered what impact the day would have. Certainly there would be some very angry officials in the German Democratic Republic that evening, with Honecker the angriest. Would Gorbachev rein in the Hungarians? Caleb couldn't imagine a repeat of 1956, but the Hungarian economy was in disarray and most of Hungary's trade was with the USSR. If Gorbachev wanted to retaliate for the opening of the border, he had plenty of ways to squeeze the Hungarians.

★ ★ ★

They drove back to Vienna through a light rain. Caleb dropped off Bettina on a street corner in Wieden and took Derek to his Landstrasse hotel before returning the van to the rental car agency. From there, he walked to the Hotel Bristol.

He had insisted on the Bristol—a sentimental gesture, because he remembered his father's stories about staying there when he wrote a feature about the Vienna State Opera.

After a quick dinner, he'd made a few calls to the States, checking in with Meilan in New York, and then he tried phoning Matthew at his Boston office. Caleb was disappointed when Matthew's assistant told him that his brother was out of the office reviewing progress at a construction site.

He wanted to describe the scene at the border, and talk about what it would have meant to their father, how delighted he would have been at the strange turn of events that summer—not only were the Hungarians inching closer to independence from Moscow, but they were also helping to undermine the East German regime.

Caleb dialed his mother in Key West, and was pleased when she answered on the first ring. He told her he was calling from Vienna.

"How are the Dodgers doing?" he asked.

"Lost to the Mets last night by a run. Blew a rundown play. Lasorda's doing his best, but I think they're done for this season. They'd need an incredible winning streak to get back to the World Series."

"I saw something amazing today, and I wanted to tell you about it. I was at the Austrian border with Hungary for this Pan-European festival today. When they opened the gate on the Hungarian side, some East Germans, maybe two or three hundred, rushed across into Austria. They were overjoyed to be free."

"That's wonderful."

"I think it could be the start of something. It seems like things are opening up in Eastern Europe. I thought of Dad because I know he was there in '56, for the uprising."

"It always bothered him," she said. "He felt that we had let the Hungarians down. He would have been pleased that you were there today to witness what happened."

"I wish Dad could have seen it himself."

"When you get back, will you and Meilan come see me?" she asked. "I'll ask Matthew to come as well."

"Is everything all right?" he asked, suddenly alarmed. "Your health?"

"I'm fine," she said. "It's just that it's been a while since we've been together as a family."

"We'll come," he said. "I'll take a week of vacation when I get back and we'll fly down."

"That would be good," she said. "There's something about your father I want to share with you and Matthew, about what he was doing in Budapest in 1956 and how he got there. I don't know the full story, but I know the most important parts. Some of it involves Virginia, your mother."

"You're my mother," he said defensively.

"Thank you, Caleb. I am, but your father had a history with Virginia that you deserve to know more about. I tried to get your father to talk to you about it, about your mother and Matthew Steele and his friend Morris Rose, but he resisted sharing the complete story with you." She paused. "There was a time when you two quarreled over politics quite fiercely. During Vietnam."

"I remember."

"I think that played a part. He didn't want you judging him harshly for what he did in the 1950s."

"I wouldn't have judged him."

"And then he made some other mistakes. Mistakes of the heart."

"I'm the one with the divorce," Caleb said. "Didn't he think I would understand?"

"Your father was a proud man. He couldn't stand the idea of you thinking less of him."

"I wouldn't have."

"When you visit, we can talk about all of it," she said. "I never should have waited this long. The days just speed by. It's hard to believe that he's been gone five years now. In the morning, I still expect to hear him complaining that he can't find the front section of *The New York Times*, and asking where I've hidden it. I miss him. Terribly."

"We all do."

"There's one other thing I'd like you to do when you come," she said. "I'd like you and Matthew to light a candle for your father at Saint Mary's. And then we'll go out to dinner at Louie's Backyard."

"Sure," Caleb said. "That would be quite fitting."

Then they said their good-byes, and after Caleb had hung up, he sat quietly for a moment, surprised at the sudden tears in his eyes, tears that were unbidden but not unwelcome.

Author's Note

By the middle of November 1956, the Red Army had snuffed out any significant resistance by the Hungarian insurgents. Although Hungarians protested by other means—an hour-long national strike and a silent demonstration by the women of Budapest in Heroes Square in December—it was clear that the dream of an independent Hungary would remain just that, a dream, for the foreseeable future.

On the Sunday of the Russian attack, Imre Nagy and members of his cabinet had sought refuge in the Yugoslav embassy. Nagy and his advisors left the embassy on November 24 with assurances of safe passage to Romania, but they were promptly arrested by waiting KGB agents. Two years later, following a staged trial, Nagy and other leaders of the revolutionary government, including Pal Maleter, were executed by firing squad in Budapest.

The estimates of the number of Hungarians killed during the uprising have ranged from 2,500 to 10,000 (with the lower estimate regarded as the most likely death total), with some 12,000 wounded; another 200,000 or so Hungarians fled to the West. Soviet military losses were estimated at some 700 killed and more than 1,000 wounded.

The Hungarian uprising of 1956, along with Khrushchev's speech denouncing the crimes of Stalinism, damaged the appeal of Marxist ideology in Western Europe and elsewhere. Albert Camus wrote in *La Verite sur L'Affaire Nagy*: "We can refuse to accept or condone what has happened, we can keep our hearts and minds alive to it, we can refuse to countenance falsehood and keep faith with innocence even after its murder."

The U.S. had adopted (in the words of historian Laszlo Borhi) a "Janus-faced attitude toward the liberation of Eastern Europe" in the years before the uprising—vacillating between public calls for rollback, and the private recognition that containment was a more realistic approach. Some Hungarians felt that before the uprising Radio Free Europe (RFE) had encouraged armed resistance to the government, and during the revolt had falsely suggested that American assistance was on the way. A CIA inquiry found that during the crisis, RFE broadcasters had sometimes overstepped the bounds, offering tactical advice to the insurgents. The CIA concluded, however, that the RFE had not incited the uprising.

President Eisenhower outlined the boundaries of American policy toward Hungary in a press conference on November 14, 1956: "But I must make one thing clear: the United States doesn't now, and never has, advocated open rebellion by an undefended populace against force over which they could not possibly prevail. We, on the contrary, have always urged that the spirit of freedom be kept alive; that people do not lose hope. But we have never in all the years that I think we have been dealing with problems of this sort urged or argued for any kind of armed revolt which could bring about disaster to our friends."

In 1957, the Soviet Union employed the R-7 missile to successfully launch Sputnik, the world's first artificial satellite, into orbit. Sputnik not only challenged the American supremacy in science and technology, but also helped offset some of the damage to the Soviet image caused by Hungary.

It seems fitting that Hungary played a pivotal role in the end of the Cold War. The defection in 1989 of several hundred East Germans across the Hungarian border into Austria at the Pan-European Picnic—which was enabled by the government of Miklos Nemeth—served as an open challenge to the hardline Communist regime of Erich Honecker. It began a chain of events that led to the fall of the Berlin Wall. West German Chancellor Helmut Kohl later said that it was in Hungary where "the first stone was knocked out of the Wall."

After switching sides just before the Soviet invasion, Janos Kadar stayed in power as Hungary's leader until 1988. The Republic of Hungary held multi-party elections in 1990, and the conservative

Hungarian Democratic Forum leader Jozsef Antall became prime minister of a coalition government.

★ ★ ★

I've told the story of the Hungarian uprising in *The Hill of Three Borders* primarily from the perspective of those Western journalists and photojournalists present during the revolt. Nearly all stayed in the Hotel Duna. They shared information, and often worked in small groups as they reported on the fighting. Many were reliant on interpreters, or on those Hungarian insurgents who spoke German or other Western European languages.

Despite these limitations, the men and women of the Fourth Estate did a marvelous job in chronicling what was happening in the streets of Pest and the hills of Buda. They kept their objectivity, not flinching from illuminating the sometimes ugly realities of a civil insurrection.

Readers may wonder where the boundary between fact and fiction lies in *The Hill of Three Borders*. I tried to take as few liberties with the historical record as possible, but the novel is, after all, a work of my imagination.

The Hill of Three Borders actually was employed as a spot for clandestine meetings in the late 1940s, according to Christopher Felix in *The Spy and His Masters: A Short Course in the Secret War*. (Christopher Felix was the pen name of James McCargar, an American intelligence officer who worked in Hungary). Harmashatarhegy was also the location for a secret meeting of Hungarian university students who helped organize the demonstrations of October 23. In one sense, then, the hill can be seen as Ground Zero for the Hungarian revolution.

Most of the journalists portrayed in the novel are fictional, although three correspondents—Endre Marton of the Associated

Press, John MacCormac of *The New York Times*, and Indro Montanelli of the *Corriere della Sera*—are not. Lester Kane is loosely based on the Hungarian-American journalist Leslie Bane.

The North American Newspaper Alliance did have close ties with the Central Intelligence Agency in the 1950s, and Ian Fleming did have an ownership interest in its London office. The lines between intelligence agency and independent journalist were sometimes blurred during the early Cold War: some correspondents regarded debriefing with the Agency after returning from an overseas assignment as part of their patriotic duty. Some CIA agents did pose as reporters, and some newspeople were used operationally. It was not until the 1970s that Congressional pressure forced the CIA to pledge to stop the use of journalistic cover (although CIA directors have been careful not to rule out the practice absolutely).

Peer de Silva and Gaza Katona were the CIA station chiefs in Vienna and Budapest respectively. (De Silva, a West Pointer, had been the Manhattan Project's head of security at Los Alamos). MI6's John Bruce-Lockhart was sent to Budapest to assess the situation on the ground. (His uncle Robert, a diplomat, was arrested in Moscow in 1918 and accused of conspiring to assassinate Lenin. The British Foreign Office traded Maxim Litvinov and some other agents for Bruce-Lockhart's release.)

There was a mole in the American legation in Budapest. The journalist and author Kati Marton learned that a warrant officer working for the American military attaché had been passing information to the AVO in the mid-1950s. After his spying had been discovered, the Army returned the man to the U.S. and discharged him.

The Hungarian State Security did employ the "Duna girls" in the hopes of ensnaring Western businessmen and journalists through the time-honored (and often effective) "honey trap." Many of the women escaped to Vienna, and Peer de Silva remarked on their beauty in his memoir, *Sub Rosa: The CIA and the Uses of Intelligence*. The Marriott Hotel now occupies the site of the Hotel Duna.

The British and American legations sent convoys of staff, dependents, and expats from Budapest to Vienna. Only in my fictional account, however, did Anna Sandor join the British evacuation. While the Russians held up the American convoy for two nights, it wasn't a delay ordered by Mikhail Durov.

* * *

In researching the uprising, I turned to contemporary journalistic accounts, including those by Leslie Bain, Endre Marton, John MacCormac, Wiktor Woroszylski, Peter Fryer, Paul Lendvai, Barrett McGurn, Ivor Jones, Erich Lessing, and Andor Heller. Janos Molnar's brief essay, "Foreign Correspondents in the 1956 Hungarian Revolution" was very helpful. Other first-hand accounts by Bela Liptak, Laszlo Beke, Michael Korda, James Michener, and Sir Leslie Fry were of great value.

For general background, I relied on broader histories by Victor Sebestyen (*Twelve Days: The Story of the Hungarian Revolution*), Reg Gadney (*Cry Hungary!*), John P. C. Matthews (*Explosion: The Hungarian Revolution of 1956*), and Bob Dent (*Budapest 1956, Locations of Drama*). Durov's cynical joke about post-Stalin Moscow was adapted from a collection of Soviet jokes curated by John D. Clare.

T.A. Heppenheimer's *Countdown* and Robert A. Divine's *Sputnik Challenge* provided an excellent overview of the Soviet and American missile programs of the 1950s.

For the events of 1989, I consulted *The Year That Changed the World* by Michael Meyer, and contemporary news coverage. I also benefited from Thomas Kleine-Brockhoff's first-hand recollections of the Pan-European Picnic and the scene at the border.

In Budapest, Tibor Frank, Laszlo Eörsi, Zoltan Töröcsik, and Keve Papp helped me better understand the events of 1956. I'm grateful for the time they generously spent with me.

Max Holland provided insights into the CIA's responses to Freedom of Information Act requests in the 1980s.

I'm indebted to Steve and Tony Flanders and Glenn Speer, who read early versions of the novel and offered helpful insights.

Any errors of historical fact or flaws in interpretation found in *The Hill of Three Buildings* are mine alone.

And, once again, I'd like to thank my loved ones for their support, understanding, and patience and for bearing with me as I fashioned this story.

Cast of Characters

In Budapest

Journalists

Dennis Collins, North American Newspaper Alliance
Felix Winters (Feliks Hawes), freelance photographer (MI5)
Lester Kane, North American Newspaper Alliance
Isabelle Lavalle, Agence France-Presse
Lachlan Ferguson, *The Daily Telegraph*
Joe Branson, *Chicago Tribune*
Abe Kaufer, United Press
*Endre Marton, Associated Press
*John MacCormac, *The New York Times*
*Indro Montanelli, *Corriere della Sera*
*Erich Lessing, Magnum Photos

Diplomats

Hans Reisinger, Swiss minister
*Gaza Katona, American political attaché (CIA station chief)
Brooks Lawrence, American press attaché
*Spencer Barnes, American acting chargé d'affaires
*Tom Wailes, American minister
*Noel Cowley, British military attaché
*Dennis "Hurricane" David, British air force attaché
*Leslie Fry, British minister
Clarissa Blackburn, British second secretary
*Yuri Andropov, Russian ambassador
Vitali Osin, Russian diplomat, (KGB officer)

Hungarians

Eva Nemeth, interpreter
Anna Sandor, "Duna girl"
Viktor Toth, insurgent
Laszlo Kosa, State Security officer
Istvan Melles, State Security officer

KGB

Maxim Rusakov (Morris Rose), colonel
Mikhail Durov, Moscow Center official
*Ivan Serov, general and chairman

Hungarian government

*Matyas Rakosi, general secretary of the Hungarian Working People's Party, de facto dictator of Hungary (1949-1956)
*Erno Gero, general secretary of the Hungarian Working People's Party (1956)
*Imre Nagy, chairman of the Council of Ministers (1956)
*Janos Kadar, minister of state (1956)
*Pal Maleter, Hungarian Army general, minister of defense
*Laszlo Rajk, foreign minister, executed (1949)

In Vienna

Cliff Wittingham, CIA official
*Peer de Silva, CIA station chief

In Washington

Matthew Steele, CIA official (deceased)
Penny Bradford Steele, wife of Matthew Steele (deceased)
Anatoli Yatov, KGB clandestine agent (deceased)
*Allen Dulles, CIA director

In New York

Maria Highsmith Collins, wife of Dennis Collins
Caleb Collins, son of Dennis
Matthew Collins, son of Dennis
Frank Collins, brother of Dennis

* indicates historical figure

About the Author

Jefferson Flanders has been a sportswriter, newspaper columnist, editor, and publishing executive. He is the author of *Café Carolina and Other Stories* and of the First Trumpet Cold War trilogy of *Herald Square*, *The North Building*, and *The Hill of Three Borders*.

Made in the USA
Middletown, DE
26 July 2016